Composing Mortals

for Denise, Esme and Patrick

Composing Mortals

20th-century British classical composers

Terry Hiscock

with caricatures by John Minnion

Foreword by Brian Kay

*'Blessed Cecilia, appear in visions
To all musicians, appear and inspire:
Translated Daughter, come down and startle
Composing mortals with immortal fire.'*

– from *Anthem for St Cecilia's Day*
(for Benjamin Britten)
by W H Auden

Thames Publishing
London

First published 1998 by Thames Publishing
14 Barlby Road, London W10 6AR

Text © 1998 Terry Hiscock
Illustrations © 1998 John Minnion
Presentation © 1998 Thames Publishing

Printed and bound in Great Britain
by Lonsdale Press, London

Contents

Introduction

VAUGHAN WILLIAMS

THIS BOOK'S AIM is quite simple: it seeks to satisfy curiosity about mainstream British classical composers working in the first 75 years of the 20th century. Where to draw the line is always a problem in such situations, not least at the beginning of our chosen period; in the end we opted against including Parry and Stanford: may we be forgiven! The book does not attempt to tackle 'contemporary' music – Harrison Birtwistle, Peter Maxwell Davies, Mark Anthony Turnage, Colin Matthews, Michael Berkeley, Thomas Ades, etc, – not out of disrespect or indifference but because this is not, we think, the kind of music our notional reader is likely to encounter frequently. Perhaps it will be covered in another book. Similarly, the book doesn't tackle 'light music' – a huge subject better dealt with elsewhere (and it has been, in Philip Scowcroft's *British Light Music*, published by Thames).

Our notional reader is, it is felt, more likely to be a casual listener than a fanatic. He/she switches on to Classic FM while driving to work, but, other than the 'Proms', is perhaps rather less likely to settle down to a full evening's concert on Radio 3, although he may well tune to one of that station's ever-widening range of feature programmes about music. He buys classical CDs but not in great numbers, and more often budget than full-price. He may not have a musical dictionary in the house and doesn't read the musical press regularly. He goes to concerts but perhaps not to more than four or five a year. His musical interests are general rather than specialist, though he is by no means devoid of curiosity or desire to expand horizons. He isn't particularly concerned with technical matters or the politics of the music world, past or present. He is not entirely disinterested in musical history but is not perhaps likely to read a substantial book on the subject or on any one composer. The 'Acknowledgements', however, indicate some of the most approachable books (currently available or recently published) about the composers featured in this book. Our notional reader knows when he likes something, and can have his interest aroused in a general way about the life and main achievements of, say, Lennox Berkeley, whose *Serenade* he has encountered on the radio, or Rubbra, one of whose symphonies he happened on by chance.

Even in these more open-minded times there is still some lingering snobbery about continental music being of more account than the home product. Neither the publisher nor the author subscribes to that view, and therefore this almost entirely non-judgmental book seeks to encourage knowledge of, and pride in, the riches to be found from Arnold to Warlock.

John Bishop
September 1998

Acknowledgements

I am most grateful for the invaluable information gleaned from the following books, periodicals and authors in the preparation of this book:

Philharmonic Concerto – The Life and Music of Sir Malcolm Arnold, Piers Burton-Page; *Granville Bantock: A Personal Portrait*, M Bantock; *Farewell My Youth*, A Bax; *Arnold Bax*, C Scott-Sutherland; *Bax*, Lewis Foreman; *As I Remember*, A Bliss; *Immortal Hour: the Life and Period of Rutland Boughton*, Michael Hurd; *Havergal Brian and his Music*, R Nettel; *Ordeal by Music: The Strange Experience of Havergal Brian*, R Nettel; *Havergal Brian: the Making of a Composer*, K Eastaugh; *Frank Bridge*, P Pirie; *Frank Bridge – Radical and Conservative*, A Payne; *Benjamin Britten: His Life and Operas*, E W White; *Benjamin Britten – a biography*, Humphrey Carpenter; *Geoffrey Bush and his Music*, Christopher Palmer; *Left, Right and Centre*, G Bush; *Whom the Gods Love – George Butterworth*, Michael Barlow; *Suite in Four Movements*, Eric Coates; *The Heritage of Samuel Coleridge-Taylor*, A Coleridge-Taylor; *Samuel Coleridge-Taylor*, W Tortolano; *Walford Davies*, H C Colles; *Delius*, Peter Warlock; *Delius as I Knew Him*, Eric Fenby; *Thomas Dunhill: Man and Music*, D Dunhill; *George Dyson: Man and Music*, C Palmer; *Dyson's Delight*, ed. C Palmer; *Edward Elgar – His Life and Music*, D McVeagh; *Edward Elgar – A Creative Life*, J Northrop Moore; *Portrait of Elgar*, Michael Kennedy; *The Music of Howard Ferguson*, ed. Alan Ridout; *Gerald Finzi: An English Composer*, Stephen Banfield; *Percy Grainger: The Man and His Music*, J Bird; *The Ordeal of Ivor Gurney*, M Hurd; *Herbert Howells – a celebration*, C Palmer; *Paddy – the life and music of Patrick Hadley*, Eric Wetherell; *Hamilton Harty: his Life and his Music*, D Greer; *Gustav Holst – a Biography*, Imogen Holst; *Gustav Holst: The Man and his Music*, M Short; *John*

Ireland: The Man and His Music, M V Searle; *John Ireland: Portrait of a Friend*, J Longmire; *Gordon Jacob*, E Wetherell; *Constant Lambert*, R Shead; *The Music of E J Moeran*, G Self; *Lonely Waters – the diary of a friendship with E J Moeran*, by Lionel Hill; *The Walled-in Garden: The Songs of Roger Quilter*, Trevor Hold; *Rawsthorne*, ed. A Poulton; *My Years of Indiscretion*, Cyril Scott; *The Memoirs of Ethel Smyth*, ed. R Crichton; *Ethel Smyth – a biography*, Christopher St John; *Tippett – the composer and his music*, Ian Kemp; *Those Twentieth Century Blues – an autobiography*, Michael Tippett; *The Works of Ralph Vaughan Williams*, M Kennedy; *William Walton – Behind the Façade*, Susana Walton; *Portrait of Walton*, M Kennedy; *Peter Warlock: a Memoir*, C Gray; *Peter Warlock: A Centenary Celebration*, D Cox and J Bishop; *Capriol for Mother*, Nigel Heseltine.

Reference was also made to articles in *Tempo, Records and Recordings, Composer, Musical Times, Music and Letters, The Monthly Musical Record, Music Review, RCM Magazine*, The *Finzi Trust Friends* Newsletters, and *The Chesterian*. Other valuable sources include *The New Grove Dictionary of Music and Musicians; Contemporary Composers*, ed. B Morton and P Collins; *Greene's Biographical Encyclopedia of Composers*, David Mason Greene; *Music in England 1885-1920*, L Foreman; *British Music of Our Time*, A L Bacharach; *The English Musical Renaissance*, F Howes; *British Composers in Interview*, M Schafer; *British Music Now*, C Palmer and L Foreman; *The Music Makers*, M Trent; *Modern British Composers*, A Frank; *A History of British Music*, P Young; *From Parry to Britten – British Music in Letters 1900-45*, L Foreman; *The Pandora Guide to Women Composers*, Sophie Fuller; and *British Composer Profiles*, Gerald Leach.

Finally, I am especially grateful for the knowledgeable and incisive comments and suggestions made by John Bishop, Eric Wetherell and Norman Humphrys.

Terry Hiscock 1998

Foreword by Brian Kay

THE TITLE of this splendid assembly of thumb-nail sketches comes
from the poem which W H Auden wrote in celebration of the patron saint
of music – words which Benjamin Britten set in his *Hymn to St Cecilia*.
It refers to the immortal fire by which composing mortals are 'startled'
– surprised, perhaps, to find that their names will live on for ever in the
creative work which their Euterpean muse inspired. If an in-depth survey
of the music of these 20th-century British composers is what you want,
then you're looking at the wrong book! What you have here is a brief
glimpse of the man behind the music (or woman, though sadly there are
only six here among nearly ninety!) which should help you to enter more

clearly his musical world, without being bogged down by structural analysis.

Great Britain used to be known throughout Europe as *Das Land ohne Musik* – the land without music. It was not easy for us to raise our heads against competition from the countries which produced the truly great composers of the 18th and 19th centuries. Then along came Elgar (who was born just 30 years after Beethoven died) and helped to rekindle the opportunity for this country once again to be blessed with a musical identity. Several of the composers in this collection have achieved major international status as well as Elgar – Britten, Delius, Grainger (we think of him as English, even though he was born in Australia!), Holst, Tippett, Vaughan Williams, and Walton, for example – and there are dozens of good books about all of those. But it's the so-called minor league that fascinates here.

The good news is that two or three top-ranking record companies have started to record a wealth of previously neglected works by so many of these composers, and I know from the enormous number of requests that I receive for my Sunday Morning Programme on Radio 3 that there's a huge audience for this kind of music – a genuine reawakening of interest in something so vital to our national heritage. The opportunity to throw a little extra light – through these short and simple biographies – on the human beings whose music enriches our lives at every turn is welcome indeed, and should whet the appetite to find out more about these Composing Mortals – the best of British!

Brian Kay

Main entries

Malcolm Arnold

b. 1921

'The idea of writing something "important" fills me with horror.'

We might say that Malcolm Arnold writes music with almost carefree ease, but that would be to deny its essential originality whose character declares itself equally in the symphonies and the lightest occasional pieces. While the former have received critical acclaim, few of his own works make him happier than *The Turtle Drum*, a BBC Schools TV commission which has been performed by children throughout the land. Neither weighed down by the heavy cargo of tradition, nor troubled by notions of musical progress, he once wrote a piece for the Hoffnung Musical Festival involving three vacuum cleaners, one floor polisher, and full orchestra, and later said that he would rather have written *Land of Hope and Glory* than the Bartok string quartets. Yet despite his bluff, nononsense approach to music and life, Arnold is no philistine and has produced works capable of fusing genial high spirits with emotional drama, ambiguity and tension.

He was born in Northampton, where his father was a well-to-do shoe manufacturer. Arnold's parents met through music, their lessons overlapping when they shared the same piano teacher in Northampton. Five children resulted from their eventual marriage, of whom Malcolm was the youngest. The family was a close one, cushioned by relative middle-class affluence thanks to the Arnold family firm, and able to indulge their mutual interests in music. Both parents had a musical background, his mother being a descendant of a former Master of the Chapel Royal, and Malcolm benefited from a variety of musical experiences from an early age. When he was four he took violin lessons

3

from an aunt, then moved to the piano taught by a second aunt. Instead of the expected period at a public school, he was educated privately at home and when it became apparent that the boy had genuine talent, his parents arranged for him to study with the organist of St Matthew's Church in Northampton. Family music-making turned increasingly to jazz, then enjoying a wave of popularity, and coinciding with Arnold's developing interest in the trumpet. He began to explore his sister's jazz records and responded to the music of Django Reinhardt and in particular Louis Armstrong, who left an indelible impression on him. *The Fanfare for Louis* which he wrote nearly forty years later for Armstrong's 70th birthday was only one of many tributes to the musician who had so influenced his childhood and entire musical direction. This enthusiasm for jazz reflected many aspects of Arnold's personality which surface throughout his life: escapism and rebellion, together with a sense of fun, improvisation and freedom to follow his own chosen course.

By the age of 15 he was travelling to London for private lessons from Ernest Hall, one of the most celebrated trumpeters of the day, and in 1937 won an open scholarship to the RCM. Though he profited from Gordon Jacob's teaching on orchestration, he gained little benefit from such formal musical training, and on more than one occasion incurred the displeasure of the College authorities, especially when he once stuffed fish down the organ pipes in the Great Hall. He also wrote an abusive letter to the Principal, Sir George Dyson, derided by many students at the time as being remote and old-fashioned. Dyson, to Arnold's subsequent admiration and gratitude, sent a courteous reply, praising the young trumpeter and imploring him to complete the course. Even so, Arnold was virtually self-taught, and was little influenced by any of the main post-war compositional trends, preferring to go his own way rather than to ally himself with any group of composers.

When the unexpected opportunity arose for him to join the London Philharmonic as second trumpet in 1940, he leapt at the chance, so that before he was even 20 he had joined the ranks of one of the country's great orchestras. Within the year he was promoted to principal, an experience which had a decisive effect upon his own creative work; by placing him as a working musician in the midst of an orchestra, it acquainted him, as no amount of theory could have done, with the quality and personality of all instruments as well as the manipulation and feel of orchestral ensembles. In the years that followed he became known not only as one of the finest orchestral trumpet players in the country, but also consolidated his reputation as a composer, having already won the Cobbett Prize in 1941 for a one-movement string quartet.

At the outbreak of war, Arnold was within six weeks of his 18th birthday and, appalled by the human suffering witnessed during the Spanish Civil War, his inclinations were towards pacifism. When eventually he received his call-up papers he determined to register as a conscientious objector, but within the year he was devastated by the death of his brother Philip, who had joined the RAF and was shot down on a raid over Berlin, so immediately reversed his earlier decision and enlisted. He volunteered for the Buffs and underwent full infantry training, only to suffer the indignity of being placed in the Regimental Band, playing parade-ground marches and selections from Gilbert and Sullivan for the entertainment of officers. By 1944 he had become so disillusioned and embittered by what he saw as a deliberate humiliation that he shot himself through the foot and spent a month in hospital before the army discharged him early in 1945.

For a short time he played second trumpet to his teacher Ernest Hall in the BBC Symphony Orchestra, but returned to the LPO in 1946, where he remained for two more years. He had married in 1941 and, together with his wife and two children, settled first in Richmond. He had been composing privately for a long time but that year the orchestra recorded his overture *Beckus the Dandipratt*, and other compositions were beginning to be noticed and performed by important conductors. Even though the LPO was generous in allowing him time away from orchestral duties to compose, it was becoming obvious that the clash of interests would need to be resolved. As it was, matters were taken out of his hands when he was awarded a Mendelssohn Scholarship which enabled him to travel to Italy, after which he decided to give up orchestral playing for a career as a full-time professional composer.

At first he supported himself largely by writing film music, where his natural ability soon catapulted him to fame and fortune, culminating years later in a string of distinguished scores such as *Whistle Down the Wind*, *The Inn of the Sixth Happiness* and *The Bridge on the River Kwai*, which won Arnold a Hollywood Oscar. He was himself a keen film fan and for the most part learned his trade by writing music for all kinds of short documentaries, but by the mid-fifties he was in great demand for feature films and for nearly twenty years maintained a prodigious output, often working far into the night.

Over the years the demands on his stamina as well as his family and friends were enormous. His first marriage wilted under the strain and ended in divorce, though he quickly married Isobel Gray, who was some twelve years younger than her husband. The couple moved to Cornwall, choosing the village of St Merryn, not far from the seaside town of Padstow, and set up home in Primrose Cottage, where for a while they lived an idyllic life. The place inevitably began to affect his music and the popular *Four Cornish Dances* were completed at the end of 1966, followed by *The Padstow Lifeboat* for brass band, in which the foghorn keeps interrupting the music. Tragically it became apparent that their son born the previous year was autistic – an illness little understood at the time – and the consequences put their marriage under considerable pressure.

In 1972 the family moved to Ireland, settling just outside Dublin at the port of Dun Laoghaire, where he hoped to find more sympathetic support for his son. Having written well over a hundred film scores, he also looked for a fresh start creatively and wrote a number of works exploiting the wider emotional range that had already surfaced in his Cornish pieces. Not for the first time in his life there were tensions which

repeated the pattern of his first marriage, and following his increasing bouts of depression, alcoholism, and an attempted suicide, Isobel left for London, taking their son with her. They were divorced the same year. Arnold also moved to the capital, where he continued to drink heavily until in 1981 he was forced to spend some months at a recuperation centre near his home town of Northampton. When he was finally discharged, he was unable to pick up the threads of his life. Performances and reputation were at a low ebb, recordings ceased altogether, and the death of his close friend William Walton in 1983 increased his depression. He became difficult to deal with, sometimes irrational and often aggressive, so that the loyalty of friends was sorely tried. He became dependent on medication for any degree of stability and his affairs were eventually placed under the jurisdiction of the Court of Protection. At one point his doctors gave him just two years to live.

In 1984 he moved to Norfolk under the care and attention of Anthony Day, a friend of a BBC producer living in Norwich who wanted to make a film about the composer. Day's intention was initially to see Arnold through some sort of rehabilitation period and provide stability in his affairs, but the relationship became permanent and gradually Arnold was able to re-assemble his broken life. Commissions and conducting engagements were still not possible, but slowly performances, recordings and broadcasts of his music began to pick up.

Day also began quietly to encourage Arnold to compose again and in the autumn of 1986 he took up his pen and after tentative beginnings emerged the 9th Symphony. Written with astonishing speed, it captured all that he had suffered and, not surprisingly, was radically different from the composer's previous works. Although greeted with caution by the BBC and his music publishers, the writing evidently marked a turning point and over the next four years he began to accept occasional commissions. A mild heart attack in 1988 set him back, but he was sufficiently recovered to write a Cello Concerto for Julian Lloyd Webber the following year, which also saw the creation of the *Four Welsh Dances* to complement the earlier sets.

With his 70th birthday in 1991 came a sudden spate of interest in the composer and his music, culminating in his knighthood two years later. When asked by his biographer Piers Burton-Page how he wanted to be remembered, Arnold replied quoting Prospero from *The Tempest*:

> *Sounds, and sweet airs, that give delight,*
> *and hurt not ...*

Granville Bantock

1868–1946

'I'd rather reign in Hell than serve in Heaven.'

Born into a prosperous family, Bantock showed no special ability or promise as a boy. He hated the obligatory piano lessons and was destined for a career in the Indian Civil Service until, aged sixteen, he began to attend concerts and discovered the possibility of his artistic expression through music. His father, a distinguished surgeon and gynaecologist, responded by enrolling his eldest son as a chemical engineering student at the City and Guilds Institute in South Kensington. Equally determined, Bantock immersed himself in the music of Liszt and Wagner and although completely untaught began his own first attempts at composition. Only when his total lack of interest at the Institute revealed itself to the Principal did his father, very unwillingly, allow Bantock private lessons in harmony and counterpoint. After three months his determination to follow a musical career won the day and he entered the Royal Academy of Music at the relatively late age of twenty-one.

He soon made up for lost time and throughout his student days poured out a profusion of compositions. Brimming with energy and confidence, Bantock was never one to hold back. Music flowed from his pen in a continuous stream and he remained an extraordinarily prolific composer throughout his life. The most widely held view is that he wrote far too much and that had he reflected more self-critically he might have composed fewer and better works. As it was he wrote large-scale choral music, including an unaccompanied *Symphony for Voices*, one-act operas and the libretti, and embarked on a plan to compose twenty-four

symphonic poems based on Robert Southey's poem *The Curse of Kehame*: all this while still a student. Another feature of Bantock's style which developed early was his preference for programme music. We are told that one of his Academy pieces was an overture about Satan, and after a passage in which the players totally lost their way, the Principal, Sir Alexander Mackenzie, asked the young composer 'Where are we now?' Bantock replied, 'In hell, sir.'

Bantock left the Royal Academy in 1893 and founded and edited the *New Quarterly Musical Review*, which survived for nearly three years. With this came an extensive period of conducting for touring theatrical companies, work which led to an offer to accompany George Edwardes's operetta *The Gaiety Girl* on a world tour. On his return, he organised a London concert of orchestral music by living English composers. It was a financial disaster but emphasised, not for the first time, Bantock's characteristic generosity and interest in supporting the music of others.

By 1897, Bantock had accepted many theatrical engagements, most of them short-lived, but about to be married he was anxious to secure a more permanent position. The opportunity came six months after he had answered a chance advertisement and he was appointed Musical Director of the New Brighton Tower Pleasure Gardens near Liverpool. This was not as grand as it sounded. It involved conducting an open-air military band and an indoor ballroom orchestra. The new Director, however, was a man with a vision. Within a short time, Bantock's energy and optimism transformed the quality and musical direction of New Brighton and he soon assembled a full orchestra giving regular Sunday concerts. It was not long before the unsuspecting couples dancing during the afternoons in the Tower ballroom found themselves waltzing to the music of Beethoven, Dvořák, Liszt and Brahms. Encouraged by the warm response of musicians and the public, Bantock went further and invited contemporary composers to Liverpool to conduct their own works. Parry, Stanford, Sibelius and Elgar all stayed at the Director's modest house in

Liscard. Meanwhile, Bantock still found time to create a successful choral society and, of course, to continue to write his own music.

In September 1900 the composer was offered a choice of two better positions: one was on the staff of the Royal Academy; the other was that of Principal of the new Birmingham and Midland Institute School of Music. He decided on the latter since it gave him the opportunity to generate a focal point for musical training in the Midlands. It was an appointment that was to have a lasting effect on his career and on music in Birmingham. He set to work at once to form an orchestra and under his ambitious leadership achieved his aim. In 1908 he also succeeded Elgar as Professor of Music at Birmingham University, a post he held until his retirement twenty-six years later.

Bantock's life during this period was extremely busy. He undertook conducting tours both at home and abroad; was in great demand as an adjudicator at music festivals; wrote an enormous number of test pieces, not only for choirs but also for solo singers and instrumentalists; and when not lecturing and composing still wrote long letters to his wide circle of friends. Only a man with huge reserves of energy could have coped with so much and yet retained such enthusiasm and drive. Of the many photographs taken of Bantock during his long life (he was not shy of cameras), few give any hint of this immense vitality. Though not a tall man he was heavily built with a thick mane of hair and an imposing beard which gave him a rather fierce expression. As a young man he did indeed exhibit an explosive temper but he is remembered mostly for his generosity and dedication to promoting the works of other composers.

Other pictures, which depict Bantock dressed in oriental costumes or bardic robes, reveal his taste for the exotic, or pseudo-exotic. His house was decorated with numerous Japanese prints and curios, and once, after visiting a Trappist monastery, he insisted that his family eat out of wooden bowls with spoons. His passion for everything oriental can be traced back to his early years, although it was the florid surface associated with Fitzgerald's loose translation of Omar Khayyam which attracted him, rather than the subtleties of Eastern life and philosophy. More fruitful inspiration was found during his 'Hebridean' phase encouraged by the folksongs collected and translated by Margery Kennedy-Fraser, who provided him with a libretto for his 1924 opera *The Seal Woman*. As an aside, Bantock seems to have been attracted to the female singer in the title role and accompanied her on a tour of America which lasted for over a year. Not surprisingly, this put a strain on his marriage from which it never fully recovered.

Bantock received a knighthood from George V in 1930 and retired from Birmingham four years later. His music, once widely performed, was now out of fashion, but he continued to write a prodigious amount of orchestral works, choral compositions and songs with almost indiscriminate ease. Aged 65, he might have looked forward to a well-earned retirement, but instead he joined the staff of Trinity College in London and threw himself into touring and lecturing. Despite being a heavy cigar smoker, Bantock was seldom ill and continued to travel widely until the outbreak of war, when he took up lodgings in Gloucester Road. He and his wife survived the bombing of London, sleeping on campbeds under the stairs, and regaling neighbours and friends with stories from *The Arabian Nights* during air raids.

In 1946, after a brief illness, Bantock was taken to hospital for an operation but fell, breaking his femur, and shortly after died of pneumonia.In a last extravagant gesture, his ashes were scattered to the winds from the top of a Welsh mountain by his sons. Under his bed was one of his small music notebooks which included an outline for yet another new work – a ballet, this time entitled *The White Unicorn*. Five days later, Eugene Goossens conducted the *Hebridean Symphony* at the town hall in Birmingham, a fitting tribute to a man who played a key part in re-establishing a tradition of British music at the turn of the century.

Arnold Bax

1883–1953

*'I'm not sure that middle-aged and unquestionably virtuous virgins
ought to play my music.'*

Fate decreed that Arnold Bax be born in Streatham to cultured and
wealthy middle-class parents, but if wishing could have made it so he
would have been born and raised in West Donegal, his spiritual haven
and musical inspiration for much of his life.

The Bax family, three boys and a sister, moved to a large, rambling
house set in almost park-like grounds in Hampstead when Arnold, the
eldest, was just ten. Ivy Bank, as it was called, was to be of great
importance to the development of Arnold and his literary brother,
Clifford. Alfred Bax, who ran a mundane but profitable business
manufacturing Mackintosh raincoats, was a mild-tempered father who
remained aloof from the running of his extensive household. He left all
domestic matters to his vivacious and determined wife, Charlotte Ellen,
sixteen years his junior, who exercised a powerful maternal influence
over her young family. In the relaxed atmosphere of Ivy Bank, its
extensive lawns and gardens, the children enjoyed an almost idyllic
childhood. Schooling was intermittent, their formal education provided
more or less by a private tutor, Francis Colmer, who readily forsook the
routine of Latin conjugations for a game of cricket on the lawn. His
sympathetic and lax regime, combined with the indulgence of their
mother, allowed the boys full scope for their creative energies. So it was
that Arnold turned gradually to music.

He had no formal musical education before 1898, but possessed an
uncanny ability to sight-read and by his mid-teens was beginning to

compose. One day, while recuperating from sunstroke inflicted by a long spell at the wicket, Arnold wrote a Sonata in two movements for piano, and Alfred Bax was prompted to send his son to the Hampstead Conservatoire, then under the direction of Cecil Sharp.When his musical interests showed no signs of abating, Alfred decided to take further advice and arranged an interview with the organist and composer Sir Frederick Bridge. Bax recalled the event in his autobiography *Farewell, my Youth*, describing their meeting as rather like an interview with a Harley Street specialist: 'Do you assure me, Sir Frederick, that my son really has this musical taint in his system?' 'I fear that I cannot hide from you, sir, that such is indeed the case. That will be three guineas, thank you, and mind the step.' Two years later, aged seventeen, Arnold entered the Royal Academy of Music.

Encouraged by the relaxed atmosphere at the Academy, Bax was supremely happy and immersed himself in all that the musical world of the day had to offer. He wrote a string of youthful works, quickly achieving an enviable piano technique, and emerged as a composer with an individual mastery of the orchestra. Yet in many ways he was still only a talented amateur. Financially secure, he only wrote or played when the mood suited him, and was content just to enjoy the easy life of the wealthy middle-class to which he belonged.

At nineteen, opening a volume of poetry during a dull afternoon, he stumbled upon Yeats's *The Wanderings of Oisin* and the imagination caught fire. 'The Celt within me stood revealed,' he wrote later. The discovery of Yeats was followed by visits to Ireland, where he ventured beyond the intellectual society of Dublin to the remote corners of ancient Donegal and the windswept Atlantic seaboard. There, in the village of Glencolumcille, Bax revelled in the savage gales and dramatic coastline while endearing himself to the locals, much in the same way as Moeran was to do after 1918 in Kenmare. The impact of Ireland was recorded first in notebooks before emerging in verse and prose written under the name of 'Dermot O'Byrne'. Influenced by this so-called Celtic Twilight,

Bax's music immediately found direction. In the summer of 1905 he left the Academy and turned to Ireland, from where he was to mould his mature style. A succession of scores flowed from rather inferior upright pianos in various pubs and lodgings where Bax would compose oblivious to his surroundings.

In 1909, while staying with friends in Swiss Cottage, London, Bax was introduced to a young Russian girl, Natalia Skarginski, and not for the first time embarked upon a passionate love affair which took him on a hastily arranged journey to Russia. The relationship was one-sided, however, and when Natalia announced her engagement to another, Bax returned to England, bruised in spirit but having absorbed important musical influences to complement Ireland. Awaiting him was the news that the family had decided to leave Ivy Bank to take a house in Cavendish Square. His great friend, Godfrey Baynes, was also engaged, and Clifford had made an impulsive marriage, leaving Bax without the stability of the family home or the immediate company of his closest companions. He turned instead to Elsita Sobrino, an attractive and generous natured girl whom he had met through family friends at the Hampstead Conservatoire. Events moved quickly and, perhaps on the rebound from his Russian experience, a wedding was arranged and the couple moved to a handsome house in Regents Park.

Within a few months they had moved to Dublin, where they set up home and Dermot and Maeve were born. In between periods of apparently happy domesticity, however, Arnold preferred a bachelor existence and took to going off with friends to Donegal. He could not settle to the routines and pressures of married life and his nomadic inclination, complicated by a growing affection for the young pianist Harriet Cohen, was to invite disaster. In the end, he and Elsita agreed to separate, she moving to Golders Green with the children, while Arnold took rooms in Hampstead and threw himself into his work.

For other young composers of his generation (Bax was 31 in 1914) the war interrupted the emerging English musical renaissance which had been gathering momentum for over a decade. While many put aside their pens and enlisted, Bax wrestled with his conscience. He was undecided whether to enter the army or, as he confided to a friend, to 'plunge into a narcotic ocean of creative work.' In the opening months of the war, Bax certainly did not identify with the conflict. Instead, he devoted himself to composition and within days of the outbreak of war had written the first of a number of works dedicated to Harriet Cohen.

In 1916 he received his call-up papers, but succeeded in establishing his unfitness for military service and continued to lead a fairly normal life untroubled by events in France. He was thus able to spend the war, as indeed he spent most of his life, doing exactly what he wanted to do. Meanwhile his attraction to Harriet was undimmed and she took precedence over everybody and everything. During the summer and autumn of 1917 he wrote two orchestral poems, *Summer Music* and *Tintagel*, followed by *November Woods*, which reflect the rival claims of domestic responsibility and romantic passion. A year later the war ended and Bax, now free from the restraints of marriage, seized the opportunity to establish himself with the large body of music written during the war years. By 1920 the composer was regarded as a figure of national stature on the musical scene.

The social round continued with endless weekends and parties which found Harriet in her element. She was his constant companion and her infectious enthusiasm for causes and people drew around the couple many diverse and interesting personalities of the day. Bax himself spent a good deal of time with the younger composers who emerged after the war: EJ Moeran in particular became a close friend. Although Ireland fascinated Bax for the rest of his life, he was now diverting his energies into other paths which were opening up for him, and for a brief period in the early 1920s he was at the height of his powers, regarded as one of the great British musical figures of the age. After this, although he was still to produce his seven symphonies, he gradually ceased to enjoy the serenity that had followed his separation from Elsita. The reason appears

to have been his deteriorating relationship with Harriet. She was becoming possessive and attempted to dominate his music as well as his
friendship with other musicians. In 1925 he escaped for a while with
Heseltine (Peter Warlock) and Moeran at their cottage in Eynsford, Kent,
and enjoyed the best and the worst of their company. The period of his
stay was musically very productive, but also introduced him to alcohol
on more than a social scale. During the 1930s and '40s Bax drank
increasingly and his growing intake of whiskey undoubtedly had much
to do with the considerable physical change he underwent during his last
twenty years.

Around this time Bax developed a close friendship with Mary Gleaves, a twenty-three-year-old girl, which quickly deepened into a real and lasting affair. Harriet remained his public companion, but was unaware of Mary's existence until 1948 – a remarkably kept secret. Her reaction to the news is to be imagined. In 1930, Bax started to make regular visits to Morar on the west coast of Scotland. Established at the Station Hotel, he recalled in his autobiography sitting 'in a dingy, unheated room, working in an overcoat', orchestrating works previously sketched out in London. As the decade progressed, he travelled more often and more widely, writing constantly to Mary when they were apart. In fact he was now writing more letters than music. He harboured an almost pathological dread of turning fifty and by 1935 there was a gradual waning of public and critical interest in his music. Curiously for one who always shrank from the limelight, Bax was nevertheless knighted in 1937 and just four years later accepted the invitation to succeed Walford Davies as Master of the King's Musick.

One weekend in the early days of the war, Bax went for a brief rest to the White Horse Hotel in Storrington, a small village in Sussex, and remained there for the rest of his life. Music began to play a less prominent role (he once said he had as much right to retire as a grocer), and he enjoyed a leisurely existence reading detective novels, drinking with the locals, presiding over the village cricket club and, every day, doing *The Times* crossword. It was during this last period of his life, however, that he wrote the music for the 1942 film *Malta GC* and the 1948 version of *Oliver Twist*. (When asked by Laurence Olivier if he was upset by the combination of dialogue and music, Bax replied 'Yes, I jolly well am – chattering all over my music.') It was on trips to Morar with Mary that he wrote his celebrated autobiography referred to earlier, but he was unable to visit Ireland again until after the war. It was while there on holiday in 1953 that he was taken ill and died in Cork quite suddenly of a coronary thrombosis, a month before his 70th birthday.

Lennox Berkeley

1903–1989

'I know quite well I'm a minor composer, and I don't mind that.'

Sir Lennox Berkeley's title is honorary – it was bestowed upon him in 1974 – but he would have inherited an earldom had his father not fallen out with his parents, joined the Royal Navy, and married a Frenchwoman. His childhood was spent near Oxford and thanks to his father's influences enjoyed an early interest in classical music, especially the Beethoven sonatas, which were played via the family's pianola. Despite this, he received little musical guidance and on leaving Gresham's School in Holt, Berkeley went up to Merton College, Oxford, to read philosophy and French literature.

Apart from some organ lessons, he received no formal instruction in music and had shown no outstanding musical abilities at school (though a friend remembers him playing the piano with much flourishing of hands). It was during his years at Oxford that he had several of his compositions performed and eventually decided to make music his career. He showed some of his early attempts at composition to the visiting Ravel, who encouraged him to study with Nadia Boulanger in Paris, and Berkeley spent the next five years developing a style orientated towards French logic, precision and clarity rather than English romanticism or modalism.

Boulanger gave him a thorough professional grounding, at first insisting he did nothing but counterpoint exercises, a discipline which often reduced him to tears at the time, but for which he was to remain grateful all his life. As with many of her pupils, Boulanger showed a real understanding of his talents. In return, Berkeley lost or destroyed most of the music he wrote under her tutelage, but her influence was profound and can be felt in much of his later music. In addition to their lifelong friendship, Berkeley met Stravinsky as well as the leading French composers of the day and formed a close relationship with Poulenc. A further influence reflected in his sacred music was his conversion in 1928 to Roman Catholicism.

In 1936 Berkeley met Benjamin Britten for the first time and they, too, became firm friends, writing a joint composition called the *Mont*

Juic Suite in 1937 and later collaborating in performances for the Aldeburgh Festival, founded after the war. Among the first of his many orchestral works to gain distinctive recognition was the *Serenade* for string orchestra in 1939, followed by other instrumental and piano music, before his move towards vocal music in the 1950s. During the war years he was a music producer under Arthur Bliss at the BBC and it was there that he met his wife, Freda Bernstein, whom he married in 1946. Their son Michael (b.1947) has made a name for himself as a composer and a distinguished broadcaster on music. In the year of his marriage, Berkeley also began twenty-two years of teaching composition at the Royal Academy, retiring in 1968. He was, in the words of one of his pupils, 'too kind' to be a very effective teacher, although he was certainly influential, numbering Nicholas Maw, John Tavener and Richard Rodney Bennett among his more successful students.

In the 1940s and '50s he turned out several stage, film and radio scores, and the first of his four operas, *Nelson*, was produced by Sadler's Wells in 1954. Britten produced two of the others at Aldeburgh: the one-act comedy *A Dinner Engagement* and *Castaway* in 1967. By this time, Berkeley had moved away from clear tonality towards more dissonant harmony, although his compositions usually preserved a tonal point of reference. Recognition and honours were received in his later years, including a knighthood in 1974, the year he became honorary professor of the new department of music at Keele University. Until succumbing to Alzheimer's disease in the early 1980s, Berkeley produced a succession of works which won him many friends and admirers. He was modest about his compositions, but if the history of 20th-century music has not been greatly affected by Berkeley, without him it would have been immeasurably poorer. He died in west London on Boxing Day 1989.

Lord Berners

1883–1950

'But praise the Lord
He seldom was bored.'
– Berners

Gerald Tyrwhitt was the only child of a younger son of an ancient Shropshire family which could be traced back to Edward III. He was educated at Eton, where he was nicknamed 'the Newt' by his peers, and understandably disliked the place except for its setting and the opportunities to broaden his mind. After graduating he studied art and languages in Europe and gained some musical instruction in Dresden. Later he had a few lessons with Vaughan Williams and received advice and encouragement from Casella and Stravinsky, though as a composer he was mainly self-taught.

In 1909 he was appointed honorary cultural attache to the British Embassy in Constantinople, moving to a similar post in Rome two years later. His first compositions of note were written there – a set of piano pieces, including funeral marches for a statesman, a canary, and a rich aunt, and a setting of Heine's *Du bist wie eine Blume* (Thou art so like a flower), a sentiment apparently addressed to a white pig, which Berners underscored with a series of intermittent grunts. Despite the influence of impressionism, there is nothing vague or merely atmospheric about this music, which is economical and direct and provides a good example of the satirical vein frequently found in Berners's compositions. He published these works under the name of Gerald Tyrwhitt, but in 1919 he succeeded his uncle as the 14th Baron Berners and 5th Baronet, and legally added 'Wilson' to his surname.

Along with his titles, he inherited a great deal of money and several estates. He made his home at Faringdon, near Oxford, and lived the life of an eccentric English gentleman, dividing his time between his country house in Berkshire and residences in London and Rome, amusing friends and disconcerting strangers with whimsical practical jokes. He put jewelled collars on the dogs, kept birds-of-paradise on his lawns, and had the doves dyed in assorted colours. His house reflected the frivolous mood of the 1920s and eccentricities were not only tolerated, but actively encouraged. A slight, bald figure with a tidy moustache, Berners was inclined to travel either in a small car of uncertain origin, or in a Rolls-Royce equipped with a spinet, sometimes wearing a mask on the back of his head, to the disquiet of following drivers. But whatever the strange excesses of his way of life, he took considerable pains over his music. To call him an amateur is correct in the sense that he did not make music his profession, and certainly he favoured parody and satirical subjects, but his art was disciplined and carefully crafted.

After writing some more songs and piano pieces, Berners was ready for a larger canvas and in 1924 his only opera, *Le Carrosse du Saint Sacremont*, was produced in Paris; but it was his ballet *The Triumph of Neptune*, composed two years later for Diaghilev, which secured his reputation. Based on the scenery and costumes sold for toy-theatre productions at Benjamin Pollock's shop in London, the characters ranged from the Fairy Queen to newspaper boys: fantasy, harlequinade, and nautical jollity are all there. In its sweep of imagination and expression, this was Berners's most successful work and was followed in 1930 by another ballet, *Luna Park*, which portrays an exhibition of freaks. The following year he held an exhibition of his own, this time of paintings, and between 1936 and 1945 he published six novels and two volumes of autobiography. On top of this he was also a renowned cook. In 1935, ignoring loud protests from his neighbours, he built a 140-foot tower on a hilltop which became known as the Faringdon Folly. A notice placed at the entrance warned would-be suicides that they jumped at their own risk.

In the 1940s, Berners turned to film scores, writing *Halfway House* in 1944 and *Nicholas Nickleby* in 1947. During his last few years he suffered poor health and wrote his own epitaph:

> *Here lies Lord Berners*
> *One of the learners*
> *His great love of learning*
> *May earn him a burning*
> *But praise to the Lord*
> *He seldom was bored.*

Though the general musical public were inclined to dismiss him as a self-indulgent dilettante, musicians and discerning critics recognised his unique talent for parody and his meticulous craftsmanship. He was certainly never boring. In *Who's Who* Berners recorded: '*Recreation: none*'. This was quite true, for though he was extremely self-critical and discarded much of his work, hardly a moment passed when he was not either composing, painting, or writing. Notorious in his day for his peculiar behaviour ('a superb instance of *real* eccentricity' as Edith Sitwell noted), he was also shy, and a man of very few words. He never made a public speech in his life, except for the three short sentences with which he opened the Faringdon cinema.

In his later years he dropped completely from public view. His autobiographies reveal that despite a sharp wit he could also be a serious, sometimes sad, man. John Betjeman once remarked of him: 'Like anybody very cheerful, he was also very gloomy, and we who had the privilege of knowing him can remember how sad it was when he just turned his face to the wall and died – died, I think, because he felt there was nothing more he could do.'

Arthur Bliss

1891–1975

*'Will Mr Bliss be able to say something when he has really got
something to say, or is he becoming a fashionable joker?'*
– The Times

Arthur Bliss began his career as a composer by being dismissed as hopelessly *avant-garde* by the musical establishment and ended up being dismissed by the *avant-garde* as hopelessly conventional. Neither view presents an entirely accurate picture of the composer's contribution to British music in the 20th century.

His father, an American of means and taste, had moved from Massachusetts to London, where Bliss was born in August, 1891. His mother, Agnes, was by all accounts an excellent amateur pianist, but her musical talent probably had little impact on her son since she died when he was four, leaving him with two young brothers, Kennard and Howard. Father and sons moved to a spacious house in Holland Park, London, which remained their home for the next twenty-seven years. As a child, Bliss showed no special promise in terms of musical ability. Until the age of eight, he went to school in Bayswater and then to Bilton Grange preparatory school near Rugby, where his music teacher introduced him to the Beethoven Sonatas. He had previously taken piano lessons for some years but gradually recognised his limitations and abandoned dreams of a career on the concert platform.

At thirteen he duly went on to Rugby, where he took up the viola and wrote a quartet for piano, clarinet, cello and timpani whose première before a small invited audience was received with great hilarity. He fared better at Cambridge, studying counterpoint with Charles Wood before entering the Royal College of Music in 1913. There he became a close friend of Herbert Howells, Eugene Goossens and Arthur Benjamin, though Ivor Gurney resisted his attempts to strike up a conversation. When Stanford wrote across an early Bliss manuscript: 'He who cannot write anything beautiful falls back on the bizarre,' their association was hardly likely to flourish.

When war broke out the following year, Bliss volunteered immediately and was in France for much of the time as an officer on active duty. In July 1916 he was wounded in the leg during the Somme offensive and returned to England to convalesce. His brother, Kennard, was less fortunate and died of shrapnel wounds in the September. After a spell as an army instructor, Bliss obtained a commission in the Grenadier Guards and returned to France, only to be gassed at Cambrai shortly before the Armistice. His injuries were not serious and early in 1919 he was released from the army. During the war years he had managed to write a string quartet and other chamber works. Though they were well received and privately published, he later disowned them and destroyed the engraved plates.

Bliss's real composing career began with a group of works written soon after the war. He received a commission for incidental music for a production of *As You Like It* at the Lyric Theatre, Hammersmith, after which he obtained permission to use the theatre for a series of concerts featuring contemporary British music by Howells, Bantock and Ireland among others. But it was the London premières of three experimental pieces for voice and chamber ensembles in 1920 – *Madam Noy*, *Rhapsody* and *Rout* – which earned Bliss the reputation of an 'enfant terrible'. This was somewhat enhanced by his celebrated storm music for a production of *The Tempest* at the Aldwych Theatre the following year (percussionists were dispersed throughout the auditorium, which kept the audience on their toes). During this time, Bliss continued to develop his experience as a conductor and at one point inherited the Portsmouth Philharmonic from Adrian Boult.

In 1922, at Elgar's suggestion, he was asked to write a work for the Three Choirs Festival. Given the opportunity to write a more ambitious piece, he lighted upon a book on heraldry which gave the symbolic meanings associated with the primary colours. The result was the *Colour Symphony*, certainly a far more romantic composition than its immediate predecessors. The first performance in Gloucester Cathedral that autumn under the composer's baton was, however, disappointing since the platform was too small to accommodate the full orchestra and several essential instruments had to be omitted. The work was well received, nevertheless, and brought the name of Bliss to a wider public.

In 1923 his father, now re-married, decided to return to his homeland, and Bliss moved with them to Santa Barbara. He wrote little music during the two years he spent in America, but continued to conduct and lecture and became the pianist of a chamber ensemble. He also tried his hand at acting and played opposite twenty-year-old Trudy Hoffman, with whom he fell in love and married in the late spring of 1925. The couple returned afterwards to London, where their daughters were born in 1926 and 1930, and Bliss once more engaged in composition, writing for commissions as well as his own oratorio-symphony *Morning Heroes*, dedicated to those killed in the Great War and in memory of his brother Kennard.

Although he travelled a good deal, both in Europe and America, in 1933 he built a home in Penselwood, Somerset, overlooking Salisbury Plain, to which the family could escape from London in the spring and summer. A year later, Bliss moved into a new domain when he was invited by the film producer, Alexander Korda, to collaborate with H G Wells on a projected film of the author's book *The Shape of Things to Come*. Bliss stated that he always found it easier to write 'dramatic' rather than 'pure' music, so it was no surprise that he was drawn to theatre and film music along with Vaughan Williams, Walton, Alwyn, Arnold and many others. Further examples of this inclination are found in ballet and opera scores including *Checkmate* (1937) and *The Olympians* (1949).

Bliss was in America when war broke out in 1939 and with the help of friends there found employment teaching at Berkeley. Within two years the burden of work and the stress of divided loyalties became intolerable and he returned to England via a dangerous voyage on a Fyffe's banana boat. Once in London he took an administrative job with the BBC, where he was appointed Music Director in 1942. During his time there, he once proposed three separate channels to cater for the differing interests of listeners and was thus partly responsible for the introduction of the Third Programme. With astonishing foresight, he also predicted a popular radio station dominated by 'a continual stream of noise and nonsense put on by untouchables with the use of records.'

Meanwhile, his wife and daughters battled against regulations and travel difficulties before finally sailing from Philadelphia in 1943 to join the composer at his flat in Cavendish Square. He continued to work at the BBC for a further six months, but resigned in order to escape the drudgery of administrative chores and to resume his own work. By this time he was already contemplating his first opera, *The Olympians*, with libretto by JB Priestley, which was eventually produced at Covent Garden in the autumn of 1949. Through no fault of either composer or writer the work was under-rehearsed, and relations between the producer, Peter Brook, and the conductor, Karl Rankl, deteriorated to the point where they were unable to speak to each other. The performance received a cool reception. By way of slight compensation, Bliss was knighted the following year and in 1953 succeeded Arnold Bax as Master of the Queen's Musick.

Thereafter, Bliss undertook many and various commissions, fulfilling the appointment's musical and official duties with the energetic professionalism which marked his whole career. Even then there were disappointments reminiscent of earlier premières when his contribution to the opening of the new Cathedral at Coventry had to be performed in a nearby theatre as the Cathedral itself was scheduled for other events – a Hammond organ was a poor substitute for the Cathedral organ and once again the stage could not contain the whole orchestra and chorus. Other commissions were more favourably performed, notably *Meditations on a Theme by John Blow* written for the City of Birmingham Symphony Orchestra. He was later to claim: 'If I were to be asked for a few works that might represent my life's music, this would certainly be one of them.' Other orchestral works include concertos for piano and violin; his cello concerto was first performed at the Aldeburgh Festival in 1970, where it was conducted by Britten. Bliss said of the work 'There are no problems for the listener, only the soloist.'

Bliss continued to travel widely and to conduct, and was still composing after his 80th birthday. His last compositions, choral works and a *Wedding Suite* for piano, were written just the year before he died.

Rutland Boughton

1878–1960

'We are dreamers, that is inevitable,
but without dreams nothing can be done.' – Boughton

Boughton began life inauspiciously as the eldest son of a modest Buckinghamshire grocer. The three children were brought up in such comfort as the family could afford and after a brief spell at a small Dame School run by two old ladies, Rutland (pronounced 'Rootland') was sent to Aylesbury Grammar School. Despite its name, the school was a simple one and provided little by way of academic learning, so right from the beginning Rutland may be said to have been self-educated. When he was old enough he became a choirboy at the local parish church, but his first actual lessons came from two girl cousins who taught him to play on the piano which his mother had struggled to buy.

Throughout his childhood it was she who encouraged his obvious gifts, and began his interest in composing by giving him a small manuscript book in which her father had written a few anthems and hymns of his own. The blank pages at the end were a magnet to the boy's musical imagination and it was not long before he rehearsed his own orchestra in his mother's kitchen: a harmonium and violin played by the two cousins, a host of school friends on penny whistles and home-made zithers, a small choir of very mixed voices, and Boughton himself as conductor. At the age of twelve he was awarded a volume of Shakespeare's plays as a school prize which aroused an immediate response and he was soon scribbling away at music for the witches in *Macbeth*. Soon after he devised a cycle of music dramas on the life of

Christ which anticipated the Arthurian dramas that were to be his life's work and his unique contribution to English music.

His education at the local school ended when he was fourteen and he became a London apprentice to the Cecil Barth Concert Agency, which promoted concert parties and brass bands. His employer was a generous and good-natured man who soon discovered that the new office boy had musical talent and arranged for him to have piano lessons, even paying to have one of his songs published. It was his first published work and he proudly dedicated it to his mother. By 1898 he had written a good deal of music and eventually caught the ear of Stanford, who decided the boy had potential and persuaded the MP for Aylesbury to fund a brief period of study at the Royal College. For all his surface confidence, Boughton was painfully shy when it came to mixing with others. He looked at his contemporaries, Ireland, Bridge, Holst and Vaughan Williams, and considered his own rudimentary education and working-class background. Guided by Edgar Bainton, his one close friend at the time, Boughton started on the process of self-education that was to last throughout his life. His feelings of inadequacy and lack of privilege made him a difficult pupil and when the money set aside for his studies was used up, he struck out on his own to make a living as a musician in London.

The next few years were among the most difficult of his whole life. He moved into cheap lodgings in Harrow and lived for a time on the edge of starvation before applying for a post as music critic for the *Daily Mail*. Having no presentable clothes to wear for the interview, he wore only things he could get hold of – a pair of white flannels and a white shirt, deceiving the editor into thinking he had come straight from the tennis court without time to change. He got the job but within a short time of joining the paper he came up against a problem that was to recur throughout his life. He discovered that he was expected to compromise his own ideals in order to comply with the expectations of his employers. He found this completely repugnant and ultimately impossible to accept. Sacked from the *Mail* he found work as a conductor and accompanist and, prompted by discussions and arguments that went on in the orchestra, he turned increasingly to politics and embraced the socialist ideal. It is not surprising that he should have turned in this direction since he had certainly experienced poverty and had felt the lack of privilege, but it was a conviction prompted more by his reading of Whitman, Morris and Ruskin than with any Marxist doctrine. It nevertheless played a crucial part in his own development and career as a composer.

In 1903 he made a disastrous marriage to a neighbour's daughter, Florence Hobley, in a naive attempt to protect the unfortunate girl from her drunken parents, and in doing so condemned himself to more years with the pit orchestra in order to support her. Help arrived after a chance encounter with Granville Bantock, who offered him a post at his Midland Institute of Music in Birmingham, where he remained until 1911, working as a singing teacher, conductor and composer of choral and orchestral music. He found the work stimulating and enjoyable and his pupils responded enthusiastically. His conducting eventually led to choral writing and there followed a series of works that helped to establish his reputation as a composer of importance. Chief among these was his cycle of music dramas on Wagnerian lines depicting the Arthurian Legends.

Less grandly, but closer to home, his marriage had begun to sour, Florence having no interests of her own and incapable of sharing her husband's. Boughton, in the meantime, had turned to a young art student, Christina Walshe, for company and support and when forced to choose between them, unhesitatingly declared his love for Christina. The idea of an open relationship outside marriage was hardly popular in 1911 and the scandal drove him to resign his post and return to London, where he was joined by Christina and his three children.

At first things were very difficult and they existed on the borderline of starvation until Bernard Shaw, with whom Boughton had earlier corresponded, found him a position with the *Daily Citizen*. Boughton continued to compose, immersing himself in a setting of Fiona Macleod's strange Celtic play *The Immortal Hour*, which he intended to perform with amateur singers in a wood by the light of the harvest moon. In the event, the moon rose before he could finish the orchestration, so the scheme for that year was abandoned, but the idea had fired Boughton's imagination and he announced plans for a festival to take place at Glastonbury in 1913. The principal work would be the first performance of *The Birth of Arthur* and the Festival Committee set about preparing for the occasion. When rumours of his relationship with Christina surfaced, however, local support was withdrawn and Boughton was forced to postpone everything for a year.

It was difficult for anyone to resist his infectious vitality and obvious sincerity for long, and the first Glastonbury Festival began at 8 pm on August 5th, with the war that overshadowed it less than twenty-four hours old. The practical difficulties of financing and organising a series of such festivals soon modified Boughton's schemes, and Wagnerian grandeur gave way to something much simpler. The Glastonbury Assembly Rooms did their best to fit the occasion, but could only seat 200 people, with no room for a conductor's baton, let alone an orchestra. Boughton was undaunted. It was this ability to turn each difficulty to his own advantage which set him apart from mere dreamers, and the first festival achieved a modest success. More importantly it provided invaluable experience and, except for a brief interruption during Boughton's military service, festivals were given several times each year until 1926. They included some 350 staged performances, with six full-scale operas by Boughton himself, together with more than 100 chamber concerts, and in 1915 he performed a setting of the nativity play which he called *Bethlehem*. The following year he received his call-up papers and spent three wholly unsatisfactory years in the army before returning to Glastonbury, where he threw himself into festival work. Once again he was tireless, carrying everybody else on the tide of his own energy and enthusiasm.

Meanwhile, a London producer had overcome Boughton's reservations about selling out to capitalistic interests and staged *The Immortal Hour* at the Regent Theatre in October 1922. To everyone's amazement its first run, of 216 performances, broke the record for any serious English opera and over the next few years was performed more than a thousand times throughout England. Despite this success, Boughton was busy digging his own grave. An affair with one of his students, Kathleen Davies, with whom he openly set up house in 1923, added fuel to the fire already ignited by his communist stance in the press, and when he tried to involve the Festival company in actively supporting the 1926 General Strike, he effectively brought to an end any further association with Glastonbury.

Never one to compromise, Boughton severed all ties with the Festival and moved to a small farm at Kilcot, a village on the borders of Gloucester and Herefordshire. Here he remained with Kathleen and his eight children for the rest of his life, earning a small living from his farm and writing critical articles. His main activity was still composition, often working far into the night, and in 1945 he completed his Arthurian cycle. Boughton remained politically active as a member of the Communist Party and continued to make unnecessary enemies, which frustrated attempts to have his music performed. In 1937, Bernard Shaw and others succeeded in obtaining for him a small regular income through the Civil List which he grudgingly accepted, although later acknowledged the debt he owed to the tolerance and generosity of his many friends. He lived another twenty-three years, a militant communist to the last, and died in his sleep two nights after his eighty-second birthday.

Havergal Brian

1876–1972

*'I care for nobody, no, not I,
and nobody cares for me.'
– from The Miller of Dee*

It will be for audiences in the 21st century to decide if Havergal Brian was a significant figure in the resurgence of British music, or, as he is generally regarded today, an interesting eccentric standing in the outer circle of those composers whose work is rarely performed or listened to. Were it not for fellow composer Robert Simpson, Brian may well have faded into complete obscurity; instead, his music is now being recorded and may well find new audiences in the future.

William Brian was born in the village of Dresden, Staffordshire, in January 1876. He was the eldest surviving child of seven children, four having died in infancy. Benjamin Brian, a twenty-four-year-old worker in 'the pots', and his young wife, Martha, gave their son no other name. 'Havergal' was one William adopted in his late teens (probably from a family of Worcestershire hymn-writers) – it had a more artistic ring than 'Billy', as he was generally called. Billy attended the village school until 1886, when he was old enough to attend St James's Elementary School at nearby Longton. His conversations and letters frequently recalled his happy childhood, and the close relationship with his father in particular. Benjamin Brian was an independent man who lived life his own way, and William took after him. Despite the cramped conditions of the small terraced house in Ricardo Street, it was a warm and secure family home: working-class, certainly, though more culturally inclined than most.

One of Brian's earliest recollections was following a brass band in which his father played, but it was at St James's that his musical life

36

began in earnest. The school enjoyed a considerable reputation in the county and its schoolmaster, James Smith, lit up the lives of his pupils with music. Brian loved singing. Both his parents sang in the Dresden choir and took him to music evenings on Saturdays, so within a few months he became a member of the St James's church choir, and soon after that, a soloist. Brian's father was a cautious man, anxious for his son to have a secure job behind him, but he also believed in nurturing talent in his children and found from somewhere the fees and rail fares for William to take violin lessons in Fenton. Organ and cello lessons followed and Brian became set in his own mind upon a life in which music would predominate over everything and everybody.

As far as his parents were concerned, however, a musical career was out of the question. People from terraced houses in little Midland towns did not earn a living from composing music. Faced with their insistence that he should seek a practical job, William, aged twelve and a half, accepted work at a colliery, weighing coal trucks as they arrived loaded from the pit. He hated it. It was the first of many such jobs, but the music always intervened in some way, and he was asked to leave. By the time he was sixteen, Brian had been appointed organist at Holy Trinity Church and from then until his late twenties he was a member of one local orchestra or another, attending concerts, parties and balls, getting to know a lot of girls, and having one of the happiest times of his life.

In 1896, Brian encountered his first piece of music by Elgar, the cantata *King Olaf*, being rehearsed at Stoke-on-Trent town hall. It was one of the cornerstones of his musical development. He wrote to Elgar, enclosing an anthem he had composed and asking for Elgar's advice on the best way to receive musical training. Elgar's reply was guarded but encouraging: the anthem was original, if somewhat convoluted, but keep on writing. As for tuition, Elgar could offer no guidance – he had had to do without it. In fact, this was inspirational advice to Brian, knowing that a formal musical education was beyond his family's means, and gave him the courage of his convictions to go on with music in his own way.

Brian was fortunate in that the Staffordshire Potteries provided a rich musical heritage. Brass bands, amateur orchestras, choral societies and visiting shows were within easy reach, and on Thursdays, Brian skipped work and travelled to Manchester to hear the Hallé Orchestra play works by his idols, Wagner and Richard Strauss. There was plenty of music to be heard for those interested and able to afford it. By this time his means had improved: working for a local timber merchant, writing critical reviews for the newly-revived *Musical World*, and continuing his post as organist, now at Odd Rode Parish Church. Brian was a busy man, but a happy one.

When he was twenty-two, he met Isabel Priestly, a local teacher, and married her the next year when she was three months pregnant with the first of their five children. They moved into 11 Gordon Street and for a while all appeared to go well. Increasingly, he took time off work to concentrate on his music which was attracting attention, not only in Stoke but further afield. Elgar extended a warm and influential offer of support, and Bantock became an admirer and close friend for the rest of his life. As a man earmarked for higher things, Bantock's support was supremely important to an unknown composer from a small provincial town. He took Brian everywhere and with the confidence of Bantock's considerable presence and prestige, Brian's own circle of influential friends widened.

It was not surprising, then, that the year 1907 brought a rapid increase in Brian's popularity. It saw the first performance of three important works, including his *First English Suite*, at Queen's Hall, conducted by Henry Wood, which was well received. Even non-concert goers in the Potteries were by now aware that they had among them a most promising composer. Brian's growing reputation was soon noted by Herbert Minton Robinson, whose middle name reveals his connection with the wealth of the pottery world. He had no special interest in music, but suggested to Brian that he leave the timber yard and receive an annual patronage of £500, nearly four times his present salary, so that he might devote himself to composition and eventually support himself through his music.

Under this new financial arrangement, Brian left his job and moved his family to a larger house in a more exclusive part of Trentham, on the other side of Stoke. He was on the edge of the most prosperous years of his life, the like of which he was not to see again until the 1960s. He had arrived. He was secure. Nothing in fact was further from the truth.

Now that he had all day in which to compose, Brian became self-indulgent and lazy. He employed maids, cooks and gardeners, sent his children to be educated privately, and assembled a large and impressive library. He also began to drink heavily, which did little to moderate his temper. If something was not completely to his liking, he flew into a rage, throwing plates across the room. His children were terrified of him, especially when his drinking increased in 1912 and his marriage began to disintegrate. Even so, he cherished his family without being very good at showing it. He needed the security of the home life he had grown accustomed to in his own childhood, but felt trapped that he had to rely on Robinson for the income he had expected to be earning from writing music. He had anticipated a flood of invitations following his London debut, but the success and performances of his larger works did not materialise. In truth, Brian had more originality, imagination and daring than many of his contemporaries, but despite his overbearing confidence among family and friends, he abhorred what he called 'sucking up' and often presented the other extreme to outsiders – outspoken, critical and tactless. He could rarely bring himself to ask a conductor to consider performing his work. On one occasion he sent several of his compositions to Henry Wood, who thought highly of them and asked what he wanted him to do with them. Brian's reply was, 'Oh, nothing. Could I have them back?' So Wood sent them back.

Brian's unpredictable moods resulted in a quick turnover of staff at their house. One of the maids hired by Isabel was a slim, pretty girl called Hilda Hayward, who stayed with the family for several months before leaving for London. Brian found women irresistible and had several affairs during his marriage to Isabel. He quickly fell in love with Hilda and continued to see her after she had left Stoke in 1912. When she became pregnant, he decided to leave behind the ruins of his marriage and join Hilda in London. He returned to Stoke only once – in 1916 – in a futile attempt to persuade Robinson to increase his monthly allowance.

His circumstances immediately suffered a radical change, from proud home owner in one of the more exclusive districts of Stoke to a squalid room behind Euston Station. He had risen high and fallen far. He wrote dozens of letters each week applying for jobs, from clerk to gardener, and even took to hanging about outside the RCM in the hope of meeting Parry, who might offer him a position. His only income was derived from song-writing and when that ceased, Brian briefly contemplated the Foreign Legion before deciding to enlist in the British Army in August 1914. The decision had little to do with patriotism since his first thought was that a change in routine would provide the spark needed to ignite his floundering musical imagination. He proved to be a poor soldier, unwilling to obey orders and hopeless with any sort of gun. As a volunteer, Brian was not obliged to serve overseas at that time, which was just as well since he was fearful of even the slightest injury. He was eventually discharged in 1915 because of flat feet (not, as he claimed, because of an injured hand), much to the relief of himself and the Army.

He found work in the Audit Office and began to work on *The Tigers*, an operatic burlesque on power and ostentation, and the first of his greatest works. By the end of the year he had resigned his post and moved his new family to Birmingham, where he worked in munitions and various factories until the end of the war. In 1919 he was again dismissed by his employers for staying away from work, this time to concentrate on his opera, and after a brief return to London, Brian and Hilda, now pregnant with their third child, moved to Lewes in Sussex. Michael was born there and was the first of Brian's children to benefit from a mellowing in his personality. He still hoped for performances of his work, but by 1924 began to worry less about this. Instead he devoted himself to developing the depth and scope of his musical gift, and with the acceptance that fame and prestigious performances might never come, achieved a more relaxed attitude towards his family.

He was to move twice more in Sussex, once to Brighton and in 1922 to a modest council house on the Downs at Moulsecoomb, although his circumstances remained desperate. A lot of time was spent looking for work, often accepting low rates of pay which kept him labouring far into the night in order to make a barely adequate wage. What sustained him during these difficult years was a work to which he clung tenaciously; his response to the tedium of his daily life. He called it *The Gothic Symphony*, and with no thought of performance, employed whatever elements were necessary to achieve the effect he wanted. It was a glorious enterprise and became the world's most colossal symphony, calling for 200 players and 500 singers, as well as four soloists, an organ, a thunder machine and a bird-scarer – all of this created, for the most part, in a council house between shifts as a fruit-picker.

At the age of fifty-one, Brian alone knew that his greatest works were yet to be written. He finally obtained a more suitable position as assistant to the editor of *Musical Opinion* and, until the outbreak of war, wrote reviews by day and symphonies by night. Though weary and depressed by events in Europe, he took a job with the Ministry of Supply and gave what time he had to another gigantic work: a four-hour cantata, *Prometheus Unbound*. When Brian played the nearly-completed cantata through to him, Bantock was enthusiastic and contacted a publisher, who was similarly impressed and insisted that Brian contact them the moment the work was finished. When that time came, Brian couldn't be bothered. Nearly seventy years old, he was at his lowest ebb. The war continued to drag on; his son, Michael, was a prisoner-of-war; and he had virtually given up hope of ever hearing any of his major works performed. He could not have known then that he would live for another twenty-eight years, during which time he would write four operas, a cello concerto and a further twenty-seven symphonies – eight of them after his 90th birthday.

A significant factor in this tidal wave of creative energy arrived in the person of Robert Simpson, at that time a young music producer with the BBC. Harold Truscott introduced him to Brian's compositions and he at once set about organising performances, including the mighty *Gothic* at the Albert Hall. In 1958, Brian and Hilda returned to Sussex, this time to a bungalow in Shoreham, where he completed the remaining symphonies – nineteen in all – the last being written in a small flat where they lived until his death in 1972, aged 96.

Frank Bridge

1879–1941

*'His loathing of all sloppiness and amateurism set me standards to
aim for that I've never forgotten.'* – Benjamin Britten

Born well within Brahms's lifetime and outliving Berg, whose music he
deeply admired, Bridge seemed to look back to one and forward to the
other, revealing an amazing development over some forty creative years.

He was born in Brighton, where his father conducted a theatre
orchestra. The young Frank would often join them, usually playing
violin, but sometimes other instruments and even, when required,
conducting. This early experience was of tremendous value to him,
providing insights into the range and colours of the orchestra, and
generally laying the foundation of the remarkable skill and knowledge
which became his hallmark. It was as a violin student that he entered the
Royal College of Music, winning a composition scholarship in 1899
which enabled him to work under Stanford for four years. During that
time he quickly established a professional reputation as an outstanding
conductor and chamber player. So exceptional were his qualities that
when the celebrated viola player Emanuel Wirth was prevented by illness
from playing in the Joachim Quartet in 1906, Bridge was chosen to take
his place and earned from Joachim and his colleagues their enthusiastic
praise.

In these early days, Bridge earned his living by playing in theatre and
other orchestras; he was, in fact, an expert and versatile musician who
soon made a name for himself as a conductor capable of taking on a
difficult work at short notice and good at reading modern scores, a
strength recognised by Henry Wood, who was quick to call on him for
Promenade Concerts when he himself was indisposed. During this period,

Bridge also undertook many important conducting engagements, presiding over repertory rehearsals for the New Symphony Orchestra, conducting opera at the Savoy Theatre and at Covent Garden, as well as appearing with such major orchestras as the LSO. It is interesting to note that many of those who played under him said that he was one of the few conductors who really interpreted the works instead of merely beating time. But as a shy and retiring man, he never cared for the limelight and was reluctant to accept a permanent conducting post. His one regular position as a conductor was with the Audrey Chapman Orchestra, formed chiefly of amateurs but whose standard of performance under Bridge reached a near professional level of musicianship and sensitivity.

It is, however, as a composer rather than as conductor that Bridge is chiefly remembered. His early music, some of which he later disowned, actually became very popular but if songs like the familiar *E'en as a lovely flower* are no more than drawing-room ballads, his true abilities emerged in his chamber music of around 1905 with a string quartet, a piano quartet, and a piano trio, all designated as *Phantasies*. In his orchestral music, Bridge absorbed something of the influence of Delius rather than surrendered to it, although his spacious four-movement suite *The Sea*, written in 1910, has something more in common with the Bax of *Tintagel* and *November Woods*.

Listening to his music of this period, it is difficult to reconcile its easy-going romanticism with the searing intensity of his post-war style. As a devout pacifist, Bridge did not enlist in the services, but the war still inflicted profound psychic scars. Beginning with the Piano Sonata, completed in 1924, his music grew more abstract, darker, and more daringly experimental. The pragmatist with a flair for tailoring his music both to the tastes of his audience and the capabilities of his performers, now saw the need to travel beyond previous conventions. Herbert Howells recalled how, almost without warning, Bridge issued 'not the old easy invitation, but a disconcertingly new and unexpected challenge.' Those who had enjoyed the early work were quick to dismiss the later

efforts as being deliberately *avant-garde* for the sake of keeping up, whereas modernists were unable to forget Bridge's initial conservatism. If this marked transformation of his musical style put him at some distance from popular taste in the 1920s and '30s, now, at the end of the century, there is a renewed regard for these more personal works.

It was in the 1920s that Bridge built a house in Sussex where he and his Australian wife Ethel, a fellow RCM student, lived a simple but lively existence until his death at Friston Field near Eastbourne in 1941. There were no children of the marriage, but seventeen years earlier he had met the 11-year-old Benjamin Britten and taken him on as a private pupil. He treated the boy like a son and Britten could remember being driven around various parts of the south of England, 'opening my eyes to the beauty of the Downs and the magnificence of English ecclesiastical architecture.' For a while it seemed as if Bridge would only be remembered for the theme which lies at the heart of Britten's popular *Variations*, but a growing awareness of his true talent has emerged in recent years which is reflected in the extensive recordings and not infrequent broadcasts of his music.

Benjamin Britten

1913–1976

*'The road, now near, now distant, winding led
By lovely meadows which the water fed...'*
– George Crabbe

Edward Benjamin Britten was born at Lowestoft in Suffolk on November 22, appropriately enough on St Cecilia's Day, which celebrates the patron saint of music. His father was a successful dental surgeon and his childhood home was a place where his musical talents were encouraged from an early age. He was, in fact, a remarkable child who began composing at the age of five, attracted, on his own account, by the exciting patterns that music made on paper.

He began studying the piano from the age of seven and took up the viola three years later when it became evident to his parents that his musical gifts would need to be taken very seriously. His early attempts at composition were conventional enough – miniature tone-poems inspired by domestic events and the usual adventures which crowd a small boy's life – but even at this early age, marked characteristics could be seen which were to remain with him until the end of his days. He was, for example, taking great care to express himself exactly, indicating that he already knew clearly what he wanted to say. For the young Britten, it was as normal a thing to express himself in music as in ordinary everyday speech, so that by the time he was 14 he had written ten sonatas, six string quartets, an oratorio and any number of songs and piano pieces. Writing music was much more interesting than his prescribed piano practice, and when he had to work at scales he could often be seen simultaneously reading a novel or a book of poetry which he propped up on the music stand in front of him.

As a day-boy at his preparatory school, Britten worked hard in class and was particularly good at mathematics. Cricket was another strength and in fact he showed all-round promise as a sportsman, but nothing could deflect him from music, which was already a way of life. He read a good many scores and by the age of 12 had developed a strong interest in orchestral music, but it was hearing Frank Bridge conduct his own composition *The Sea* at the 1924 Norwich Festival that, in his own words, 'knocked me sideways'. When Bridge came to East Anglia he used to stay with Britten's viola teacher, and three years later Bridge became the boy's first and most inspiring instructor in the art of composition. It was a happy encounter, for Bridge was to become Britten's prime mentor. To a boy barely in his teens, seething with ideas and eager to tackle ambitious projects, Bridge provided valuable discipline for his precocious pupil, teaching him to insist on 'the absolutely clear relationship of what was in my mind to what was on the paper' and to 'think and feel through the instrument I was writing for'.

In 1928 he entered Gresham's School at Holt, some 35 miles from his home. Almost the first person he met was the school music master, whose ominous greeting, 'So you are the little boy who likes Stravinsky!' foreshadowed a virtually non-existent musical education at the school; but he was able to continue composition studies with Bridge and began piano lessons with Harold Samuel in London. Quite apart from music, Britten was an unusually thoughtful and sensitive boy, probably unsuited to the robust environment of an English boarding school, and after just two years he was relieved to have won an Open Scholarship to the RCM. His expectations were high. Throughout his time at Gresham's he had looked forward to a full-time music course in London to satisfy his creative energies, and was composing as freely as ever. But he was out of line with the RCM, who actively discouraged his attempts to break out of their rather narrow approach to composition. His teacher, John Ireland, though sympathetic, evidently taught him little and in his three years at the RCM only one of his compositions was performed there. Bridge's

argument that a student composer should have a chance to hear what he had written was refuted on the grounds that the singers were not up to the standard of difficulty of the music. In truth, Britten's interests were much wider than those considered proper by the RCM, who even opposed his wish to spend a travel award on a period of study with Alban Berg in Vienna, fearing his contamination by twelve-note music. All in all the RCM completely failed to recognise the talent that it had within its walls and in 1934, at the age of 20, Britten left to earn his living simply and solely as a composer on his own terms.

He was lucky on at least two accounts. Ralph Hawkes, of Boosey and Hawkes, gave him a publishing contract which showed a steady faith in the young composer during the earliest and most difficult stages of his career. His second opportunity came when he was invited to work on documentary films for the GPO Film Unit, and for five years until 1939 he contributed to eighteen films, of which at least two, *Coal Face* and *Night Mail*, have become classics of their kind. He was fortunate in both films to enjoy the literary collaboration of the poet W H Auden, who became one of Britten's most important artistic associates, and an influential friend during a period of about seven years. Though temperamentally quite different, Auden exercised a liberating influence on the younger man's outlook, and while his upbringing conditioned him to disapprove of his less inhibited companions, Britten found himself both attracted and repelled by their company. Britten's homosexuality was never publicly discussed in his lifetime: only after his death was it referred to by the tenor Peter Pears, who was the composer's constant partner for some forty years and for whom Britten wrote much of his greatest music.

In the meantime, he had begun to produce the works that were first to bring him to the attention of the public. *A Boy was Born* was given its first performance in a BBC broadcast early in 1934, followed later that year by the *Simple Symphony* for string orchestra. Both were well received but it was the symphonic cycle for soprano and orchestra *Our Hunting Fathers*, written in collaboration with Auden, which aroused hostility and admiration in equal measures. Describing it as 'uncomfortable music ... spiky, exact and not at all cosy', Pears understood its underlying quality, but for some the suspicion took hold that young Benjamin Britten was too clever for his own good and bound to come to a sticky end. It was a reputation that he never entirely escaped.

There were, of course, other projects under way besides his work with Auden, and his next success, *Variations on a Theme of Frank Bridge*, carried his name throughout Europe and America. There could be no doubt now of the quality and brilliance of his talent, but for many reasons he was not settled in England. He moved from London, where he had shared a flat for two years with his sister Beth, and with an inheritance of £1000 bought the Old Mill at Snape near Aldeburgh. There were many happy days, entertaining friends and keeping busy with incidental music commissions, but he remained disturbed by much of what he saw around him. At home the shadow of mass unemployment lengthened and the winter of 1938-39 saw a steady darkening of the European political scene. Like many intellectuals in the thirties, Britten wondered if it would be more honest to adhere to his humanitarian principles, and in May 1939 he and Pears followed Auden's example and sailed for Canada and then shortly afterwards moved to New York. Except for a visit to California, and a short stay in Brooklyn with the American composer Aaron Copland, Amityville on Long Island remained his home for the next two-and-a-half years.

Britten's stay in the United States was immensely productive in terms of his music but it was not to be the answer to his problems. At 25, he had lost both his parents and New York seemed far removed from the happy landscape of his childhood. In his own words he felt 'muddled, fed up and discouraged', a feeling reflected in a long and serious physical illness which laid him low during 1940. In truth, he never enjoyed robust health. He had suffered pneumonia when only three months old and though he recovered was never to grow into a strong boy. There were also suggestions of a heart murmur which called for a number of tests, and if he kept reasonably well for periods of his life, the impression of

51

Britten as an energetic composer who liked to swim, play tennis and take long walks with his dog, does not give a true picture of the man.

Although he had earlier contemplated taking American citizenship, he came to realise that his roots lay in English soil and in 1941 he chanced upon an article in *The Listener* by E M Forster about the poet George Crabbe which defined the way his thoughts were moving. What also emerged from Crabbe's poetry was the idea which a few years later was to become *Peter Grimes*, but first Britten and Pears knew they had to return to England, and after several frustrated attempts to find a passage, they eventually set sail aboard a small Swedish cargo boat. As pacifists, both knew that their situation would not be easy, but Britten was optimistic and during the slow month's voyage he felt sufficiently confident to write the *Hymn to St Cecilia* and *A Ceremony of Carols*. On arrival in Britain, both were exempted from military service on condition that they gave recitals for the Council for the Encouragement of Music and the Arts, and in between concert tours up and down the country, Britten settled once more at Snape to concentrate on composition. These tours ranged from crowded lunch-hour recitals held at the National Gallery in London to remote tin-roofed village halls housing twenty or so. Whatever their numbers, audiences delighted in the performances which confirmed Britten's long-held belief in the importance of the artist's place in society.

By the beginning of 1944 work was under way on the music of the opera *Peter Grimes* and a year later the score was complete and given its famous first performance by Sadler's Wells in June 1945, with Pears singing the title-part. The opera was a triumphant success and put the seal on all that had gone before in his career. No comparable English work had been greeted with such acclaim since Elgar, and Britten was finally established as a major musical figure in his own country. The opera's success was soon to be repeated in countries throughout the world, and audiences everywhere held their breath to see what Britten might do next. There followed *The Rape of Lucretia*, *Albert Herring*, *Billy Budd*, *Gloriana*, *The Turn of the Screw*, *A Midsummer Night's Dream*, *Curlew*

River, Owen Wingrave, Death in Venice – a truly impressive list of operas and many other works, particularly sets of songs like *Winter Words* and the *Holy Sonnets of John Donne*.

In 1945 he had begun to toy with the idea of founding an opera company of his own for which new works would be written along chamber lines, to avoid the expense of a large chorus and orchestra. Among the enormous range of activities that he undertook after the war, Britten therefore established a really professional body of operatic performers, at first in conjunction with Glyndebourne and then on its own as the English Opera Group. His apparently endless energy also founded, with others, an annual festival at Aldeburgh, an event which grew from modest beginnings to major proportions. Fifty years on it is now a fixture of English cultural life, as familiar and as permanent as Covent Garden or the Royal Shakespeare Company. It is difficult, therefore, to imagine the sheer eccentricity, the seeming impossibility, of creating a festival in a remote fishing village looking out on the vast horizons of the chilly North Sea – a landscape captured so vividly in the poetry of Crabbe and which had drawn Britten home from America. In the tiny building of the Jubilee Hall, on a pocket handkerchief stage where you would think twice before putting on a village pantomime, Britten assembled players and singers of extraordinary quality to perform works which have since been presented in the world's great concert halls.

If his energy and vision were formidable, so was his stubborn determination, as on the occasion when he got soaked through while sitting at his desk, oblivious of the rain sweeping in through an open window. Though his large catalogue of works may be attributed to his musical fluency, it had more to do with this dogged perseverance and his craftsman's discipline. Sticking to a firm timetable, he would invariably sit down to work at nine in the morning and go straight through to lunchtime, followed by an afternoon walk and tea, after which he would carry on until about eight o'clock: after an early night the routine would begin again the next day. Such meticulous working habits applied equally to practical and administrative matters, where the same rigorous professional standards were brought to bear. Collaborators and musicians who were less inclined to compromise their own views found that their services were no longer required, and although encouraging with amateurs, he could be ruthless with professionals who fell short of his exacting standards.

Yet if he showed an inflexible determination towards others, of nobody did he demand more than himself. He was often greatly stretched by the amount of work he undertook, and besides composition travelled widely both as a performer and as a conductor. He was also responsible for much of the detailed planning of the festivals at Aldeburgh, where he achieved almost mythical status among visitors and the local inhabitants. But there were lighter moments as well, as when Peter Pears recalled their amusement watching a gauze curtain, representing mist in a scene from *Billy Budd*, becoming caught up and coinciding with the line: 'I don't like the look of the mist, Mr. Redman.'

Britten was clearly a man of considerable personal charm, able to get on well with the local people, the fishermen and workmen who helped him build his concert hall, and he was able to communicate particularly well with children. One of his most popular works, *The Young Person's Guide to the Orchestra*, is dedicated to the four children of a friend, and his operas *Albert Herring* and *The Little Sweep*, as well as the cantata *Saint Nicholas*, all have children's roles. So, too, did his chamber opera *The Turn of the Screw*, which silenced any lingering scepticism among the critics, to be followed in 1957 by the equally successful three-act ballet *The Prince of the Pagodas*.

Five years later, the City of Coventry celebrated the consecration of its new cathedral, which had risen alongside the ruins of the original building, destroyed by bombs in 1940. The *War Requiem* was commissioned to mark the event and created a remarkable and deep impression, crowning Britten's position as England's greatest living composer. Later that year he was made an Honorary Freeman of Aldeburgh in recognition, not of his worldwide reputation, but of the part he played in the local community. Even with the astonishing success of the *Requiem*, Britten claimed not to write for posterity: 'I write music now, in Aldeburgh ... for anyone who cares to play it or listen to it.' While continuing to travel abroad for extensive periods, Aldeburgh remained the fixed point on his compass. New works germinated there and the Festivals flourished, particularly that of 1967, when the new concert hall at Snape was opened by the Queen.

His heart operation was still three years away, but from 1970 onwards Britten's recurrent illnesses of varying kinds increasingly handicapped and depressed him. That year he began work on a new opera, *Death in Venice*, which resonates with his own craving for lost innocence and is felt by many to be the most personal of his operas. Visconti's film, made the same year but not seen by Britten, changed the central character from writer to composer, modelled on Mahler, who died of heart disease. While writing his opera, Britten was told a heart operation was essential if he was to live. The news was half-expected, and he worked feverishly to finish the huge score before the operation in May 1973 which was only partially successful, and after a slight stroke, suffered during surgery, he was left without the full use of his right arm.

From 1974 he had a constant companion in his Scottish nurse Rita Thomson and during the next year felt a little better, but during 1976 his health once again deteriorated and he died at home in Aldeburgh in December that year. Three days later the funeral took place at Aldeburgh Parish Church. The choir sang the *Hymn to the Virgin*, which he had composed as a sixteen-year-old schoolboy with a lifetime of achievement before him.

Alan Bush

1900–1995

'His neglect, whether on ideological grounds or otherwise, is genuinely surprising.' – Musical Times

Born in London into what he described as an 'ample Victorian middle-class family,' Bush later reflected on his early life with a degree of discomfort: the family's affectations embraced nudism, teetotalism and dietary whims as well as a fascination with the occult (spiritual messages once persuaded some of his family to undertake a search for hidden treasures which took them half way round the world.) As a young man he, too, had dabbled in theosophy and horoscopes, but recovered a sense of purpose by reading widely and developing an interest in philosophy and politics.

The early encouragement he received from his mother eventually came to the fore, and in 1918 he went to the Royal Academy of Music, where he studied under Corder for composition and won numerous scholarships. In 1921 he met John Ireland and had six years of private tuition with him before going to Berlin University as a student of philosophy and musicology. The time he spent here was probably the most significant factor in his development as a composer for it equipped him technically to deal with a vision which was at odds with most of his English contemporaries. Berlin at that time was a breeding ground for radical ideas which included music as a political force for propaganda purposes, and while living for a while in a house next to Brecht, Bush nourished sympathies with the Communist Party, eventually becoming a member in 1935.

In the 1920s, before his commitment to political ideology completely dominated his work, Bush was regarded as a promising young composer. His first success came when his String Quartet of 1924 won a Carnegie Award, while another work for quartet, *Dialectic*, did much to establish his reputation abroad. In 1925 he was also appointed a professor of composition at the RAM, where he was the first to lecture on musical history, and in 1929 he succeeded Rutland Boughton as music adviser and conductor to the London Labour Choral Union before founding the Workers' Music Association a few years later. He served in the army from 1941 to 1945 but it was following the war that a major shift of style took his music towards a more popularist, tonal idiom which reflected artistic ideas current at the time in the Soviet Union. Ironically, his belief in this specific form of national music resulted in his compatriots treating his efforts with complete indifference, and although his works were in great demand on the other side of the Iron Curtain, none of his four full-scale operas received a professional English production.

While his passionately-held political convictions probably stifled his musical career in this country, many of his contemporaries among English composers greatly admired Bush's talents. Vaughan Williams, for one, protested vigorously on Bush's behalf when the BBC temporarily banned his music during the war on account of his political affiliations, and there were many others who supported his music if not his views. Today, Bush's music is seldom heard, but the composer himself is remembered by his pupils and those ordinary people for whom he was an inspirational champion of music for a common purpose.

George Butterworth
1885–1916

'All sounds have been as music to my listening.' – Wilfred Owen

George Butterworth was born in London on 12 July, 1885, and killed by a sniper's bullet on the Somme on 5 August, 1916. He was 31. As in all cases of unfulfilled promise, it is fruitless to consider what he might have achieved had he lived, but he was perhaps the finest of the many musical talents whose lives were claimed in that conflict. Before he went off to the war, he sorted out his papers and destroyed anything he thought unworthy, writing nothing more until his death except a diary which made no reference to anything musical.

Little is known of him now and, apart from a memorial volume privately published in 1918, little has been written about him since, except for a centennial tribute by Ian Copley and Michael Barlow's biography, *Whom the Gods Love*, published in 1997. Yet his untimely death was mourned by all who knew and worked with him. They were certain that here was an outstanding man whose loss to British music was severe. His reputation today rests upon a handful of surviving works spread over only three or four years, yet their delicately scored pastoral simplicity beautifully evoke an English countryside which he was never to see again.

It was from his mother, a professional singer *née* Julia Wigan, that Butterworth inherited his love of music. From time to time he sent home small piano tunes written while at prep school, but it was later at Eton, where he was a King's Scholar, that he began to develop his musical ideas, and his first composition – a *Barcarolle* written during a holiday in Scotland – was played by the Eton orchestra in 1903. His father, Sir Alexander Kaye Butterworth, planned for his only son to go into law, but at Oxford he met two men who were to have a deep influence on his music: Cecil Sharp and Vaughan Williams. It was through these two that Butterworth became interested in folksong and dance, and they remained close friends until his death. Before leaving Oxford he had decided, against the wishes of his father, to pursue a career in music. This late start may have been a blessing as his training was very informal and the chance interest in folksong ignited his enthusiasm. Had he had a more academic training, or not been at Oxford at the right time to meet Sharp and Vaughan Williams, he might not have achieved anything worthwhile.

The chief problem on leaving Oxford was how to make a living at music. He first supported himself as a reviewer for *The Times* and then as a music teacher at Radley College, where he seemed to have been very much liked during his brief stay. But self-confidence was not Butterworth's strong suit and within a year he left to enrol in the Royal College of Music to improve his technique. Even this he gave up after a few months and became instead increasingly active in the English Folk Song and Dance Society, often accompanying Vaughan Williams on trips to the country to collect songs. It is known that he became something of an expert in the dances themselves. A friend at the time recalled Butterworth jotting down dances from an ancient villager who stumbled and hobbled his way through long disused and almost forgotten steps. Both men had been surrounded by an astonished crowd and Butterworth stood, oblivious of them, calmly noting the intricacies of the neglected dances and occasionally providing refreshment for the dancer from a jug of beer. In spite of all this activity, Butterworth was restless. Neither teaching nor criticism gave him personal satisfaction, but composing, which did, would keep him busy for a month or two and then, when the piece was finished, a barren period would set in and dissatisfaction with life in general. Even Vaughan Williams confided in a letter to a friend that Butterworth had not quite 'found himself'.

The war, when it came, seemed to provide a solution. It was entirely characteristic of Butterworth that he should have enlisted at the earliest opportunity and promptly banish all thought of music. It seems typical of the man that he threw himself headlong into his new occupation, in this case soldiering. Unlike Wilfred Owen, whose poetry was formed through the experience of war, Butterworth allowed himself no distractions, so that after his death a fellow officer could write: 'I did not know he was so very distinguished in music ...' On the morning of August 4th, 1916, another officer recalled how Butterworth had escorted him to the farthest point of a newly captured trench, urging him always to keep below the parapet:

George Butterworth

I had only reached the Battalion Headquarters on my return when I heard poor Butterworth was shot dead by a bullet through the head. So he, who had been so thoughtful for my safety, had suffered the fate he had warned me against only a minute before.

His diary reveals a typically understated perspective on the ravages of the war surrounding him, though his own military career was highly distinguished: he won the Military Cross for bravery in action, and was recommended for it again on the day he died for leading a bombing party behind enemy lines.

Butterworth's untimely death was mourned by all who knew him. Vaughan Williams, Parry, Sharp, Dunhill, Rootham, Colles, Dent, Hadow, Ernest Walker, Henry Wood, Hugh Allen and many other musician friends expressed their sorrow that such a promising young composer should be taken when so little of his work – a few songs and orchestral pieces – was done.

It has been said of Butterworth that few men can have been worse at making an acquaintance, or better at keeping a friend. Gruff and honest always, he would probably have agreed.

Eric Coates

1886–1957

'The man who writes tunes' – Ethel Smyth

For two decades at least it was Coates's achievement to occupy the middle ground between music pursued by serious composers which few wanted to hear, and the more banal end of the light music spectrum. In the 60s and 70s his work was to be regarded with faint amusement, portraying an age long since past. Like Farnon, Binge and Haydn Wood, his crime was to be light, tuneful and accessible in an age of dissonance. Yet his best music is far from being transient. Vaughan Williams delighted in a 'big tune', Elgar bought all of Coates's records, and more discerning audiences today are less inclined to worry about musical pedigree. The current revival of interest in the genre is evident. If they like it, they listen to it, and for many, British light music evokes the essence of a past age which has all but vanished.

Born in the small mining town of Hucknall near Nottingham, Eric was the youngest of five children. His father was a respected local doctor, but it was his mother who played the piano and encouraged her son when, from an early age, he showed remarkable musical talent. He began to teach himself the violin at the age of six and within ten years was playing chamber and orchestral concerts with local musicians in and around Nottingham. In the autumn of 1906 Coates entered the Royal Academy expecting the viola to be his principal study, but his inclination was to write tunes and he found a capable teacher in Frederick Corder. Although he became an accomplished violist, Coates was even then constitutionally frail, suffering from both asthma and chronic neuritis, and he knew that as soon as was practical he should earn his living as a composer rather than as a player. In the meantime his enviable sight-reading ability, matched only by his reputation as a fine viola player, led to many invitations from orchestras, including those of Beecham and Wood. Here he encountered an exciting new repertoire of music by Strauss, Elgar, Glazunov and Edward German which exercised enormous influence on his own work.

The remaining years before the 1914-18 war saw Coates consolidating his position as a promising young composer while fulfilling his duties as a viola player. He had married Phyllis Black in 1913 and was determined to provide a comfortable life-style for them both, but the outbreak of war led to the cancellation of many performances and his income from the sales of sheet music was beginning to fall off. He was unable to enlist on health grounds and employment as a player seemed likely to be erratic when he became a founder member of the Performing Right Society in 1914. Despite initial opposition from concert promoters, the Society flourished and as a result the balance of Coates' income tilted away from sheet music towards performing fees.

He began to acquire a reputation as a 'commercial' composer, but his main motive in writing in a frankly popular style was a desire to have his music played at all. Songs poured from his pen and were heard everywhere. By 1917, Coates was doing some teaching at the RAM, was principal viola of the Queen's Hall Orchestra, and remained in demand as a freelance orchestral player. Two year later came the blow, when Henry Wood decided not to re-engage him to lead the Queen's Hall violas. No reason was given, but it may be assumed that Wood disapproved of members of his own orchestra enjoying so much independent success. Coates' reaction was abrupt: he never again played the viola and indeed only handled it 22 years later when he gave the instrument away.

He and Phyllis moved to the top floor of her parents' house in St John's Wood, where they lived for the next three years, she going from strength to strength in her stage career while he stayed at home writing. They lived an enchanted life largely undisturbed by the horrors of war and its aftermath. Absorbed in each other, their social life flourished and they danced the night away, beautiful people living beautiful lives. The birth of their only son Austin in 1922 was initially an intrusion into their dream world and he was dispatched as soon as possible to boarding school in Hampshire. From time to time the family moved to Hampstead and Sussex, but Coates really needed to be in town and felt cut off if out of London's West End for any time.

By the mid-twenties he had become a celebrity and was now financially secure. He was under contract to Chappells to provide a modest output of orchestral music and ballads each year to fit the playing time of the old 78 rpm records. In 1930 he wrote a short *Valse-Serenade* inspired by a still summer evening looking across the beach towards Bognor Regis. To the rest of us this music evoked the coral reefs and turquoise waters of an ideal Pacific atoll when used eventually as the signature tune to the radio programme 'Desert Island Discs'. The piece, *By the Sleepy Lagoon*, was among a number of popular works which benefited from the new age of radio broadcasting. In 1933 his *Knightsbridge March* enjoyed a spectacular success when the BBC used the music to introduce its new weekly programme 'In Town Tonight', capturing for ever a sharply defined London mood for every listener over a certain age. *Calling All Workers* also achieved instant success when broadcast in 1940 and within a few weeks was adopted by the BBC as the signature tune for the new 'Music While You Work' programme. It was heard thousands of times during the war years and became one of the most potent musical symbols of its time.

Despite his considerable output during these years, including what was arguably his most enduring work, *The Three Elizabeths*, the time and energy expended took its toll on Coates's already waning health. He was plagued by bronchial trouble and between prolonged periods of recuperation was only able to write incidental music from 1948. When he was asked to write the film score for *The Dam Busters* in 1954, he at first declined. He was 68, in delicate health and not prepared to subject himself to the rigidity of deadlines. He was eventually persuaded on the grounds that only a single march would be called for, which in fact he had already sketched out the year before. By August 1956 a quarter of a million records of *The Dam Busters' March* had been sold, for which Coates received the Ivor Novello Award.

The following year he and Phyllis drove down to Sussex. On 17th December he suffered a stroke and died four days later in hospital at Chichester. While symphonies and oratorios by serious and worthy men gather dust on shelves, Coates wisely kept within his limitations and, as he asserted in his autobiography, *Suite in Four Movements*, wrote music that people wanted to hear.

Samuel Coleridge-Taylor

1875–1912

'... far and away the cleverest fellow going among the younger men'
– Edward Elgar

Samuel Coleridge-Taylor was born in London and enjoyed musical popularity and fame previously denied in English-speaking countries to people of black ancestry. His mother, a white Englishwoman, was left to bring up the boy after his father, a medical doctor from Sierra Leone, returned there for good when Samuel was a small child. He grew up in Croydon, where it seems a local theatre conductor, Joseph Beckwith, took an interest when he saw him playing marbles on the street with a violin case at his side. Beckwith taught him to play the instrument and from the age of 10 Samuel extended his musical education by singing in a local church choir.

At 15 he was accepted at the RCM as a violin student and wrote his first important composition, a *Te Deum*, in that year. He became a pupil of Stanford and by 1893 had written further choral and chamber works, some of which were given public performances. He was awarded an open scholarship for composition and over the next four years completed a symphony, won two prestigious prizes, and gained the advocacy of Elgar, who recommended the young composer for a Three Choirs Festival commission. The result, the *Ballade in A minor* for orchestra, was well received at its first performance in Gloucester in 1898.

This success was eclipsed, however, by his cantata, *Hiawatha's Wedding Feast*, which was conducted by Stanford in November that year at the RCM. Recalling the concert some years later, Parry wrote:

It had got abroad ... that something of unusual interest was going to happen, and when the time came the hall was besieged by eager crowds, a large proportion of whom were shut out, but accommodation was found for Sir Arthur Sullivan and other musicians of eminence. Expectation was not disappointed.

The production of the work at the Albert Hall in 1900 set the seal on the composer's achievement and he was asked to compose for one festival after another. The work, on which the composer's fame now largely rests, soon became widely acclaimed in England and America, both audiences and singers attracted to it through the popularity of Longfellow's poem and the current vogue for the exotic. Coleridge-Taylor tried to capitalise on its popularity with *The Death of Minnehaha*, a *Hiawatha Overture* and *Hiawatha's Departure*, all written within eighteen months, but none of them attracted as much attention; nor in fact did anything he wrote afterwards, although the 1911 cantata *A Tale of Old Japan* achieved a measure of success.

At the end of 1899 he married Jessie Walmisley, a fellow student who came from an English musical family, and supported her and their two children – Hiawatha and Gwendolen (later Avril) – by teaching and conducting. He was conductor of the Westmorland Festival for 1901 and professor of composition at Trinity College in 1903 and at the Guildhall School of Music in 1910. In 1904, the year in which he made the first of three successful visits to the United States, he became conductor of the Handel Society. A very shy child, Coleridge-Taylor grew in confidence over the years and learned to respond effectively to racial prejudice, bearing condescension with patience and dignity. Yet there was always an innocence about him which made him vulnerable to criticism. On one occasion as a student, Stanford had amended a piece which was later found thrown aside in the college waiting-room as not worth carrying home. Success made him happy, but he was easily discouraged and tried in vain to recapture the glories of *Hiawatha*.

It was only after his best work had been done that he conceived a desire to study African negro music and to become its champion by composing works on native folk themes. His visits to America no doubt did something to awaken his racial sentiment and he came to see it as his mission in life to help establish the dignity of black people. He went on to achieve celebrity status in the United States and was received by President Roosevelt at the White House, where the two men talked at length. But as Coleridge-Taylor's first biographer, W C Berwick Sayers, noted: '*Hiawatha* was at once his glory and his bane. It had genius and novelty combined; and thereafter the critics demanded novelty of him rather than music.'

He was contemplating emigrating to the USA when he died suddenly from pneumonia at the early age of 37.

Frederick Delius

1862–1934

*'I would have hated an English village with institutes
of this and that and the vicar for ever on the doorstep.'*

James Gunn's famous portrait, Eric Fenby's moving biography, and Ken
Russell's BBC film made for 'Omnibus' in 1968 all show the composer
as a crippled, blind invalid, devoid of humour and consideration for
others; a bitter, unattractive man who had turned his back on the world.
It may be true that this was the person he became for the last eight years
of his life but it reveals little of his dry wit, enjoyment of detective
stories, or the elegant adventurer with a fondness for fine clothes and
good food. Delius was one of the most remote and isolated figures in
recent music history and of all English composers may well be thought
of as the most cosmopolitan.

For all that, Delius was born in Bradford, the fourth child and second
son of a wealthy immigrant wool merchant and was brought up in solid
Victorian comfort at No 1 Claremont, a substantial property which in
those days backed onto open moors. This was the age of large families
and Elise Delius provided her husband with fourteen children, mostly
girls, who were brought up to speak both German and English. Julius
Delius had emigrated from Bielefeld in the North-Rhine province to
Bradford, where he prospered in the wool trade. Despite the quiet,
provincial world of West Riding he remained a true Prussian and within
the family his word was law. He brooked no contradiction, no
disobedience and also insisted upon a strictness of routine which was to
surface later in his son's approach to composition.

Fritz (as they called him) managed to enjoy a carefree childhood and
became a robust and hardy boy, equally good at both cricket and football

until prevented from playing such ungentlemanly games by Julius. He had violin lessons from the age of seven and played the piano by ear, making up little descriptive pieces to amuse the family and their friends. Since Julius was fond of music in a purely amateur way, he did not discourage his son's interest, but any notion that he might one day pursue a professional career in music was entirely out of the question. After three years at a prep school in Bradford, Fritz and his brother Max attended the local grammar school, where he failed to make any

impression, disliking all subjects except geography. The brothers were soon moved to the International College at Isleworth to prepare themselves for the family wool business, where instead Fritz took advantage of his proximity to London to attend as many concerts and performances as possible; he also increased his batting average.

When the two brothers left Isleworth, Delius found himself an unwilling apprentice to the wool trade. Max was regarded as completely unsuitable for the demanding occupation of wool-brokering, while Ernst, their elder brother, had escaped to be a sheep farmer in New Zealand. Though evidently reluctant to follow in the family business, Delius seemed to have all the attributes of a successful representative of the firm. He was anxious to please, keen to learn, and his appearance and manner endeared him to everyone. For almost five years he made fitful attempts to apply himself but his trips abroad as his father's agent always ended with an abrupt recall to account for his lapses in business acumen. From his own point of view, a brief visit to Scandinavia in 1882, where he glimpsed the high and lonely places of Viking and Norse legend, was enough to convince him that there he would find the spiritual freedom that had so far eluded him. But again he was recalled to Bradford and after further futile attempts to direct his mind towards business, during which father and son were barely on speaking terms, Delius persuaded his father to set him up as an orange-grower in Florida. He had no more intention of cultivating oranges for a living than dealing in wool, but it allowed him an escape from Bradford and hopefully many leisurely hours to study music. So it was that at the age of 22, Delius and an old school friend, Charles Douglas, sailed to Florida and freedom.

From New York the pair took a small boat to Solano Grove, a remote spot about forty miles south of Jacksonville, where they found a desolate shack and a wilderness of overgrown orange trees. Delius was not disappointed. The tropical air and general surroundings intoxicated him and oranges were forgotten, if they were ever thought of. He saw clearly for the first time where his life's work lay and for a time things went well until he began to neglect his share of the chores, which led to arguments with Charles. After three months their future seemed less certain as Delius was impatient to get to grips with the craft of music itself. He had already composed one or two short pieces but his efforts had hardly progressed beyond the stage of improvisation. He needed a piano. When Charles fell ill with malaria, Delius set off by steamer to Jacksonville, intending to return with medicine, but instead visited a music store to negotiate the hire of an instrument.

What followed was a stroke of remarkable good fortune. While trying one of the pianos being offered to him, a passer-by was attracted by the unusual textures of the chords he heard and went into the shop to investigate. He introduced himself as Thomas Ward, organist of a Jesuit church in Brooklyn, who was in Florida to restore his health. The two were quickly on friendly terms, staying together for several days until Delius managed to persuade Ward to return with him to Solano. Charles in the meantime had sufficiently recovered to part company with his unreliable partner, leaving Delius and Ward to concentrate on music and over the next six months he developed rapidly, working with amazing energy far into the night. Ward was a natural and gifted teacher whose impact on Delius's musical development was incalculable; the composer even said in later years that only Ward taught him anything worthwhile.

At home the impression that music, not fruit, was the entire occupation of those at Solano Grove was confirmed with the news of the breach between Delius and Charles. Julius despatched a representative to make enquiries, but in an unexpected turn of events Ernst arrived from New Zealand and was delighted with the opportunity of taking over the plantation. Fritz meanwhile determined to work his passage to Bradford in stages and make a final appeal to his father to be allowed to study at the Konservatorium in Leipzig. For several months he earned a living giving music lessons in Danville before a private detective sent by Julius eventually tracked him down in New York. The news he received was unexpected. Julius had been impressed by reports of his son's reputation as a music teacher and had agreed to an eighteen-month course at Leipzig on condition that on completion he must return to America to exploit his teaching skills still further. At the end of June 1886, Delius sailed for England and after only a few days in Bradford he made straight for Leipzig.

Were it not for the stimulating company of fellow students and the endless opportunities for hearing music in the city's concert halls and opera house, Delius considered the years spent in Leipzig to have been largely a waste of time. After the first few months he abandoned organised instruction and followed his own musical instincts, completing his first orchestral suite, *Florida*, in the early spring of 1888. In return for a large barrel of beer he received the services of a small orchestra and was able to hear the piece performed, which he later said taught him more in half an hour than all his months at the Konservatorium.

Prior to this he visited Norway on a walking tour where he was introduced to Grieg, then at the height of his powers, who recognised at once Delius's singular qualities and the two soon became inseparable companions. It was Grieg who persuaded Julius to support his son for an extra year in Europe, and with additional help from his uncle Theodore, who lived in Paris, Delius was able to concentrate solely on composition. In the summer of 1891 he settled in the neighbourhood of the Lion de Belfort and for the next six years got through a prodigious amount of work. Three operas, a string quartet, a sonata for violin and piano, two orchestral works as well as a large number of songs and smaller pieces date from this period.

In the artistic life of Paris that was open to him, however, Delius inclined more to the society of painters and writers than to that of musicians; he was on close terms with Strindberg and especially Gauguin, from whom he later bought the large canvas 'Nevermore' for the modest sum of £20. Already a man given to extremes, Delius greatly enjoyed every side of Parisian life, alternating between the decorous society of his uncle's circle and the low life of Montmartre. It was there that he may have contracted syphilis, which was then incurable and which led to his eventual paralysis.

Returning from a visit to Norway in a more sober frame of mind, he was to be seen more often in fashionable society where he first met Jelka Rosen, a young painter from a distinguished family. Although she knew of his relationships with a number of women, Jelka felt an immediate bond and was secretly delighted with their deepening friendship. He accompanied her one summer to a little village beyond Fontainebleau called Grez-sur-Loing, where she loved to paint in the overgrown garden of a rambling house belonging to the eccentric Marquis de Caryeaux. Delius, too, was immensely taken with the village and the surrounding area, and confided to Jelka that this would be his ideal as a place in which to live and work. The following year the Marquis was forced to sell his estates at Grez and Jelka was just able to raise the cash to buy the house. Delius had meanwhile deserted her, either in the unlikely attempt to secure an income from growing tobacco at Solano Grove, or perhaps to trace an illegitimate child. On his return he sent a postcard to Grez announcing his arrival the next day. This was the first Jelka had heard of him for months and we can only imagine her state of mind when she heard the news. Even so, she gave him a room to work in, complete with a piano, and Grez was thereafter to be his home for the rest of his life.

Delius was now 36 years old yet only one of his works had received a public performance. He had long since established the habit of working on a composition only when guided by the instinct of the moment, and as soon as it left him he would put the score aside and take up another until he felt ready to continue with the original. Considering the way in which his compositions were being finished only to collect dust on shelves, anyone less confident of his own genius would have soon given up. He did not even try to attract the interest of a publisher and seemed only to want to go on composing. However, with the aid of a small legacy left to him after Theodore's sudden death in 1898, Delius was able to give a concert of his own music in London the following year. Critical reaction was favourable but no immediate impact was made and he had to wait another eight years before anyone showed further interest in his work. The event had also depleted his financial resources and there were no royalties to sustain him while he worked on his fourth and best-loved opera, *A Village Romeo and Juliet.*

There was also at this time a strain in his relationship with Jelka. He was jealous of his independence and insisted on retaining his Paris flat for as long as possible, which led to blazing arguments. During these quarrels Delius could be spiteful and wickedly cruel, yet Jelka always remained faithful and supportive. When Julius died in 1901, refusing to acknowledge his son's musical progress, or even mentioning him in his will, only Jelka continued to have unbounded confidence in him, and in 1903 they married. After this Delius's fortunes took a turn for the better. *Sea Drift* was performed in Essen, catching the imagination and starting a vogue for his music in that country, while in England *Appalachia* and *Brigg Fair* were premièred in London and Liverpool. The young conductor Thomas Beecham had also become one of his principal champions and in 1909 gave the first performance of *A Mass of Life* at Queen's Hall.

Delius, uncharitably, reacted by growing even more remote, aloof and intolerant of others. The cause probably lay in his state of health, which began to deteriorate while he was in London in 1910, so that by the end of the year he began the endless tour of sanatoriums in a search for a successful cure. Philip Heseltine, still a schoolboy at Eton, visited Delius for the first time that summer and found his musical hero already thin and haggard but continuing to work hard composing and correcting proofs. Yet his music retained its freshness and vitality, and the delightful *On hearing the first cuckoo in spring* was written at this time, dispelling any notion that he was hardening his musical voice.

In 1915 Delius and his wife buried about a thousand bottles of wine in the garden, rolled up their most precious paintings and left for England to escape the German advance. They returned to Grez after the war to find their home turned upside down but the wine still undiscovered. The conflict, however, had played havoc with his affairs. All German royalties had ceased and because a large proportion of his wealth was invested in Germany, Delius suffered a great financial loss which was to involve him in litigation and constant worry for years to come. To add to his difficulties, he began to lose the use of his hands and by the end of 1921 he was fast becoming a helpless invalid, at times impossible to live with because the mind within his diseased body was unimpaired. Nothing that cures or doctors could do made any permanent impression and he eventually lost his sight as well the use of his lower limbs. In less than a year he became the myth that he was to remain for the next fourteen years, imprisoned in an emaciated body that spent most of the time in a wheelchair.

There were brief moments of light relief when Percy Grainger visited Grez and brought a welcome sense of fun and mischief to the household, taking Delius for walks and pushing the wheelchair at great speed along the roads with Delius calling him to stop, yet enjoying it all the time. All the running of the house was centred around him, every event timed to suit his convenience and everything managed according to a strictly observed routine. Jelka knew there was a real need for people like Grainger to stand up to Delius and turn his ill-temper into good humour by ignoring or teasing him until the real nature of the man emerged again. It was a shrewd judgement.

While he was undergoing another cure in Wiesbaden he received a letter of sympathy from a young Yorkshireman called Eric Fenby which he answered personally. Encouraged, Fenby wrote again to offer his services as his amanuensis and was duly taken on for a trial period. Not only did this completely unknown and musically self-taught twenty-two-year-old possess genuine talent, but he also managed to withstand Delius's rough treatment. Over the next six years Delius and Fenby committed to paper such lasting compositions as *A Song of Summer*, *Idyll*, the *Irmelin Prelude* and *Songs of Farewell*.

77

In 1929 Delius was made a Companion of Honour to the bewilderment of the British public, most of whom had never heard of him. Beecham decided that this was the time to launch a Delius Festival in London and co-opted as his assistant Philip Heseltine, who managed to persuade the composer to appear in person during the three-week series of concerts. The Festival was a great success and in recognition of his achievement, Delius was later invited to become a Freeman of the City of Bradford. With some irony he accepted the honour on the condition that he need never set foot in the place.

In the late autumn of 1933, Jelka was knocked down by a cyclist and forced to retire to bed. Shortly after this she was admitted to hospital with cancer. They sent for Fenby, who arrived to find Delius distressed and frail, struggling against pain which kept him awake most of the night. All he wanted was the continuous murmur of Fenby reading *Huckleberry Finn* until, on June 6th, he had a decided relapse and sank into a coma. In a last effort to revive him Jelka was brought home from hospital but he died shortly after in the early hours of June 10th. He had hoped all along to be buried in his garden at Grez but a change in French law had recently forbidden it and Jelka was persuaded that Limpsfield in Surrey would be a suitable resting place. He was buried there the following year, two days before the death of his wife.

George Dyson

1883–1964

*'I am really what the 18th century called a Kapellmeister –
a musician equipped to compose such music as is needed.'*

At a time when it seems many of his contemporaries were blessed with the advantages of a private income, Dyson came from a working-class background – his father was a blacksmith, his mother a weaver – and knew the problems of early poverty. His childhood was spent in a busy industrial town of the West Riding in the days of the butterfly gas-burner and the horse omnibus, but there was a good local choral society and from the age of 13 he was playing the organ at church services. His parents encouraged his interest in music and three years later he won a scholarship to study at the RCM under the exacting eye of Stanford. Among his friends there were Frank Bridge, Rutland Boughton, Thomas Dunhill and John Ireland and he made the most of their company during his four-year stay.

In 1904 Dyson travelled abroad on a Mendelssohn scholarship and spent a further four years in Florence, Vienna and Berlin before returning to England. Unable to secure a living as a composer, he embarked upon a career in teaching, beginning with the Royal Naval College at Osborne and a little later moving to Marlborough. When the war came he enlisted in the Royal Fusiliers and by a sheer accident of officialdom found himself training men in the use of hand grenades. Finding no book on the subject, he set to in characteristic fashion and wrote a *Manual of Grenade Fighting* which was not only adopted by the War Office but sold in such numbers that he earned both an income and a military reputation strangely at odds with his gentle personality. Although a victim of shell-

79

shock, he emerged relatively unscathed from the Great War and for a while confined himself to administrative work for the Air Ministry. At the same time he prepared the establishment of RAF military bands, edited a set of bugle calls, and assisted Walford Davies in composing the *Royal Air Force March*.

In 1921 he was invited to take charge of the music at Wellington College, a task he combined with lecturing posts and musical journalism which culminated in his principal book, *The New Music*, an examination of modern compositional technique. Within three years he was married and appointed director of music at Winchester College for the handsome salary of £1,000, a post he held for the next thirteen years. He loved the place and confessed that he spent his happiest years there, eventually returning in retirement to end his days. The College itself embodied 600 years of English tradition which perfectly coincided with Dyson's personal outlook on life. His brilliant all-round qualities were particularly evident in these teaching appointments for he had the rare gift of communicating and maintaining enthusiasm, and his dry humour would round off a performance of a complex contemporary piece with 'Anyway, it's a lovely piano isn't it.' At Winchester he exercised benevolent despotism, not only in the college but in the country round about. He could coax a choir or orchestra to rehearse a two-hour programme in half that time and give a performance better than was thought possible, even if he did remind them 'You are supposed to be a symphony orchestra, not an elastic band!' Whilst there he lived in two beautifully spacious houses from where he devoted his time to teaching, conducting, writing, lecturing and broadcasting, as well as bringing up his two small children.

There was no doubt that he fulfilled every expectation. The school orchestra was resuscitated, choral and organ scholarships to Oxbridge were won for the first time, and the Winchester Music Club was founded. Above all, Dyson began again seriously to compose. *In Honour of the City*, a choral setting of Dunbar's poem, came first, followed by *The Canterbury Pilgrims*, written for his friends of the Winchester Festival, which established a place for him in the programmes of English choral societies. By the time he left in 1937 to take over directorship of the Royal College of Music, Dyson had gained a prominent place in Winchester musical life as conductor of the choral society and amateur orchestra of the town. Even so, his RCM years exerted a tremendous pressure which he could not have foreseen.

With the outbreak of war and the subsequent bombing of London, he was urged by the government and his own board of trustees to evacuate the College to some safe place in the country. He refused to budge and converted one of his offices into a bedroom that he might stay there to keep the place open. Helping to put out fires on the roof at night and conducting student orchestras by day, he remained in London nourishing fresh talents through the six years of the war. His ability in administration and his financial acumen were outstanding, and his innovations in government grants, buildings, syllabuses and pensions proved of lasting benefit. He employed a rigorous style during his term of office which firmly established the College's high professional and international reputation.

On retiring from the RCM in 1952, Dyson settled once more in Winchester among old friends and enjoyed a wonderful Indian summer as a composer, even though, on his own admission, he wrote only to please himself and his friends. He continued to lecture, broadcast, chair committees and conduct until deafness began to be a problem. He grew frail but was never seriously ill and as the end approached was nursed comfortably at home.

Edward Elgar

1857–1934

*'We are the music makers,
And we are the dreamers of dreams,
Wandering by lone sea-breakers,
And sitting by desolate streams'*
– Arthur O'Shaughnessy

Edward William Elgar was born at the village of Broadheath, three miles from Worcester in the country cottage where the Elgars briefly lived until 1859. He was the fourth of seven children, spending his early years living over his father's music shop, Elgar Bros, in Worcester High Street, now engulfed by a modern shopping development. Although not ambitious for his children, William Elgar ensured that they all had at least a rudimentary knowledge of music, and Edward took up the piano, violin and organ, receiving lessons first at a 'dame school' and later from Frederick Spray, a respected local musician. His proper schooling took place at Littleton House, an establishment of about 30 pupils where he was contented enough, but always solitary, nervous and lonely by nature. A friend at the time remembered him as 'a miserable-looking lad – legs like drumsticks – nothing of a boy about him.' Even so, he enjoyed a carefree childhood and from an early age, as was to be evident from his music, responded to the landscape and countryside of rural Worcestershire in all its moods.

Unremarkable in many ways, in one thing he was exceptional – his ability to read and understand printed music without recourse to sound. It was a remarkable facility which later enabled him to avoid the academic constraints of the London colleges, and to develop his own individual and distinctive voice. He wanted to go to Leipzig to study

music, but family finances were stretched and instead he left school at 15 to work in a solicitor's office. As with everything he did, Edward took his work seriously but his apprenticeship lasted only a year, after which he turned wholly to music, helping his father in the shop while pursuing every musical opportunity open to him. As well as deputising for William in the organ loft of St George's church, there was plenty of local work. He led the Worcester Amateur Instrumental Society and the Worcester Philharmonic, first accompanied then conducted the Glee Club, played the bassoon in a wind quintet, established a violin teaching practice and, in an unlikely undertaking, coached musicians among the staff of the County Lunatic Asylum. Throughout the 1870s Elgar was learning his craft and having relinquished the idea of becoming a concert violinist, turned more and more to composition.

By the end of 1882 he had saved enough to visit Leipzig and though he couldn't afford to study, he did attend concerts and rehearsals, often in the company of a young English girl called Edith. He was always attractive to women: tall, handsome and lean, from his early twenties sporting a fashionable and luxuriant moustache, his volatile moods combining with his ambitions as a composer to catch the romantic imagination. In Leipzig he also met a German girl who visited him for most of that summer in Worcester, and the following year's holiday in Scotland saw another brief romance which came to nothing. In 1883 he became engaged to Helen Weaver, daughter of a local shopkeeper, but even that relationship ended after a few months, leaving him lonely and dejected. Musically, however, this was an excellent period for Elgar. His compositions were attracting local attention and an orchestral work, *Sevilliana*, became his first composition to be heard in London when Manns conducted it at the Crystal Palace.

He was also much in demand as a soloist and augmented his meagre earnings by teaching a group of young, middle-class ladies in Malvern. One of these was Caroline Alice Roberts, daughter of a Major-General in the Indian Army and nine years his senior. Despite her family's opposition, they married in a brief ceremony at Brompton Oratory in

May 1899. The Roberts family at the time were horrified. They regarded Edward as no more than a local music teacher, a tradesman's son and a penniless one at that. Their reaction left an indelible impression on his personality and an outsized chip on his shoulder.

Part of him attempted to become all the things he was not. Adopting the clothes and posture of the country gentleman, he appeared to be happier at the racecourse or with his dogs than in the concert hall, even refusing to carry a violin case because it betrayed the low status of a professional musician. It was a sadly deceptive image. Wanting to be accepted and liked by Alice's Malvern set, he also despised them for their snobbery and religious bigotry, for as a Catholic he offended the largely Protestant conservatism of the Severn Valley in the 1880s. Meanwhile, his own insecurity revealed itself in rudeness and insensitivity to the feelings of others, and he hid his shy nature behind a gruff, abrupt facade. On one occasion an invitation to attend a formal luncheon party received the curt reply: 'You would not wish your board to be disgraced by the presence of a piano-tuner's son and his wife.'

Alice's approach was very different. Never in all the years that followed did she once waver in her faith and belief that her husband was a creative genius of the highest order. She persuaded him, without much resistance, to abandon his teaching and choir practices and to set up home in London, the centre of music-making. Once there he tramped the streets around Piccadilly and Soho, seeking out publishers who accepted the odd piece for violin and piano, until Schotts jumped at *Salut d'Amour*, which made the company a small fortune. Elgar, however, had sold it to them outright for about £5; had he not done so perhaps the financial problems which were to complicate so much of his life might have been avoided. Many years later, he was strolling through London with a friend when they passed an itinerant fiddler giving a fairly good rendition of the piece. Elgar paused and then offered the bewildered musician half-a-crown and asked if he knew what he was playing. 'Yes', the man replied. 'It's *Salut d'Amour* by Elgar.' 'Take this,' he said, 'it's more than Elgar ever made out of it.' As it was, Alice had to sell her jewellery to maintain their standards, while Edward suffered from nervous headaches and the eye and throat complaints that often troubled him when the weather was bad and morale was low.

Events took a turn for the better when he composed his first major work, the overture *Froissart*, in response to an invitation from the Three Choirs Festival in 1890, the year in which their only child Carice was born. The music was favourably received but it was not taken up in London and depression once more set in. A septic tooth added to his other ailments and after a cold, hard winter the Elgars retreated, disappointed and bitter, to Malvern. To his mind it was an humiliating defeat, but with several London performances and published works to his credit, he was gaining a small reputation as a composer.

Once established in Malvern, he settled down to serious composition almost immediately and over the next few years went from comparative obscurity to national fame. Between holidays in Germany he wrote *The Black Knight* – a work for orchestra and chorus – and completed the *Serenade for Strings*, his own favourite composition, and certainly one of the most popular works for string orchestra ever written. Despite growing recognition, money was still scarce and Elgar was obliged to concentrate on playing chamber music and to pursue commitments other than writing music. It was through his teaching, however, that he became acquainted with all the local music-lovers, some of whom are familiar through their portraits in the *Enigma Variations*. One in particular, August Jaeger, became a close friend, not only dealing with the publication of Elgar's music in London but also providing a sympathetic outlet for the composer's repressed frustrations. His championship of Elgar, as well as his sound professional criticism, probably had a greater influence on his friend's music during this period of his finest work than that of any other man. If so then Variation IX, 'Nimrod', the most famous of all the movements, is a worthy tribute.

In 1896 he wrote to Jaeger complaining as usual about his state of health and lack of money, but enthused about his second cantata, *King Olaf*, which was to be given its first performance in Hanley that autumn.

He was always a keen sportsman, thoroughly enjoying golf and cricket as well as supporting Wolverhampton Wanderers, so the prelude to the evening concert was a happy afternoon watching football. If the match failed to produce any goals, the impact of the cantata on its audience was more decisive and the work was successfully repeated in London, Liverpool and Birmingham over the coming months, lifting Elgar from local to provincial fame.

It was not this work, however, which made Elgar a household name. The country threw itself vigorously into party mood for the Queen's Diamond Jubilee, and Elgar, a monarchist and life-long conservative, wholeheartedly joined in. His patriotic cantata *The Banner of St George*, and in particular the *Imperial March*, caught London's imagination in 1897 and made Elgar's name well known. Now entering his forties, he was enjoying a reputation equal to the most admired musicians in the country, although his finances were in as desperate a state as ever and if it had not been for Alice's small private income, things would have been even harder. His frustration and anger sometimes attached itself to his treatment of contemporary musicians. Always ready to help young and struggling composers by recommending commissions and performances of their work, he could also be dismissive and downright unkind once they became a potential threat to his own position, as both Coleridge-Taylor and Bliss found to their cost. Some of his other acquaintances suffered a similar rebuff followed by months of silence, and for whatever reason there is no doubt that for years on end he was not on speaking terms with one or another of his fellow musicians. Yet confirmation of Jaeger's faith in his friend's genius lay just around the corner.

One evening in October 1898, Elgar was improvising at the piano and played something new. Alice sat up and asked what it was. 'Nothing,' he replied, 'but something might be made of it.' The *Enigma Variations* is perhaps still the best known of all his music. There are fourteen variations in all, twelve headed by the initials of a close friend, the first depicting his wife, and the last revealing himself. Elgar loved puns and puzzles but the origin of the work's 'Enigma' subtitle remains the subject of fascinating speculation. He wrote in a programme note: 'The enigma I will not explain – its "dark saying" must be left unguessed' and referred to a larger theme in the music which 'goes' but is not played. Efforts have been made to establish *Auld Lang Syne, God Save the Queen*, even *Pop goes the weasel*, but the secret, if there is one, died with him, and anyway it seems almost irrelevant to the music, which received its first performance under Hans Richter in St James's Hall, 1899. It was a huge success and even Elgar, with his obsessive sense of neglect, could not fail to be pleased with the reaction. He was elevated in the public's mind from a moderately successful composer of salon pieces and provincial commissions to the leading musical figure of his generation.

The *Variations* were soon being performed all over the country, and after the song-cycle *Sea Pictures* he accepted a commission for the Birmingham Festival of 1900, which led to his next main creative work, *The Dream of Gerontius*. It was an auspicious beginning to the twentieth century. Elgar poured his heart and soul into the work, matching himself to his great subject, and writing against the last double-bar line 'this is the best of me ...' But the first performance of *Gerontius* fell short of the work. A combination of factors resulted in a chaotic final rehearsal and inadequate performance, and though many musicians managed to grasp the work's stature, to most of the audience it was a disappointment. Not surprisingly, Elgar was devastated and to make matters worse his financial position was as insecure as ever. Determined not to resort to teaching, which he loathed, his only way forward was to concentrate once more on composition, this time with the cheerful overture *Cockaigne*, a tribute to Londoners, which he described as 'stout and steaky'.

One Sunday afternoon a few weeks later, he sketched a tune on the back of an envelope and played it to his friend Herbert Brewer. 'Listen to this,' he said. 'This'll make them sit up.' It did, and when performed in concert King Edward is said to have remarked to Elgar: 'You have composed a tune which will go round the world.' With A C Benson's words added it has certainly done that. Being so thoroughly familiar with the tune nearly a century later, it is difficult for us to imagine its impact when first played at those early concerts. *Land of Hope and Glory* swept the country in 1902 and became a second national anthem, setting the seal of Elgar's 'official' status.

He received honours such as no previous English composer had accumulated in so short a time, including a knighthood in 1904. Still not wealthy, he reluctantly accepted the Peyton Professorship of Music at Birmingham University, but was glad to hand over to Bantock following a series of controversial lectures. The strain of being a celebrity affected his ability to concentrate and he was prone as ever to bouts of depression. Early in 1905, however, he was working on the *Introduction and Allegro* and a new *Pomp and Circumstance* march. In the same year he was given the freedom of the city of Worcester, an honour which meant more to him than all his honorary degrees. As the civic procession filed down the High Street to the Cathedral, they passed Elgar Bros where the composer paused to acknowledge his father, who was too ill to attend but sat watching from the upstairs window of the shop. It must have been an intense moment for both men.

Following *The Apostles*, written three years earlier, Elgar spent the latter part of that year and the beginning of the next working on a second oratorio, *The Kingdom*, only to lose interest in completing his intended trilogy. Now, when he was not fishing, kite-flying, or building a hutch for Carice's rabbit, he was sketching not only a symphony but also a violin concerto. Late in June he played his family the theme which was to become the great 'noblimente' opening of the First Symphony and the ideas progressed steadily throughout the rest of the year. Its première in Manchester was an immediate and overwhelming success and in the year that followed the Symphony was acclaimed in Europe, Australia and America, as well as on seventeen occasions in London. For Elgar personally the work placed him irrevocably at the head of his profession but, true to form, he could not resist at least a semblance of indifference, and retreated to the 'Ark', a converted shed at the back of his house. From here he indulged a boy's passion for chemistry sets and was completely happy concocting more or less explosive substances, often to the alarm of startled neighbours.

The Violin Concerto which followed achieved similar success and Kreisler played it throughout the land. Although the work had been dedicated to him, the score also contains the quotation, 'Here is enshrined the soul of . . . . .' The five dots are deliberate and could refer to Julia (Worthington), an American friend to whom Edward became deeply attached, or Alice (Stuart-Wortley), daughter of the painter Millais and a devoted follower of Elgar's music. He wrote hundreds of letters to her over the years in which he revealed glimpses of the man as few knew him, an attraction which was discreetly tolerated by Lady Elgar and greeted with polite indifference by the lady's husband.

By 1912, with his Second Symphony behind him, Elgar had largely achieved all he had set out to do. He was the country's greatest living composer and, at the age of 55, had become a national institution. Living once again in the capital, Edward enjoyed the theatre and his London clubs, spending as many hours in the billiard room of their new home in Hampstead. The house was definitely beyond their means, but Alice was determined to maintain a gracious life-style, entertaining the great and the good and reaping the social rewards of her years of devotion to her husband's music. Although few original compositions flowed in these years, he enjoyed touring with the LSO and conducting at the major provincial festivals, where he felt more at home with the orchestral players than with any other group of people.

With the outbreak of war, Elgar exchanged his conductor's baton for that of a special constable and became a staff inspector, too old to enlist but willing to serve his country. A fervent patriot, he represented the strong sense of national pride throughout the war years, always ready with occasional pieces for fundraising or exhortation. On the other hand, he was fully aware of the horror of war and found nothing in it to glorify. His notorious comment about the slaughter of horses being a greater tragedy than the loss of human life should be seen in the context of a man whose sensibilities were profoundly shocked by physical cruelty to any living creature. Like so many of his contemporaries he, too, lost close friends in the conflict.

The war did not stop music-making altogether but concerts were severely curtailed and, despite his public image, privately Elgar was deeply unhappy and frequently ill. As often as he could he escaped to Worcestershire or the Lake District, but by the end of 1917 his nerves were strained to breaking point and Alice realised the need for tranquillity and solitude away from London. She and Carice found a secluded thatched cottage, 'Brinkwells', at Fittleworth in Sussex, which had a dilapidated but refurbishable studio in a large garden surrounded by woods and fine views. The move was little short of miraculous. He immediately began work on four major scores at the same time and still found time to indulge his enthusiasms for bicycling, fishing and woodcraft as well as burning huge fires in the nearby woods. Alice once welcomed their friend W H Reed saying: 'I am so glad you have come: it is lovely for him to have someone to play with.'

The Cello Concerto was written at this time, evocative of woodsmoke and autumn bonfires, the evening of life. It is sometimes said that this work is Elgar's war requiem but, while partly true, it is rather an elegy for Elgar himself, a survivor from a past age. To all intents and purposes this concerto was Elgar's last word. Six months later Alice died after a short illness and was buried at Little Malvern. With her death, Edward's will to compose collapsed. Without her much needed encouragement and belief in his musical gifts, he remained a lonely figure adrift in the post-war years where so much of his familiar way of life had been swept away. There was still a protective circle of friends to whom he could turn and he settled once more in Worcestershire, but music seemed to be a forgotten occupation, discarded with the rest of his past. Apart from theatre music, suites and arrangements, his attention turned more to the studio, where valuable recordings of his major works were made by The Gramophone Company, later HMV. His sadness at the passing of an era was often laced with bitterness and he defended himself from the prevailing indifference to his music by taking the offensive, once remarking to Vaughan Williams at a rehearsal of the Cello Concerto: 'I am surprised that you come to hear this vulgar music.'

In truth, the gulf between the world of late Victorian Worcestershire and post-war Britain was too wide for Elgar to encompass and to the younger generation he was becoming a museum piece in his own lifetime. In 1930, however, the beginning of a new decade saw a change in mood and the public renewed its interest in his work. Thoughts of new compositions were also stirring and there were fragmentary sketches for a third symphony, a piano concerto and an opera at various stages of completion. Work was interrupted in May 1933 when he visited France to conduct Menuhin in the Violin Concerto before setting out to visit the ailing Delius at Grez-sur-Loing. For the first time in his life Elgar had travelled by aeroplane and couldn't wait to describe his exhilaration, even comparing the experience to a passage of Delius's music: '... a little intangible sometimes, but always beautiful. I should have liked to have stayed there for ever.' Delius was impressed and called for champagne all round.

Later that year, Elgar suffered a severe bout of sciatica and an exploratory operation discovered a malignant tumour. Although he recovered somewhat and was able in his last weeks to listen to gramophone recordings of his own music, he grew steadily weaker and died in February 1934. It was a sad year, for within a few months English music also lost Delius and Holst.

Howard Ferguson

b. 1908

*'Though the thought would never have entered his head,
Howard Ferguson as a composer was concerned
with the writing of masterpieces.'* – Alan Ridout

Howard Ferguson was born in Belfast, the fifth and last child of Stanley Ferguson, a banker, and his wife Frances. Neither of them was musical, though the composer can remember his mother playing piano pieces she had learnt as a schoolgirl in Brussels. He began piano lessons at the age of six given by a patient local teacher before encountering F H Sawyer, one of the two best piano teachers in Belfast at the time, who provided four further years of excellent grounding in basic piano technique. As a thirteen-year-old he was heard playing at the Belfast Musical Competitions by Harold Samuel, fresh from his remarkable series of Bach recitals; Samuel persuaded Ferguson's parents to let the boy go to London without delay to study piano with him prior to entering the Royal College of Music.

On arriving in London in the summer of 1924, Ferguson attended Westminster School for 18 months before enrolling as a student at the RCM sometime before his 16th birthday. While there, Samuel introduced him to George Dyson and R O Morris. He took an instant dislike to Dyson but warmed to Morris, a remarkable teacher whose name is constantly being met in connection with the early training of young British composers. Not only did he teach Ferguson counterpoint and composition but also invited him to meet the young Gerald Finzi, to whom he was giving private lessons. The two became firm friends and for the next eight or nine years, until Finzi moved permanently to Ashmansworth after his marriage, they would meet every week to play through each other's compositions. Neither man was to know that 30 years later Finzi's family would be asking Ferguson to complete the orchestration of a work left unfinished at Finzi's death – *The Fall of the Leaf*, subtitled Elegy for Orchestra.

During the winter of 1926-27 Ferguson accompanied Samuel to America, where the pianist was booked for a four-month tour. Morris also began a two-year lecturing post at this time in Philadelphia, so Ferguson was able to continue taking lessons with both men. When not working on a Mass (long since destroyed), he went to concerts, operas and galleries, heard Rachmaninov give the first performance of his

Fourth Piano Concerto, and listened to the orchestras of New York, Boston and Chicago under conductors such as Toscanini and Koussevitsky. It was a memorable experience for an 18-year-old, but absence from home reinforced his attachment to England and he was pleased to return to the RCM, this time as a pupil of Vaughan Williams.

On leaving the College, Ferguson divided his time between composition and playing chamber music. It was an arrangement which worked well. Despite tuition at the RCM with Malcolm Sargent, he had decided against conducting, nor did he seriously contemplate a solo pianist's career. Not being a prolific writer, however, he earned an enjoyable living playing chamber music and as an accompanist, fulfilling engagements at the many music clubs which then existed, and with the infant BBC at Savoy Hill. Ferguson first drew serious attention as a composer with his Violin Sonata No 1, performed in October 1932 at the Wigmore Hall by Menges and Samuel. The favourable impression was confirmed the following year by his *Octet*. Thereafter his composing career continued steadily and though his output was modest, each new work demonstrated its own unmistakable character.

In the summer of 1936 he again accompanied Samuel on a concert tour, this time to South Africa, but on the return voyage Samuel suffered a serious coronary attack and died a few weeks later. For a while Ferguson lived in a gardener's cottage belonging to the house which Joy and Gerald Finzi were building at Ashmansworth, but despite the excellent company and surroundings, he knew that a rural retreat was not for him and looked to return to London. One advantage of the Munich crisis was that the widespread fear of bombing sent house prices in the capital plummeting and Ferguson was able to afford a property in Hampstead which even boasted a single-storied music room. He moved in to 106 Wildwood Road in 1938 and remained there for the next 34 years.

When war broke out the following year, Ferguson was staying with his parents in Belfast, trying to finish his Piano Sonata before joining the RAF as one of the groups charged with the task of providing entertainment for the forces. After a year-and-a-half he was officially released in order to continue working full-time on the daily lunchtime concerts at the National Gallery which he had successfully started with Myra Hess. Over a thousand people queued for her first concert. Others followed and continued without a break on five days a week for more than six years. By the time they ended in April 1946, 1,698 concerts had been given, attended by more than 800,000 people. During those years Ferguson not only assisted Hess in the organisation and planning of the repertoire, but also performed as a pianist in 66 of them himself.

By 1944 the pressure of wartime responsibilities had made composing virtually impossible for Ferguson, though he did manage to write the *Five Bagatelles* for piano which were premièred at the Gallery concerts. When the war ended he determined to resume composition and told friends that he was going away for several months in order to write. Only Finzi and Hess knew that he was working comfortably at home on his Second Violin Sonata. When he 'returned', he was invited to do some composition teaching at the RAM and though he only taught for one day a week and retired after 15 years, he numbered among his pupils a surprisingly wide variety of distinguished composers, including Richard Rodney Bennett and Cornelius Cardew. Already during the 1950s, Ferguson had begun to do some editing of music which particularly interested him and it was not long before the OUP and the Associated Board invited him to produce series of editions of an educational nature. Editing was first done in the intervals between composing. He was a fastidious rather than a prolific composer and, modest though his output was, it was of a consistently high standard. But a couple of years after completing *The Dream of the Rood* in 1959, he found to his alarm that whenever he tried to write anything new, it turned out to be no more than a reworking of what had already been done. Rather than persist he decided that he had said all he wished to say as a composer and courageously determined to write no more.

Ferguson turned his attention to musicological work and in particular the editing of keyboard music, which has been his chief musical occupation for the past 37 years and more. He actually began this work before the war when collaborating with Finzi in the publication of songs by Ivor Gurney, but it was in the 1950s that editions of his began to appear with some regularity. These early editions were prepared during the last ten years of his composing career, and as composition was then still his major preoccupation they are relatively few in number. Since 1960, however, the sheer quantity of music he has edited is enormous, not least the complete edition of the Schubert piano sonatas which he undertook between 1972–76. Living now in Cambridge, surrounded by libraries, friends and beautiful buildings, Ferguson's contribution to British music this century is a distinguished one, yet he remains one of a small band of single-minded composers who is all too easily overlooked.

Gerald Finzi

1901–1956

'But at my back I always hear
Time's winged chariot hurrying near'
– Andrew Marvell

In an early press notice *The Times* critic mentioned a work 'by one Finzi, who set us wondering why a composer of his name dealt so confidently in a definitely English idiom.' No doubt Holst, Delius and van Dieren suffered similar fates in their time; yet Finzi was as English as the rare native apples he cultivated in his small orchard at Ashmansworth, Berks.

His Italian grandfather had married a British girl, and his father, born in London, founded a successful shipbroking company but died just before Finzi's eighth birthday, leaving a widow and five children. Shortly afterwards two of his brothers also died, the eldest in India, another of pneumonia. Finzi himself spent four miserable years at boarding school but was finally withdrawn after feigning illness, and was taken by his mother to Switzerland for a year's cure.

By now the young Finzi had decided that he would be a composer, and when the family settled in Harrogate he managed to avoid the restrictions of a formal education and instead began lessons with the organist and composer Ernest Farrar. Within a short time, however, Farrar enlisted in the army and in 1918 both he and Finzi's remaining brother were killed in action. Already withdrawn and shy, the death of his father, three brothers and Farrar in so short a space of time had left their mark. For solace he turned to literature and studied sporadically with Edward Bairstow at York until 1922, when he and his mother moved to an old mill at Painswick in Gloucestershire. In the solitude of the countryside, Finzi began writing music in earnest, including some orchestral pieces and the first of what was to become an extensive series of settings of Thomas Hardy.

Despite this idyllic retreat, life became too claustrophobic for a young man of Finzi's temperament and on the advice of Boult he moved to London in 1926, to a small house on his own near Sloane Square, where for a while he took lessons in counterpoint from R O Morris. For the first time in his life, Finzi was moving among people of his own age and interests and for the next few years enjoyed the company of other young musicians, met Holst and Vaughan Williams, went to concerts, galleries and theatres, and spent any spare time in London's second-hand bookshops. Howard Ferguson recalled his first meeting with Finzi at this time, which took place just outside the Albert Hall. Richard Strauss had been conducting his *Alpine Symphony* when the wind machine had

toppled over and crashed into the middle of the startled orchestra. As the audience left the hall the two men, helpless with laughter, had cannoned into one another by chance, and from that moment had become firm friends. To those who knew him during those London days, Finzi was indeed robust, warm-hearted and energetic, bursting with idèas, and forthright in his opinions. Shortish, good-looking, with black curly hair, he was entertaining and charming, a perfect companion for those who tramped untold miles with him during many walking holidays in Cornwall, East Anglia, Wiltshire and Hardy's Wessex.

Yet for all his warmth and vitality, a brooding sense of melancholy and life's brevity was deeply ingrained in Finzi's character, which was revealed in the quiet intensity of so much of his music. When composing, his earliest ideas were invariably measured and lyrical; it was also the slow movements of his instrumental works which suggested themselves first. It was, for instance, characteristic that he should withdraw his violin concerto of this period, but retain the slow inner movement which he later revised as the hauntingly beautiful *Introit*.

The reflective side of Finzi's nature became even more acute after he lay for several months in 1928 recovering from a mild attack of tuberculosis. Two years later he joined the Royal Academy of Music to teach composition but found himself unsuited to the pressure and withdrew. Concerned about his health and knowing himself to be a slow worker, Finzi's apprehension of 'The too short time' became almost tangible. 'He lived', said a friend of those early days, 'as if he somehow knew he was going to live briefly.' It was then that his marriage to the artist Joyce Black rescued him from what he later described as near collapse. Her practical efficiency and ease of manner provided the stability and space for Finzi to compose in peace, and in 1937 they built for themselves a retreat at Church Farm in the high and isolated hamlet of Ashmansworth, south of Newbury. There they made a life together which captivated their many visitors. They were content to forgo what many would think were necessities, preferring the indulgence of good taste: the craftsmanship of the house, the garden, the apple orchard, local walks, picnics and the happy atmosphere of children and cats – all combined with the ever-growing library of music and literature to create a cultured haven in the middle of a rural village.

As an agnostic and devout pacifist, Finzi was horrified at the outbreak of war but, judging it to be a 'damnable necessity', he put duty before belief and worked as a civil servant for the Ministry of War Transport. As a composer and family man he hated the weeks spent away from Church Farm, so to fill the gap when all concert-going stopped at the beginning of the war, he assembled a group of mainly local amateur players to take music to army camps, village halls, schools and churches where people had perhaps never heard a live orchestra before. His conducting, like his music, was not predominantly rhythmical, waving his arms in an enterprising manner while the players did their best to follow him. In 1940, he wrote to Ferguson:

> *I shall never make much of a conductor, but I'm glad the players want to carry on, as it's something to fill the terrible hollow feeling that the absence of music and music-making gives to me.*

Away from London at weekends, Finzi continued to rehearse and give concerts, and began to spend weekday lunch-hours exploring little-known byways of string music suitable for amateurs to play. In this way the Newbury String Players revived many previously neglected English composers of the 18th century. Altogether typical was Finzi's constant concern for composers whose work he felt had been overlooked. He refused to perform his own music with the Players, but took endless trouble to foster the work of those who would otherwise remain anonymous. He worked tirelessly, for instance, on behalf of Ivor Gurney – whom he never met – almost forcibly extracting the manuscripts from the protective family who guarded them. Though not by nature a committee-man, Finzi was always the first to support any organisation whose task it was to administer funds to a talented beneficiary, and as chairman of the Berkshire County Music Committee fought many a battle on behalf of local music-making.

The war over, commissions began to flow in: a festival anthem, *Lo, the full final sacrifice*, in 1946, and the following year an altogether bigger work, the *Ode for St Cecilia*. It was soon after setting Wordsworth's *Intimations of Immortality* that Finzi was brought to face his own mortality when he learnt he was suffering from a form of leukaemia and had at most ten years to live. Characteristically, he felt that if he was to carry on with his work, the fewer the people who knew of his illness the better, and between frequent hospital visits he simply continued to compose. In the middle of all this came a request from Barbirolli for a major work to be performed at the 1955 Cheltenham Festival. Finzi had long had a cello concerto in the back of his mind and at this time of apprehension, of medical treatments and a major operation, he produced a work on a bigger scale than anything he had done before. The slow movement, as with so much of Finzi's quiet music, reveals something of his deepest thoughts at this time. Howard Ferguson wrote of his friend's 'bubbling sense of fun, his humour and electric nervous energy ... always striding restlessly about the room', but also knew of the fundamental sadness which lay beneath the buoyant exterior.

In 1956, Finzi walked with his great friend and father-figure Vaughan Williams up Churchdown Hill near Gloucester and looked in on a family living in a local cottage. The children, it turned out, had chicken pox and with his own resistance to infection weakened, Finzi developed shingles and died shortly afterwards in a nursing home at Oxford. His work stood quite unselfconsciously outside the thrust of 20th-century music. So, too, did the composer. During the war, he once gave a lift to an American airman who was bemoaning the lack of fridges in England. When Finzi retorted that Bach had managed very well without one, his passenger wanted to know who this man Bach was: they completed the rest of the journey in silence.

Peter Racine Fricker

1920–1990

'He exerted a strong influence at a time when British composers were turning from the insularity of the war years.'
– Grove's Dictionary

Though closely followed by Searle, Fricker was the first British composer to establish a reputation entirely after the Second World War and by 1951, the year of the Festival of Britain, his position already seemed assured. Prizes, performances and commissions came pouring in, and in the decade which followed his reputation spread and acquired international status. Yet within a remarkably short space of time that recognition gradually diminished, at least as far as widespread performance of his music was concerned, and to the majority of today's listening public his name means little.

A direct descendant of the French dramatist Jean Racine, his family came originally from Wiltshire, though Fricker himself was born in Ealing and educated at St Paul's School, Hammersmith. Poor eyesight prevented him from joining the merchant navy, his original choice of career, and having studied the organ as a schoolboy, he entered the RCM instead, where he took counterpoint and composition under R O Morris and organ with Ernest Bullock. He also attended classes at Morley College, where he first met Tippett, but this formative period was interrupted by the war and in 1941 Fricker joined the RAF and served for a while as a radio operator. He married two years later, only to be posted to India as an intelligence officer, following an intensive training course in Japanese at London University.

On returning to London he tried to resume his studies at the RCM, but was refused on the grounds that he had already spent four years there.

Instead, he returned to Morley College, where Tippett, now director, suggested he study with Matyas Seiber, the Hungarian-born composer and teacher. In 1947, horn virtuoso Dennis Brain and his chamber group played Fricker's wind quintet in a BBC broadcast and from then on, for a time, his ascent was rapid. He joined the faculty of Morley College, working closely with Tippett, whom he succeeded in 1952 as director, and from 1955 also taught composition at the RCM. All this time he was writing radio and film music, lecturing, conducting, taking commissions and accepting a variety of administrative jobs to make ends meet. In 1958 the Leeds Centenary Festival commissioned an oratorio on a large scale and Fricker responded with his powerful *The Vision of Judgement*, composed in the tradition of Walton's *Belshazzar's Feast* written 27 years earlier.

Gradually, however, the demands of earning a livelihood by means other than composing became too time-consuming and in 1964 he seized upon the offer from the University of California to join the music staff at Santa Barbara. Originally the post was for one year only, but when offered a permanent appointment he readily agreed since he was provided with the means and leisure to compose in peace. In 1965 he was appointed professor and moved to nearby Goleta with his wife, and remained there for the rest of his life. He was a dedicated and patient teacher who provided guidance to many composition students over the years. A tall, imposing figure, he was nevertheless somewhat shy and reserved. In his spare time he managed to enjoy the company of cats while remaining a keen bird-watcher. He had since turned out some large works and a good many chamber pieces for local performance, but nothing that had the impact of his earlier efforts.

In 1989 he was appointed composer-in-residence of the Santa Barbara Symphony Orchestra, for which he composed the orchestral work *Walk by Quiet Waters*. It was while working on a second composition for them, and looking forward to retirement, that he fell ill with cancer and died early the following year.

Edward German

1862–1936

'Young England is full of splendid promise, but there is danger ahead in sacrificing the beauties of art to mere sensation.'
– German

Edward German began life as a Shropshire lad called Edward German Jones, the second of five children, all musical, to be born in Whitchurch. His father was organist at the local Congregational church and taught his son both piano and organ from an early age, so that Edward was occasionally able to deputise for him at Sunday services. He taught himself to play the violin well enough to join a small orchestra when he was 14 and, encouraged by his mother, cultivated an early interest in the theatre. A serious illness forced him to drop out of boarding school in Chester before the age of 16 and after his recovery it was suggested that he train as an engineering apprentice. Fortunately his musical talents were recognised by Walter Hay, conductor of the Whitchurch Choral Society, who coached him for the entrance examinations to the Royal Academy of Music, where he was admitted in 1880.

He spent seven years there studying the violin under Alfred Burnett and won a number of awards, including the Charles Lucas Medal in 1885 with his *Te Deum*. By this time he was teaching violin at the Academy and elsewhere, and the following year his first operetta, *The Two Poets*, was given a successful London production and toured the provinces. He also had a symphony performed at St James's Hall in the year of his graduation. It was during his RAM period that he dropped his surname to avoid confusion with another Edward Jones.

After leaving, German continued to teach and to perform as an orchestral player, often in the theatre orchestras at the Savoy, and within the year he was conductor of the orchestra at the Globe Theatre, where his incidental music for *Richard III* won him notice. Thereafter he was in great demand for such scores, writing music for several Shakespeare plays, most notably for a production of *Henry VIII*. A set of three dances from the score gained wide popular acclaim and earned him a reputation as a composer of music in a quasi-Tudor style. His most successful years were those after the death of Sullivan in 1900, when he was commissioned to finish Sullivan's score for *The Emerald Isle*. To follow it, a libretto was written to exploit his popular old-English style, and the comic opera *Merrie England* became an established part of the repertoire of amateur companies everywhere. For a time German concentrated on other genres and wrote the *Welsh Rhapsody* and a number of songs, among which *Glorious Devon* achieved particular success, but in 1907 he returned to comic opera with *Tom Jones*, which also proved popular and led to an invitation to conduct the work in America.

Although only 47, German then virtually retired from composition, adapting only his *Henry VIII* music for the coronation of George V, and a *Theme and Six Diversions* in 1919 for the Royal Philharmonic Society. Though he continued occasionally to conduct, he primarily amused himself as a bachelor country gentleman, pursuing his recreations of walking, cycling, fishing and watching cricket at Lord's, a short distance from his home in Kilburn. He was increasingly troubled by rheumatism and in 1927 lost the sight of his right eye. He was knighted the following year, not, one suspects, for his contribution to serious music but for the lasting appeal of his lighter works. The *Welsh Rhapsody* and the *Norwich Symphony*, however, suggest a more subtle composer than history remembers and what he lacked in originality was balanced by a gift for melody and simplicity.

Percy Grainger

1882–1961

'It is no use living merely not to die. One should live to really live.'
– Grainger

If he could have sat still for more than two minutes, Percy Grainger would have made a fascinating subject for any psychoanalyst. To call him eccentric would be kinder, but that would detract from the man of stature that he undoubtedly was. He lived in that strange realm where madness and genius merge imperceptibly and which often produces great art. Remembered mainly for his folk-derived pieces like *Molly on the Shore* and *Country Gardens* (which he once said had more to do to with turnips than flowers), he died a bitter and frustrated man. At his most creative Grainger was a serious, not to say wholly independent and even revolutionary, composer. An idealist, with boundless energy, compassionate and generous to a fault, regarded by many as a buffoon, he was also a complex and misunderstood man whose contribution to the music of the 20th century is only now beginning to emerge.

Grainger was born in Melbourne, the only child of Rose, an overbearing and possessive mother, who became the dominant force in his life. His whole personality was shaped from the cradle by their extraordinary relationship, so that even on the rare occasions when they were apart her influence was almost tangible. He had no formal education, his entire schooling lasting no longer than three months, and he was allowed only selected adult company. Under his mother's guidance, the young Grainger devoured a huge array of literature, cultivated a mastery of foreign languages, acquired a talent for painting, and from the age of five studied piano. This 'hot-house' upbringing produced deeply ingrained habits and attitudes which were always to be part of him. His passion for long hours of hard and frenzied work, his curious naivety and his unsophisticated humour, and the fact that in so many ways, like Peter Pan, he never grew up, could all be traced back to his strange childhood. By the age of ten it was felt he had outgrown Rose's piano lessons and thereafter he received professional tuition, giving his first public performance two years later. This was by all accounts an assured debut and signified Grainger's future as a concert pianist.

In 1895, Rose and her son sailed to Frankfurt, where he would continue his studies at the Hoch Conservatorium of Music. During his years there, Grainger fell in with four English students, Norman O'Neill, Roger Quilter, Cyril Scott and Balfour Gardiner, and with the exception of O'Neill, they remained his friends for life. Scott in particular provided support when the more eccentric of his young friend's suggestions brought upon him the ridicule of academic superiors. One of these was to replace the baton-waving conductor with an 'orchestral supervisor' who would operate by remote control mechanical music desks through which the score would pass. He had indeed a penchant for mechanical contraptions which in later years led to the construction of machines for the creation of his Free Music. Though he was not taken seriously at the time, it is tempting to ponder on what he might have achieved given access to today's generation of synthesisers and multitrack recording facilities.

His contact with other musicians, however, introduced him to a wide selection of composers and musical thought, and the Frankfurt years were decisive in his development as a composer. He rejected the belief which equated length with profundity, and light-heartedness with frivolity. His music got to the point, a style which ensured his popularity with the wider public but often at the expense of his being taken seriously by the musical establishment. Many of these enduring compositions he later regarded as artistic liabilities, in the same way perhaps that Conan Doyle rued the success of Sherlock Holmes. Nevertheless, by 1901 Grainger had mastered a selection of solo piano items and a few piano concertos,

including that of Grieg, and in order to provide a more comfortable existence for his mother, he decided to seek a living giving recitals in London. At the age of twenty-one Grainger stood poised on the brink of his most active years as a composer and concert pianist.

Once settled in Kensington, Grainger quickly became established as a concert pianist of note and performed throughout Britain. His charm, striking good looks and prodigious talent attracted an almost hysterical gathering of society hostesses and he soon became a favourite in London music circles. Never comfortable in this role, Grainger saw the endless touring and recitals as a means of supporting himself and his mother while concentrating on his passion for composing. Proud of his Anglo-Saxon heritage and seeking a relief from his onerous public life, it wasn't long before he became caught up in the growing enthusiasm for folksong collecting, an activity which provided him with the basis of many of his best-known pieces and arrangements. He had an approach which put folk singers at their ease and he was able to collect a wonderful repertoire of some 500 songs. He was also the first member of the Folk Dance and Song Society, founded in 1898, to tramp about the countryside with an Edison Bell cylinder phonograph making live recordings of his singers. Unfortunately, his concert life kept him away from the task of transcribing many of the cylinders into manuscript form, but his typically energetic attitude to folksong collection during this period is one of his most important contributions to the history of British music.

After a decade and a half of energetic composing, arranging and performing (increasingly his own music), Grainger arrived in New York in 1914 and when war broke out in Europe he decided to stay on and he became an American citizen in 1918. His most intense and productive compositional activity was behind him, but America welcomed him with open arms and glowing reviews. He was soon earning a good living from touring, both as an accompanist and a concert pianist. When the USA entered the war, he enlisted in the Coast Artillery Corps as a bandsman and, thinking that he might be posted to France, he promptly made piano rolls of his unfinished music. In fact, he was sent no further than New York, near enough for Rose to go on making his favourite brown sugar sandwiches every morning.

After the war Grainger continued touring America, travelling everywhere by train, a form of transport he always enjoyed. He did not need peace and quiet to compose and found working on trains ideal. (Later, when radio arrived, he was frequently to do his best work with the radio turned up to its fullest volume.) He would always travel second class, often alighting from the train at the station before his destination and running the rest of the way - donating the difference in fare to a local charity. Photographs show him striding off with a rucksack and on one occasion he walked sixty-five miles between Friday and Saturday evening concerts. He preferred to be in a state of nervous and physical excitement before a recital and would often run to the town before a performance wearing running shorts, with his evening dress rolled up in a bag on his back. During his first concert tour of South Africa, he misjudged the distance to his next destination and the audience were already taking their seats when Grainger's friends, searching the horizon with binoculars, saw a cloud of dust. It cleared to reveal a tribe of Zulu warriors heading for the township accompanying Grainger jogging along in their midst. (He was not at all pleased when his travelling companions were refused seats for the recital.) Walking wasn't his only interest: he continued to paint, wrote copious letters and articles, and made himself clothes out of towels. These didn't catch on.

Meanwhile, Rose's health was deteriorating; her mental stability received a further blow when a rumour spread that her relationship with her son was incestuous. In 1922, a friend returned to the 18th floor of the Aeolian Building in New York, where she had left the now frail Rose sitting, to find an empty chair beside the open window. Her body was found on the roof below. Grief-stricken, Grainger left America for a punishing tour of Europe, where he walked eighty-six miles in three days carrying a heavy rucksack and sleeping mostly under the stars. Returning to America by ship he met Ella Viola Strom-Bundelius, a Swedish

112

woman, who curiously resembled his mother, and whom he later married at the end of a concert on the stage of the Hollywood Bowl before an audience of 20,000. Needless to say, the honeymoon was a hectic climbing and walking tour in the Glacier National Park.

He continued to perform, compose and walk enormous distances until, at the age of seventy-one, he developed prostate cancer. With his accumulating wealth he had bought a fine house in White Plains, his home for forty years, and it was there on 20th February, 1961, that he died with Ella at his side. Generous to a fault, boundlessly energetic, tirelessly pioneering, modest about his impressive talents, Percy Grainger was an anarchist by nature with a bewilderingly original mind. He deserves a longer epitaph than *Country Gardens*, and fortunately in the 1990s the release of a CD series devoted to his entire output is giving us the chance to hear the full range of his work.

Ivor Gurney
1890–1937

*'He'll stay untouched till the war's last dawning
Then live one hour of agony.'* – Gurney

Gurney wrote these lines in the trenches in 1917 during a lull in hostilities. They were frighteningly prophetic for in them, darkly, he glimpsed his own fate. His musical career was, like George Butterworth's, cruelly foreshortened by the Great War, but perhaps even more tragically, he died not from gunfire but from tuberculosis in a London mental hospital some nineteen years later.

The second of four children of a Gloucestershire tailor, Ivor Gurney experienced a good deal of hardship in his early years. His father ran his own business and was moderately well off, but despite some success and his wish for a quiet life, his wife's temperament was more volatile and critical, creating a tension in the cramped house in Barton Street with little room for childhood to flourish. When six years old, Ivor started Sunday school at All Saints Church and two years later joined the choir, attracting the attention of the curate, Alfred Cheesman. Their relationship was to have a profound effect on Gurney's future. Cheesman was twenty-five, a kind and gentle man with few ambitions of his own but a sincere desire to nourish enthusiasm in others. Under his watchful eye, Gurney secured a place at the King's School which served the needs of the Cathedral Choir. In such an environment a sensitive boy might be expected to have flourished and to have received a thorough grounding in musical education. In actual fact, the musical standards were not particularly high and the quality of teaching was decidedly average, so that Gurney's own recollections of those days concern cricket and football rather than academic stimulation.

Nevertheless, throughout this time Gurney was encouraged by Cheesman, who provided a welcome alternative to the restrictive atmosphere of home. He introduced the impressionable boy to a range of literature far beyond the few books he found in his own front parlour and encouraged him when he first began to write songs. The influence of this benevolent man can scarcely be exaggerated, not least in introducing Gurney to the sisters Emily and Margaret Hunt – Emily played the violin and Margaret the piano. A generation older than he, these spinster ladies provided a haven of inspiration which echoed through the dark years which lay ahead.

At seventeen, Gurney left the school and enrolled as a pupil of the Cathedral organist, Dr Herbert Brewer, who did his best to instil in his headstrong pupil the rudiments of counterpoint and harmony. As teacher and pupil they did not get on. Gurney was undisciplined and opinionated, swept along by all that his inventive mind was discovering. It was significant that when Dr Brewer later published his autobiography, he made no mention of Gurney, although he reminisced fondly about Herbert Howells. He and Gurney were fellow pupils of Brewer and became firm friends for life. Not only were they of a similar age and background, but both were captivated by Gloucestershire, its city and countryside.

It seems, however, that they were markedly different in temperament and appearance. Howells, elegant and strikingly handsome, stood in complete contrast to the awkward, bespectacled and somewhat shuffling Gurney, whose indifference to clothes and personal appearance was astonishing. His behaviour, too, was disconcerting. His family saw little of him and understood him even less. He would take himself off for long walks, sometimes for days on end, sleeping in the open or on the floor of a friend's house. Digestive problems plagued him all his life, exacerbated by his erratic eating habits involving long periods without food followed by excessive quantities of cakes and left-overs. But if his family saw little of him, his friends saw a great deal and he would walk in unannounced at any time of the day or night. The Hunt sisters kept open house for him, as did Alfred Cheesman, for no matter how unconventional his behaviour may have been, his talent and enthusiasm were infectious and he possessed an unworldly charm which could not be resisted.

By the age of seventeen Gurney was writing music to some purpose and it was clear that he stood in need of more advanced training than Gloucestershire could offer. In the autumn of 1911, with the help of the Rev Cheesman, Gurney enrolled as a student at the RCM and began lessons in composition under the critical eye of Charles Stanford. He did not get on with his new teacher, who looked aghast at Gurney's confused and almost illegible musical scores which suggested a mind already out of touch with reality. The songs, however, were a different story. Written with an innocent spontaneity, they revealed genuine originality beyond the teachings of Stanford and even the influence of Vaughan Williams. In later years, Sir Charles declared that, of all his pupils, Gurney was potentially the greatest of them all, but also the least teachable. With his instinctive feel for the power of words, it was only a matter of time before Gurney was drawn to the writing of poetry himself and by 1913 he was devoting almost as much time to this as to his music.

At the outbreak of war, Gurney was initially rejected on the grounds of defective eyesight, but by 1915 the authorities were less fastidious and in February he was drafted into the army. Within the year he was sent to France with the 2nd/5th Gloucesters. To escape the boring routines of army life, he wrote copious letters to friends, in particular to Marion Scott, once secretary at the RCM, and to his old friend from Gloucester whom he addressed affectionately as 'My Dear Erbert Owls'. Starved of the opportunities of writing music, Gurney took to writing poetry, scribbling in pencil in small notebooks that would fit into his uniform pockets, and 1917 saw the publication of his first collection, *Severn and Somme*. Despite the horrors of trench warfare, the poems often share with the letters a curious detachment. The comradeship, physical endurance and release from having to think for himself all provided an unexpected tranquillity, enabling him to achieve the near impossible feat of composing music on the battlefield. Needless to say, there was no piano to hand, which argues an exceptional degree of concentration made all the more impressive by the fact that the first of five songs, a setting of Masefield's *By a Bierside* – written in a disused trench-mortar emplacement – is an undoubted masterpiece.

While his thoughts remained in Gloucestershire, Gurney was not impervious to the hazards of the front line and he was eventually wounded in the arm and hospitalised in Rouen for six weeks. He recovered in time to be involved in the fighting that autumn at Passchendale, but was caught this time in a mustard gas attack. After a year in military hospitals, during which his mental health began to deteriorate, the army declared him to be past rehabilitation owing to 'deferred shell shock' and he was discharged in October 1918.

Returning to Gloucester, Gurney was unable to find the peace and security he needed and it became increasingly evident to his friends and family that he was still deeply disturbed. He found some relief in physical hard work and lengthy walking tours and the following year he felt well enough to resume his studies at the RCM, this time under the tutelage of Vaughan Williams. The second half of 1919 saw Gurney writing some remarkable songs, several short piano pieces and an extended orchestral work among other items. This brief period of intense creative activity lasted a year, when again mental instability reappeared. He thought nothing of walking from London to Gloucester, sleeping under the stars and earning a few pennies singing folksongs in country inns. On more than one occasion he was picked up by the police, only to be released again as a harmless eccentric. He remained a nominal student in London until the summer of 1921; after that it was impossible for him to continue. He returned to Gloucester but soon after began to suffer delusions, and after twice attempting suicide was eventually admitted to Barnwood Mental Hospital in the town.

Just before Christmas in 1922, Gurney was moved to the City of London Mental Hospital at Dartford, Kent. There, though he experienced periods of lucidity, he spent the rest of his life. Many of his best poems emerged through the muddle and genius of his mind during this time, but he finally gave up composition around 1928.

During this last period of his life, Gurney's friends – notably Finzi and Ferguson, though they were never to meet him – collected and preserved his manuscripts, evaluated them and prepared the best for publication. Gurney himself was unaware of this activity on his behalf and late in 1937 he fell ill and died. His body was taken back to Gloucester and towards the evening on the last day of the year he was buried at Twigworth.

Patrick Hadley

1889–1973

'All the trees they do grow high,
The leaves they are so green,
The day is past and gone, my love,
That you and I have seen.'
– folksong

Hadley was the younger of two sons born in Cambridge, where their father was Master of Pembroke College. After attending the King's College School, he was educated from 1912 to 1917 at Winchester. His brother had already been mortally wounded in action when Patrick, aged 18, joined the Royal Field Artillery and was commissioned as a second lieutenant. Within a few weeks of going into action on the western front he was wounded, losing one leg above the knee, but whatever the psychological damage, he refused to accept any physical limitations and bicycled, swam, played tennis and remained an active hill-walker until well into middle-age. (He would often wear his artificial leg back to front to amuse friends and confound strangers, and gave tuition with it standing at his side, saying 'mind my leg' as pupils arrived.)

After the war he resumed his education with three years at Pembroke College before enrolling at the RCM, where he studied composition with Vaughan Williams and conducting with Adrian Boult. Together with fellow pupil Ivor Gurney, he became an enthusiastic supporter of English folksong, inspired naturally by Vaughan Williams, who became a close friend of the young man (despite receiving quirky telegrams from him at all hours of the night), and his finest work, *The Trees so High*, uses a Somerset tune to make a fully fledged four-movement choral symphony in its own right. This was written in 1931, six years after he was elected

119

to a college lectureship in music at Cambridge with the somewhat vague job description of 'encouraging the musical activities of the young men'. By this time he had to his credit nine major compositions which had all received important public performances, while his own work with the College Chorus, for which he both composed and arranged music, became justly well known in the university and outside it.

During the war he deputised for Boris Ord as conductor of the University Musical Society and was subsequently elected to the Chair of Music, remaining there for the next twenty-six years. His hospitality and humour were well known and generations of undergraduates, who knew him affectionately as 'Paddy', would regularly visit his rooms to enjoy his amusing company. He was also an influential friend and mentor to the likes of Bax, Lambert, Warlock, Moeran, Rawsthorne, Howells and Walton, though he always found composition a laborious process and his own output remained disappointingly small. What there is reflects his own meticulous standards where every note is weighed before being committed to manuscript in order to achieve exactly the desired effect.

Over the years, Hadley had taken refuge in large quantities of alcohol which exacerbated his often wayward and unpredictable behaviour. Colleagues and friends were sympathetic, but in 1960 he decided on a sabbatical and retired as Professor the following year at the age of 63. The next few years were spent travelling in a vain attempt to alleviate his increasing loneliness before the onset of throat cancer in 1972.

Hamilton Harty

1879–1941

'Was it a vision, or a waking dream?
Fled is that music: Do I wake or sleep?'
– John Keats: *Ode to a Nightingale*

Hamilton Harty was one of the first British conductors to win international fame, though he preferred to think of himself as a composer. He was born at Hillsborough, County Down, and had a Northern Irish upbringing. His father taught him to play the viola and piano and by the age of 12 he was organist at a church in County Antrim, moving on to posts in Belfast and Dublin, where he was advised and helped by the Italian composer Michele Esposito. In Dublin he gained a reputation as a particularly sensitive piano accompanist to singers, and arriving in London in 1900 he soon consolidated his standing, being heralded as a promising composer in his own right. Four years later he married the soprano Agnes Nicholls, to whom he dedicated his setting of a Keats poem, and won approval for his Piano Trio and Quartet, but even more significant was the success of his *Comedy Overture* at the Proms in 1907. His tone poem *With the Wild Geese* enabled him to take a distinct place among the rising number of young British composers in the first decade of the century, and more than one of the great provincial festivals produced his works, notably his Walt Whitman cantata *The Mystic Trumpeter*, given at Leeds in 1913.

It was about this time that Harty began to make a name for himself as a conductor and during the war years he frequently appeared in Manchester with the Hallé Orchestra. When, in 1920, the Hallé Society decided to appoint a conductor exclusively devoted to the orchestra's interests, they looked no further than Harty, who quickly restored its

fading reputation and for the next thirteen years made the orchestra one of the best in the country. Although his impetuous and sometimes capricious personality courted controversy on occasions, he introduced many new works and composers to his audiences. The music of Bax, Sibelius, Berlioz, Moeran, Walton and Strauss featured largely in his programmes, and in 1929 he played the piano part in the first performance of Lambert's *The Rio Grande*. His manner with an orchestra was quiet, and his unquestioned authority was derived from his outstanding musicianship combined with the warmth and exuberant humour of his personality.

Knighted in 1925, his fame spread through the series of recordings he made with the Hallé, and he was increasingly in demand as a guest conductor. His frequent absences, however, did not meet with the board's approval; they took him to task and he promptly resigned. He spent the rest of his career conducting elsewhere, principally with London orchestras, and premièred Walton's First Symphony in 1934 with the LSO. He had already toured America and visited Australia, where his skill in welding together an orchestra from assembled collections of players served to create a new era in orchestral playing in Melbourne and Sydney.

Harty's last years were chequered by ill-health, but he continued to accept conducting engagements and his delicate transcription of *A John Field Suite* in 1939 was hailed as a highly original contribution to the challenging art of orchestral arrangement. Two years later, poor health overtook him and he died at Hove in February 1941.

Joseph Holbrooke

1878–1958

'Nameless here for evermore' – Edgar Allan Poe: *The Raven*

Earlier in this century Holbrooke was seldom absent from the main festivals and symphony concerts, and any serious discussion of contemporary English music would have included his name. Now he seems largely forgotten and his music, once so much in demand, is rarely heard today.

He learned the rudiments of music from his father and made his debut as a pianist at a London music hall when he was only twelve. Later he attended the RAM, where he won both a prestigious scholarship and the Lucas Prize. He was already composing before he left in 1898, supporting himself by taking occasional conducting jobs and playing the piano, generously devoting a series of concerts to publicise the music of his fellow English contemporaries. He was once called 'the Cockney Wagner' and, like his hero, Holbrooke seems to have preferred to live on patronage. In his early 'twenties he was sponsored by the German conductor August Manns, who produced his symphonic poem *The Raven* at the Crystal Palace in 1900. Holbrooke favoured large orchestras and big subjects, and was fascinated all his life by another hero, Edgar Allan Poe. Wagner, Poe, the Celtic twilight – the singularity of his tastes was obvious enough and he soon completed another tone poem in the same idiom, *The Viking*, which was produced by his friend Granville Bantock.

Like Rutland Boughton, Holbrooke had socialist leanings and talked of writing music 'for the people', but his only work to achieve real popularity was a set of orchestral variations on *Three Blind Mice* played at the Proms. He later attempted to capitalise on this success with his variations on *Auld Lang Syne* and *The Girl I Left Behind Me*. When the

124

Irish poet Herbert Trench commissioned Holbrooke to set his curious poem *Apollo and the Seaman* to music, the result was a huge symphonic piece whose first performance also failed to impress, partly for want of an indispensable player of a bass-sarrusophone. At the performance, conducted by Beecham at the Queen's Hall, the occasion was made all the more outlandish by means of a magic lantern projecting the poem on a screen so that the audience could follow the work's progress.

All this provided welcome publicity and Holbrooke's next patron, Lord Howard of Walden, was willing to pay handsomely for the composer to set his vast poem derived from the Welsh epic *The Mabinogion* as an operatic trilogy. Beecham conducted the première of *The Children of Don* in 1912, and Nikisch that of *Dylan* two years later. Performances followed in Vienna and Salzburg, indicating the appeal of Holbrooke's music in the first quarter of the century. However, the third work, *Bronwen*, was not completed until 1922 and had to wait another seven years for its first performance, in Huddersfield, by which time the situation had deteriorated sharply and Holbrooke, once notorious for courting violent controversy, gradually lapsed into silence. He lived to be 80, but in his last years he was hampered by growing deafness and disillusionment, settling deeper and deeper into eccentricity and solitude. For over half his life Holbrooke wrote prodigiously and uncritically, perhaps at the expense of too much exposure and notoriety, so that long before his death reaction had set in and his music was largely ignored. It remains to be seen if his present complete neglect is quite justified.

Gustav Holst

1874–1934

*'The three chief reasons for gratitude were music, and the
Cotswolds and Ralph Vaughan Williams.'* – Holst

Gustavus von Holst was born at a small house in Pittville Terrace,
Cheltenham, on 21 September, 1874. Three generations earlier, his
Swedish great-grandfather Matthias, also a musician, had arrived in
England, where he managed to earn a living teaching the piano. His son
grew up to be a composer as well as a pianist and eventually settled in
Cheltenham with his English wife. Both he and his brother were gifted
musicians, but when the eldest left to take up a musical appointment in
Glasgow it was his brother Adolph who became well known locally as
an outstanding pianist and organist; he married Clara Lediard in 1872 and
two years later their first son was born.

From an early age Gustav practised the piano every day under the
stern eye of his father. It was a strict upbringing not helped by the boy's
poor eyesight and asthma, neither of which received any medical
attention at the time. When, at the age of 7, his mother died suddenly,
Gustav and his younger brother Emil were looked after by a well-
meaning but incapable aunt until their father remarried a few years later.
It was as a pupil at the Cheltenham Grammar School that Gustav first
began to compose. His father gave him little encouragement, determined
that his son should be a really good pianist, but he was already suffering
from the neuritis in his right arm which was to trouble him for the rest of
his life, and at 17 he was with some reluctance allowed to spend a few
months in Oxford studying counterpoint. He then tried, unsuccessfully,

for a composition scholarship at the Royal College of Music and had to wait a further two years before he won a place in 1893.

Stanford thought Holst to be hardworking but not exceptional; fellow students found him easy enough to get on with, though forthright and uncompromising in his ideas on music. Solitary by inclination, disliking any display of sentiment, he nevertheless enjoyed a boisterous sense of fun and was given to fits of loud laughter when confronted with ideas which were unexpectedly humorous. It was a trait which remained with him through life and partly accounts for the lasting friendships he made. One such was with Ralph Vaughan Williams, whom he met about this time. They became close friends and began what was to be a lifelong habit of playing their compositions to each other while still working on them. They called them their 'field days'. Vaughan Williams conceded

that on occasions he dared not reveal to his friend a complete score because he 'could not face the absolute integrity of his vision'. It was this very honesty and directness of thought which enabled Holst to assimilate diverse elements into a style which fused vitality, clarity and austere mysticism.

For a long time he had been struggling against the pain in his arm and soon after joining the RCM was forced to give up the piano. He took up the trombone instead and was soon paying for his board and lodging playing on the pier at Blackpool and Brighton during the summer holidays or at London theatres during the pantomime season. On leaving the RCM in the autumn of 1898 he joined the Carl Rosa Opera Company and later toured with the Scottish Orchestra. He was not a brilliant trombonist but was competent and found the experience of orchestral playing invaluable when scoring his own compositions.

In 1901 he married Isobel Harrison, a young soprano he had met four years earlier. They lived for a while in lodgings at Shepherds Bush, but he soon realised that touring left no time for composition and he decided once and for all to earn a living by writing music. They were hard times during which Isobel kept things going by dressmaking, but in 1903 he was offered a teaching post at the James Allen Girls' School at Dulwich and his career as a teacher began. Two years later he was appointed director of music at St Paul's Girls' School in Hammersmith, a post he kept until the end of his life.

1905 was an important year in another way: his discovery of folksong. It is not difficult to see the appeal to a man of Holst's sensibilities who recognised at once the simplicity and economy of the tunes which he felt to be an essential element in any great art. His contribution to the *English Hymnal*, being edited at the time by Vaughan Williams, was the beautiful setting of Christina Rossetti's poem *A Christmas Carol*, more widely known as *In the bleak mid-winter*, which, more than anything he wrote, revealed his gift for simple, unadorned melody.

His absorbing interest in folk music, however, was not allowed to interfere with his Sanskrit studies, which he happened upon while still a student. He had learnt about Hindu literature and philosophy when trying to set some of the poems to music and took lessons at the School of Oriental Languages in the translation of Sanskrit literature – a brave attempt for someone who was inept at European languages. But by 1907 he had finished the music of *Sita* and was beginning to work on the first group of hymns from the *Rig Veda*.

Composing was easier now that he had moved from lodgings to a small house in Richmond from where he and Isobel escaped at weekends to a two-roomed cottage on the Isle of Sheppey. The accommodation was very basic, but after hectic weeks in London the remote and solitary landscape between fields and sea was delightfully peaceful, interrupted only by the birth of their daughter Imogen in the spring of 1907. This was the year that Holst took charge of the music at Morley College for Working Men and Women, then housed in gloomy premises next to the Old Vic. His success in raising standards of music at Morley he regarded as one of the major triumphs of his life, one which characterised his whole approach to music. It didn't matter that his first orchestral class consisted of eight amateur players and a choir which had difficulty with basic sight-reading. He hated textbooks and believed in practical music-making, putting honest enthusiasm before technical accomplishment every time. It was an approach which led to the memorable series of Whitsun festivals he organised at Thaxted some years later.

Inevitably, perpetual overwork took its toll and the following year Holst was reduced to a near breakdown from which he recovered only after an unusual holiday: bicycling in the Algerian desert. Living now in Barnes, he returned to teaching and composing, but publishers were not keen to accept his works and performances were few. His teaching flourished, however, and in the summer of 1911 Morley College gave the first performance since the 17th century of Purcell's *Fairy Queen*. Holst was exhilarated by the occasion but again it left him exhausted. Another holiday, this time walking in Switzerland, restored his health and in 1913, working from his new sound-proofed music room at St Paul's, he wrote the *St Paul's Suite* for the school orchestra. Teaching still took up most of his time and he was only able to compose at weekends and during August; he had still to achieve a breakthrough as a composer, storing away his ideas until the end of each week.

Moving out of London to Thaxted provided further opportunities for long weekends of composing, and some of the orchestration for *The Planets* was sketched there. He had already finished the first draft of *Mars, the Bringer of War* when it actually arrived in 1914 and he immediately tried to enlist. His neuritis and weak sight made him unfit for war service, but in the autumn of 1918 he gave up the 'von' in his name and was sent to the Middle East as a music organiser with the YMCA's Army Education Service. As a parting present his friend Balfour Gardiner gave him a private performance of *The Planets*, which he had finished the previous year. When he returned to England the following summer the suite had already had its first complete public performance.

Holst never considered *The Planets* to be his best work and was disconcerted by its sudden success. Soon afterwards *The Hymn of Jesus* was also hailed as a masterpiece by critics and audiences, and by 1921 there were so many performances of his works that he was often unable to keep track of them. It was perhaps just as well, for he heartily disliked all the attention and when called to the platform to receive rapturous applause he would gaze at the audience in blank dismay. Photographers found him fidgety and unhelpful and he remained tongue-tied when faced with reporters, scowling through his spectacles and surrounding himself in a sullen and impatient silence. He could now afford a home in town as well as in the country, but earning more money meant little to him as long as he could escape to the silence and solitude of his music room. This reticence extended to his public life and he made it a firm rule never to accept any honours, degrees or titles. He certainly tried to keep his mind as free from distraction as possible, but there were pressures from his publishers to revise earlier neglected works, as well as adjudicating and recording commitments. He had also been appointed to the staff of the RCM and of University College, Reading, where he spent a good deal of time teaching and lecturing.

It was at Reading in February 1923, while conducting his students, that he slipped from the platform and fell on the back of his head. The concussion was not serious, but it happened during a time when he was already feeling depressed and overworked. Although he seemed to recover during the spring in time to lecture and conduct in America, on his return to England he found himself on the verge of a serious nervous breakdown. His doctor ordered him to cancel all professional engagements and with a generous donation from an anonymous patron, Holst was able to retreat to the solitude of Thaxted. Initially his nerves got worse instead of better and he would sit crouched over the fire, withdrawn and silent, unable to sleep and fearful of any loud or sudden noise. But very slowly he began to recover and despite the continuous pain in his arm, he began to compose again so that by the beginning of 1925 he was back in London.

To his immense relief Holst found himself to be out of favour as a popular composer. His newest works were too austere for audiences accustomed to *Jupiter* and the *Somerset Rhapsody*: even Vaughan Williams admitted that he felt only a 'cold admiration' for the *Choral Symphony*, but Holst was untroubled and for the next six years he enjoyed the best time of his life as a composer. He was free to take occasional holidays, exploring Sicily or northern France and walking over the Gloucestershire hills or through the unfamiliar byways of London docks. He began going to theatres and would entertain friends at the 'George' in Hammersmith, ordering large steaks and draft beer in tankards. His later compositions continued to disappoint most listeners, including *Egdon Heath*, which had its first London performance in 1928, little more than a month after Thomas Hardy's death. Holst as usual was unmoved by those who thought the music ugly and monotonous: he knew it to be the best thing he had ever written, a view he held until his death.

In 1932 he took up the post of visiting lecturer in composition at Harvard and accepted many invitations to conduct his own works. He had never known such a hectic existence, but he greatly enjoyed the work and the company, and was looking forward to a concert tour in the spring. In March, however, he was taken ill with a severe attack of haemorrhagic gastritis and although he was well enough to return to England in June, he was forced to conserve his energies. In the autumn he returned to teaching at St Paul's and even took up the trombone again, but on Boxing Day he fell ill and the next few months were spent in and out of clinics. In spite of frequent pain he was able to go on composing and besides the *Lyric Movement* for viola and orchestra, and the *Brook Green Suite* for strings, he began scoring the *Scherzo* for a new symphony.

In December he went into another nursing home to receive further treatment which proved unsuccessful. He was offered two alternatives: a minor operation which would partially cure him, but which would leave him a semi-invalid, or major surgery which, if he survived, would restore his health. Holst didn't hesitate, for life without the energy to compose was unthinkable. In the event, the operation was successful but his heart was unequal to the strain and he died two days later on 25 May. On a midsummer afternoon his ashes were buried in the north transept of Chichester Cathedral.

Herbert Howells

1892–1983

'Show us Tintern and the sunset across the Malverns and Welsh Hills. Make us see the evening stars among the trees.'
– Letter to Howells from Ivor Gurney

Oliver Howells was born in a village on the edge of the Forest of Dean and could trace his family for several generations to districts in the vicinity of the Forest. He was a general builder and decorator by trade, honest and hardworking no doubt, but with no head for business, which frequently left his large family – six boys, including Herbert (the youngest), and two girls – in financial difficulties. In later years, Herbert bitterly recalled the patronising tone of some local townspeople and former friends, who cold-shouldered his father after the business failed.

Yet despite their lack of money the family was a happy one. Oliver was musically inclined and played the organ on Sundays at the local Baptist Church where Herbert was himself a choirboy and assistant organist. His musical ability came to the notice of Charles Bathurst, the local Squire, who arranged for Herbert to travel each week to Gloucester for piano lessons with Herbert Brewer, Organist and Master of the Choristers at the cathedral. Howells did not greatly care for these lessons, but in 1908 he left Lydney Grammar School and enrolled as a full-time pupil at the cathedral, where he met the ill-starred Ivor Gurney. They became close companions and together encountered the first performance of Vaughan Williams's *Tallis Fantasia* which affected both so much that sleep was impossible and they spent the rest of the night pacing the streets of Gloucester.

Gurney, also a pupil of the dour Dr Brewer, and equally frustrated, left the cathedral the following year to go to London and study with Stanford. Around this time, Howells decided to follow suit, spending a year at home devoting himself to composition before joining his friend at the RCM in May 1912. Among the pieces he submitted to the College, in the hope of gaining a scholarship, was a song cycle which he dedicated to the singer Dorothy Dawe. Howells had taken the place of her regular accompanist one evening and was captivated first by her voice and then by herself. Throughout his college days his private life revolved around his family in Gloucester and Dorothy, whom he eventually married in 1920.

While at the RCM, Howells remained on excellent terms with his renowned composition teacher Charles Stanford (given the latter's reputation for acerbity, this was no mean achievement), who called him 'my Son in Music' and who pulled every string at his disposal to keep his young protégé out of the army when war broke out in 1914. In the event, Howells was prevented from taking any part in the conflict when Graves' disease was diagnosed and he was given just six months to live. At that time there was no known cure until a heart specialist suggested he try radium treatment, and for two years Howells went twice a week to St Thomas's Hospital for injections in the neck. For a while he still expected an early death, but by 1920 was on the road to recovery. Having been forced, through ill health, to give up an appointment as Assistant Organist at Salisbury Cathedral, he returned to the RCM, this time on the staff as a composition teacher, and remained for a further fifty years.

Arthur Bliss, Arthur Benjamin, Ivor Gurney and Francis Warren were Howells's closest friends when they were students together at the RCM and each in his own way wrote affectionate letters from the front recording his high regard for Howells's musical ability. Warren was killed at Mons in 1917 and was commemorated in the beautiful *Elegy* for solo viola, string quartet and string orchestra. Benjamin served in the Royal Flying Corps, but was captured and remained a prisoner-of-war in

Germany until 1918. He and Howells remained close friends until his death in 1960. Bliss enjoyed a less intimate relationship with Howells – they were fundamentally different in outlook and temperament – but their friendship and mutual respect endured to the end of Bliss's life in 1975.

Howells's relationship with Ivor Gurney, however, was less straightforward. Without doubt, Gurney and he were at one time the closest of friends, but following Gurney's mental collapse, Howells had very little to say about his former companion from Gloucester. Certainly his visits to the asylum were infrequent. It may have been that the memories were too painful to recall; or perhaps, as one biographer has hinted, it was that Gurney's wild and untutored genius might have eclipsed that of Howells, who was regarded as the star of his generation at the RCM. Although restrained and self-effacing, Howells did enjoy the spotlight and may not have relished the prospect of being upstaged by the emerging reputation of his wayward and unpredictable friend.

Having joined the College as a member of staff, Howells set about earning a living. Unlike his friend Gerald Finzi, he could not afford to rely solely on composition as a ready source of income, and immersed himself in teaching, adjudicating and examining. Not surprisingly, his composing activities show a marked reduction in quantity, though not quality, and for the most part, Howells' life after 1920 remained outwardly uneventful. He and Dorothy settled in Hammersmith, where they had two children, Ursula and Michael, before renting a furnished house in Redmarley, a village in Gloucestershire. From the 1950s, Howells was relatively comfortably off, though there was never much money, and he lived modestly until his death in 1983, aged ninety.

Along the way, a tragedy of momentous proportions was waiting to engulf the composer and his family. On 12 April, 1935, Michael Howells had his ninth birthday, and at the beginning of August the family set off from London for their summer holidays in Gloucestershire. On Wednesday, 4 September, Michael felt unwell and a doctor was sent for. On Friday evening he died of spinal meningitis and five days later was buried at Twigworth. Ivor Gurney was himself buried there in early January, 1938, the same year that Howells completed the first draft of a requiem for Michael, *Hymnus Paradisi* – his most ambitious and arguably his greatest work. Henceforth, Howells was never the same composer again. The prevailing orchestral and chamber works gave way to the church and organ music for which he is mostly remembered. Fifteen years later, almost to the day of Michael's death, Howells conducted the first performance of *Hymnus Paradisi* at the Three Choirs Festival, having been encouraged by Finzi and Vaughan Williams to do so. It was rapturously received by critics and public. For a man who had previously recoiled at the slightest criticism of his work, the public success of *Hymnus Paradisi* was a small triumph compared with the private fulfilment of an intensely personal, almost secret, valediction. Recordings of Howells's longer choral and orchestral works issued in the 1990s have given us a belated but welcome view of his achievement.

John Ireland

1879–1962

'What's the good? Nobody wants the stuff.'

Though Chelsea was his home for over forty years, Ireland was born on the family estate in Cheshire, youngest by seven years of five children. Both his parents were writers, his father, Alexander, being editor of the *Manchester Examiner*, and the family was an open house to eminent musicians and literary figures of the day. Despite these comfortable middle-class surroundings, Ireland's childhood was singularly unhappy. His father was already sixty when his youngest son was born and remained an hospitable but remote figure. Annie Ireland, thirty years his junior, was an affectionate mother but in delicate health, preferring to spend much of her time alone in an upstairs room. These circumstances, and the disparity in the children's ages, placed the youngest boy very much under the authority of his elder brothers and sisters, who were quick to enforce the prevailing moral code with a zeal bordering on abuse. Increasingly music brought him real repose and happiness, and by the age of eight, Ireland began to show a genuine interest in the piano. By the opening of the 1890s, he knew that music would be his future life and living.

His first step was to seek serious training. Aged only thirteen, Ireland took himself to London to audition at the Royal College of Music, where he was subsequently accepted as a full-time student. He did not tell his family of the trip until his offer of a place had been confirmed, pretending instead that he had spent the day at a motoring exhibition in Manchester. This evidence of his determination to study music overcame his mother's initial resistance to the boy's move away from home, and lodgings were found for him in Bayswater. So it was that he entered the College just a few months before his fourteenth birthday. Less than six months later both parents died, leaving him an orphan but with sufficient funds in trust for him to continue his studies. For the next four years Ireland concentrated his attention on the piano, studying with Frederick Cliffe before deciding that his future lay in composition rather than performance. He wrote his first rudimentary string quartet during a summer holiday in the Lake District in 1895 and dedicated it to Stanford, who promptly dismissed the work as being 'dull as ditchwater'. In due course he relented, and despite his innate sensitivity, Ireland came to appreciate the discipline imposed by Stanford's teaching.

In 1900 he became organist-choirmaster of St. Luke's, Chelsea, where he stayed for a quarter of a century. Chelsea remained his home and parish almost for life and there, in his Gunter Grove studio, he passed his most prolific years as a composer and teacher. During these early years, Ireland established himself firmly in the local and artistic life of Chelsea. With his inheritance to support him he was free to teach and compose, entertain friends, and enjoy the company of many acquaintances in the nearby Gunter Arms. Ireland was a man of contrasts. He liked solitude, but was a lively and convivial companion; was genuinely kind towards pupils, yet capable of sudden, if exaggerated, outbursts of temper; was small and slight of stature, but with an exuberant enthusiasm for fast cars – his first was a green Talbot 8 with bright yellow wings. When not driving around London he would set off for the sea and countryside on day-trips to Dorset, Kent and Sussex. A favourite retreat was Deal, where he had taken a flat in the High Street, and from 1905 he made frequent visits there on the slow Kentish ride from Charing Cross.

Waiting one day for his train to arrive, Ireland picked up a book from the station kiosk entitled *House of Souls* and after a brief glimpse into its pages felt an immediate affinity with its author, Arthur Machen. He already had an interest in the prehistoric, the pagan and the mystic, but

now felt that the world of his own imagination was shared by someone who could interpret this lost world in words. Machen's books exercised a strong influence on Ireland's music, most noticeably heard in *Mai Dun* and *Legend*, although clearly evident in several other of his compositions. It was a turning point for Ireland and in 1908, nearing thirty, he discarded all but a few works written before the age of twenty-one.

From about this time, Ireland made frequent visits to the Channel Islands to absorb their prehistoric and pagan associations which so intrigued him. *The Forgotten Rite* was the result of island impressions gathered over several stays and is a work permeated by an ancient mysticism. Despite its recognition as a major composition, Ireland was particularly put out by its general neglect and came to refer to the piece as 'Forgotten Quite' In later years he became increasingly sensitive to real or imagined neglect of his music and dubbed *Mai Dun* as 'May Not Be Done' when its novelty wore off on concert promoters.

After the Great War, Ireland revisited the Sussex countryside inland towards Steyning and the hills culminating in Chanctonbury Ring. Captivated by the surrounding villages he took permanent lodgings at Ashington and began gradually to leave behind the increasingly noisy Chelsea. Many ideas sprang from early morning walks among the ancient tumuli and barrows scattering these downlands: mystery and ancient rites drew him as strongly here as in the Channel Islands.

1923 brought Ireland back as a professor to the RCM, where he stayed until 1939, teaching composition to the likes of Moeran, Britten, Geoffrey Bush, and Arnell. For the most part these were good years. He was excellent company, a talented mimic, unashamedly fond of good food and wine, and a much admired and respected teacher. One of his pupils at the time was a seventeen-year-old student, Dorothy Phillips. Ireland was in his late forties, absorbed but often lonely; she was flattered by the admiration of so distinguished a musician. When her parents went abroad, their inflammable relationship resulted in a disastrous marriage.

The couple separated on the night of the wedding and the marriage was quickly annulled.

With war becoming almost certain, Ireland closed the weekend flat in Deal and shut up the Chelsea studio, before departing for what was assumed would be a safe haven in Guernsey. Several months later he was crammed aboard a tiny ferry making a desperate escape from German occupation to the mainland, where he arrived virtually homeless. He was soon rescued by the Rev Paul Walde, an old friend from St Luke's, Chelsea, and in 1942 moved into their Rectory at Little Sampford in Essex. He spent the next three years composing incidental music and indulging his favourite relaxation – cooking, which he regarded as a form of composition.

Returning to Chelsea after the war, Ireland embarked upon a demanding round of engagements, but post-war London was chaotic and his health was beginning to deteriorate. His work on the film score *The Overlanders*, though a great success, involved up to eighteen hours a day for six weeks and left him exhausted. Worse was an alarming deterioration in his sight. Just before his 75th birthday he moved into Rock Mill at Washington, a converted windmill which he had long admired. Here, at his home in the green of the Sussex countryside from where he could look out onto Chanctonbury Ring, Ireland passed the last few years of his life.

Among the few London buildings to survive the Fire of London is the ancient Church of the Holy Sepulchre – the Musicians' Church, to be found in Smithfield. Occupying part of its west wall are six pictorial panels representing John Ireland's life and work – a biography in stained glass. It includes the places which influenced his music, among them Sussex, where he died peacefully in June 1962.

Gordon Jacob

1895–1984

'... my style is deeply rooted in the traditions in which I was trained and which, by inclination, I followed.'

A glance at the dates of Gordon Jacob's life describes a composer born into the late Victorian era who lived to see man walk on the Moon. In those years, upheavals in music reflected the turmoil of this troubled century yet here was a man belonging to that lost generation of British composers whose music remained faithful to an unmistakable English tradition.

He was born in Upper Norwood, London, the tenth and last child of a middle-class family. In later years, friends discerned the military traits of his forebears – his father was an official in the Indian Civil Service stationed in Calcutta and was himself the son of an Indian Army officer, but died when Jacob was only three. The following year the family moved into a larger house in Wimbledon which stood in an acre of ground, and despite the loss of his father Jacob enjoyed a secure and comfortable childhood. At the age of seven he was sent to prep school and soon after began piano lessons, so that within two years he was rising early to compose songs before setting off for school. By the time he entered Dulwich College, at thirteen, he was already writing full orchestral scores, but an accident at this time severed a tendon of the little finger, preventing him from developing his technique at the piano or from learning a stringed instrument, and since he had also been born with a cleft palate, wind instruments were also ruled out. Yet throughout his school days Jacob engaged in every musical opportunity which presented itself and laid the foundation for his mastery of orchestration for which he was to become renowned.

In the summer of 1914 he had just reached the age of 19 and was holidaying in Devon when war was declared. Like so many of his generation, Jacob put aside his own plans and within a few months of enlisting found himself in France and in the front line. In the spring of 1916 he was sent back to England as potential officer material, the same year that his brother Anstey was killed on the Somme just short of his 23rd birthday. Jacob never really got over the loss and dedicated his First Symphony to his memory. Finishing his officer training, Jacob was himself sent to the Somme, where he led an unsuccessful attack on the German lines and was taken prisoner. At the camp in Strohen he managed somehow to acquire an old upright, and finding piano scores when looking through the canteen facilities maintained some sort of practice, even working through a harmony textbook he discovered on a shelf. Early in 1918 he was moved to another camp with more comfortable amenities and gathered around him a band of four strings and three wind with himself on piano – a POW orchestra for whom he both wrote and arranged, much to the astonishment and amusement of his captors.

The war over, Jacob was repatriated and with a gratuity of £150 and accumulated pay he was able to train for a career. At first he turned to journalism as a means of earning a living, but soon reverted to music and gained a place at the RCM, where he studied under Stanford and the young Herbert Howells. Owing to the war there was something of a bulge of students, many of them, like Jacob, of more mature years and destined to become leading figures in the renaissance of English music. More modestly Jacob trod the line between paid musical chores which were not too time-consuming and working on his own compositions. Part-time work at the RCM and for the Associated Board seemed for the moment to be the answer to his financial needs and in 1924 he felt secure enough to marry a young woman, with the unlikely Christian name of Sidney, whom he had met soon after the war. In 1927 the couple bought a house at Ewell from where he took a genuine interest in the life of the local community, something he did wherever he lived.

He was now a regular member of the RCM teaching staff and somehow managed to fit in teaching at Morley and Birkbeck Colleges. Performances of his works given at the Proms were well received by critics and audiences, while music students acclaimed his very readable books, which gave practical hints in instrumentation. In November 1931 Jacob was approached by Elstree Studios, on the recommendation of his friend Constant Lambert, and began work in films with the orchestration of Bliss's music for the film *Things to Come*. He also took on the job of Music Adviser and Inspector to the LCC, orchestrated works for Sadler's Wells, and still found time to involve himself in local music-making.

By 1935 he was renowned as a brilliant all-round musician who could be relied upon to fill practically any gap. When Elgar died the previous year his successor, Walford Davies, approached Jacob with a view to orchestration work for royal occasions, and his contribution to the Empire Day concert no doubt brought his name to the attention of court circles. Within two years he was an almost indispensable figure in the background of every royal event, arranging and orchestrating music for the coronation of George VI in 1937 and, the following year, 'By Royal Command', contributing to another Empire Day concert.

It came as something of a shock to Jacob when he received his call-up papers at the age of 44 with the declaration of war but Dyson, now Director at the RCM, assured the authorities that Jacob was doing 'work of national importance'. In spite of restrictions, professional concerts continued to thrive and after the destruction of the Queen's Hall in 1941 the psychological need for music if anything increased. A similar impulse lay behind the National Gallery concerts, where Jacob's name occurred frequently in their programmes.

Another measure of the man's selfless desire to put his 'trade', as he called it, at the service of others, not to mention his own pragmatic approach to music, was his contribution between 1942 and 1948 to the popular weekly BBC radio series 'ITMA' that did so much for war-time morale. Each programme had at its centre a three-minute musical item consisting of an orchestral piece founded on a well-known tune, an amusing contrivance which delighted Jacob and millions of listeners. Some of the musical establishment, however, were less charitable, believing he had demeaned himself by becoming involved in such low-brow activities and, what was worse, had seemed to enjoy it. Neither would they have been impressed by his willingness to assist the war effort by writing documentary film music, but his more serious output continued and broadcasts of his works were heard throughout the period. He also continued to teach at the RCM and undertook arduous examining tours as well as writing a large-scale Second Symphony.

The end of hostilities saw no let up in his output. With an apparently inexhaustible supply of energy, he undertook editorship of the influential Penguin miniature score series in 1947, followed by a *Festival March* commissioned to celebrate the birth of Prince Charles. Writing to his sister about the piece he declared: 'Don't expect anything very good, it had to be done very quickly and is a bit ordinary, though it certainly makes a good deal of noise and has bells and things in it . . .' Jacob's name was now to be seen in the programmes of the nation's most prestigious musical events and he was accepting commissions from all over the country. In addition to these his diaries show a steady teaching commitment, attendance at RCM diploma exams, membership of BBC audition panels, and visits to performances of his music in London and the major cities. By 1951 Jacob's position and authority seemed assured as representing the traditional aspect of British music, and on the death of George VI his expertise was again called upon for the Coronation Service in 1953. For the occasion he was given the option of wearing either his robes as a Doctor of Music or Court Dress: he chose the latter because, as he put it, 'You can get more sandwiches in the hat.'

Performances of his music were frequent both on radio and in the concert hall and new works continued to pour from him. He was now 63 and enjoying life more than at any time in his career when in 1958 his wife died. Despite the sympathy and affection of friends, Jacob felt very much alone and for a while was close to despair. Having no children of his own he was drawn particularly to Margaret Gray, a niece of his wife's, in whom he confided his innermost thoughts and feelings in a way he rarely allowed himself to do. The friendship eventually blossomed into something more and in August the following year they married. She was some 40 years younger and the national press had a field day.

The couple set up home in Saffron Walden and Jacob settled into a routine of composing in spite of time-absorbing teaching and examination commitments. This consisted of work directly after breakfast, a sherry before lunch, an afternoon off when he might do some gardening or go for a drive, and then work from 4.30 until the evening meal, which was always preceded by a gin and orange. Although always friendly and courteous he was not naturally gregarious and shunned publicity, creating for himself a quiet niche in the musical life of the country which even he could not have foreseen at the age of 64 would last for another 25 years. The arrival of a daughter and son at the beginning of the new decade brought new delights and for the first time the composer could enjoy a full family life.

As tastes in music leaned more and more towards the *avant-garde*, attracting a new generation of British composers, commissions from the BBC began to diminish. Over the next ten years Jacob's writing was exercised almost entirely on behalf of amateur orchestras and those in schools. Commissions for wind instruments and chamber works were in demand and earlier pieces by Jacob were played a lot in the USA, providing an unexpected source of income. He finally resigned from the RCM in 1966 to devote more time to composition, and was awarded the CBE two years later. He attended fewer prestigious venues in the late 'sixties and turned increasingly to work with youth orchestras, but he was still known as a composer able and willing to turn his considerable technique to almost any purpose. In 1970 the Band of the Royal Marines commissioned the three-minute *Ceremonial Music* in honour of the Duke of Edinburgh's birthday, and for the centenary of Alexandra Palace (1975) the GLC requested a piece which he named *Ally Pally*.

In his final years there was no falling off in his work-rate but the outlet for a composer had changed considerably by the end of the 'seventies and Jacob found himself more in demand for music within the educational system than the concert platform. Far from being disillusioned, he positively relished this new market and between 1978 and his death he wrote some 55 separate titles for orchestra, wind band, chorus or brass.

Troubled for some time by deafness in his right ear, he began also to suffer with failing eyesight and had an operation for glaucoma which did nothing to prevent him accepting further commissions, including a proposed concerto for timpani in 1982. In one of his last letters, written two years later, he wrote of his intention to hear a newly commissioned work at the Festival Hall, but was unable to fulfil his wish. He suffered a stroke in May that year and the end came swiftly.

Constant Lambert

1905–1951

'For a while … he stood alone, a single figure of genius who embodied the ideas and thoughts of his time.'
– Hubert Foss

Lambert may not have achieved lasting fame as a composer in his own right, but his contribution to music through his conducting and writing, and his development of the Sadler's Wells Ballet, is now universally acknowledged. As a brilliant figure in the intellectual and social life of London, his circle of friends was wide and varied, and included many composers referred to in these pages as well as writers, artists and dancers. Greatly gifted in so many ways, Lambert was, however, his own worst enemy, unable to handle the problems of his personal life. A prolonged childhood illness, for instance, left him in continual pain. He was compassionate and sensitive, yet found it hard to secure lasting relationships with those he most loved. Finally, encouraged by the company of Philip Heseltine (Peter Warlock), he drank to excess, and hard drinking, ill health, overwork and disappointments eventually took their toll. He died just two days before his forty-sixth birthday.

The son of one respected sculptor, George Washington Lambert, and the brother of another, Maurice Lambert, Constant was a part of the artistic world from infancy. Family finances, however, were never sound and after falling behind with the fees for Manor House School in Clapham, George was obliged to seek help in educating his children. A successful application to the Almoners of Christ's Hospital, Horsham, allowed Constant to take his place at the Preparatory School there in 1915, but he had little opportunity to participate in the life of his new school. He was plagued by ill health. There was an appendicitis, and a double mastoid which left him permanently deaf in his right ear. He appears also to have developed osteomyelitis and over the next few years underwent some eighteen operations which left him lame for life – he could never put the whole of his foot to the ground and had to walk on his toes. He eventually resumed normal school life in the summer term of 1918, only to return to the infirmary in the autumn. The long months spent there gave him plenty of time for reading and his remarkable command of English was rivalled only by his reputation as a pianist and composer. His request that he be allowed to conduct the school orchestra, however, was met with a stoney silence.

In 1922, Lambert won a composition scholarship to the RCM, where he was a student of Vaughan Williams and George Dyson, among others, and soon became noticed as an outstanding conductor of natural aptitude. Though he cared little for the English folksong school, his career might have followed a more traditional course had he not gone to the London Pavilion in May 1923 to see a show called *Dover Street to Dixie*. Seventeen years old and highly impressionable, Lambert was completely captivated by the troupe of black singers and players, acclaimed later as the 'Blackbirds'. From that day, Lambert's enthusiasm for American Negro music never deserted him. He was among the first to foster a serious appreciation of jazz in general in this country and of the work of Duke Ellington in particular.

Several student works date from this period in Lambert's life, but his studies did not prevent him from pursing his other interests. Hours were spent in the company of friends visiting exhibitions, obscure cinemas and theatres, as well as going to revues and music halls where he could indulge his fascination with all forms of popular art. Known as 'Incessant Lambert' because of his stimulating talk, he numbered among his many friends the Sitwells, who introduced him to Bernard van Dieren, Philip Heseltine, and their young protégé, William Walton, whose 'entertainment' *Façade* was dedicated to Lambert. He and Walton would visit Heseltine at Eynsford for convivial evenings of limericks, songs and passionate conversation, but as well as their shared interest in early music, there was a sinister background of unconscionable drinking which confirmed Lambert on his own road to destruction. Nevertheless, it was a remarkable piece of good luck at this time which brought Lambert, still only twenty-one, on to the international stage. The artist and book illustrator Edmund Dulac introduced him to Diaghilev, who promptly commissioned a ballet from this young, unknown English student. The result was *Romeo and Juliet*, the first English ballet to be performed by the influential Ballets Russes.

Why did Diaghilev choose Lambert? He recognised his ability, certainly, but the charm and good looks of this unknown student would also attract useful publicity. His youth, too, was no disadvantage: the young did as they were told and Diaghilev needed a compliant collaborator to replace his former associates Stravinsky and Cocteau, now established and independent in their own right. Anyone in fact other than Lambert would have been overwhelmed by the honour of working for the Ballets Russes and easily suppressed any twinges of professional integrity in order to comply with Diaghilev's wishes. Though inexperienced and remarkably young, Lambert, however, had a mind of his own. On discovering that the original designs were to be replaced, and that the choreography was to be fundamentally altered, he had an almighty row with the great impresario and threatened to withdraw his score. All his life, Lambert held strongly to his belief that ballet at its best was a successful combination of music, choreography and design, and he was not prepared to compromise his views. In the event there was little he could do, and *Romeo and Juliet* was performed as Diaghilev decreed. But it did Lambert's reputation no harm and from 1926 he was known as the young English student from whom Diaghilev had commissioned a ballet, and for the next five years Lambert was to write his best music.

In the same year, Lambert took two rooms in Oakley Street, Chelsea, before moving to Bloomsbury. Throughout the 1920s he was short of money. He had no regular income at all until appointed conductor of the Vic-Wells Ballet in 1931. Otherwise he made some sort of living by playing the piano for dancing classes, by occasional conducting engagements, and journalism. Yet despite his financial problems, Lambert was not unhappy: he had many friends and led a busy social life. Over the next few years he wrote more music than he ever did in later life, including his most famous composition, the jazz-inspired *The Rio Grande*. The work received many performances in Britain and overseas, but its success, achieved at the age of twenty-four, was hard to live up to. Although he regarded both his Piano Concerto and *Summer's Last Will and Testament* as superior, *The Rio Grande* became the piece against which all his work would be measured. Failure to recapture its irresistible blend of exuberance and nostalgia was to lead ultimately to disappointment and frustration.

1930 was a year of two extremes for Lambert. His estranged father died in Australia in May; his close friend Christopher Wood died in August; and, worst of all for Lambert, Philip Heseltine was found dead in his flat on 17th December. Lambert never fully recovered from the blow. The darkest of all Lambert's works, the Piano Concerto, is dedicated to Heseltine's memory and shows its composer at his most bitter and disillusioned. Despite these emotional shocks, he had allowed himself, not for the first time in his life, to fall hopelessly in love. He first met Florence Cutter when visiting a friend's house where she worked as a housemaid. Only fourteen at the time, she was not his intellectual equal, nor did she share his cultured background, but she was strikingly beautiful, and over the next two years they were seen together a good deal, much to the delight of the gossip columnists. They married in August 1931, and on returning from honeymoon in France, moved into a small flat above an Indian restaurant in Percy Street. It was a beginning, and stability of some sort seemed possible when he accepted the post of musical director to the newly formed Vic-Wells Ballet, a position he was to hold until 1947.

For the next sixteen years, ballet dominated Lambert's life. He gave it all he could, and devoted himself to conducting, scoring, and advising, and during the war, when no orchestra was available, he accompanied performances on the piano. But he never again achieved the density of creative activity in the field of composition that he had attained in the late 1920s. His next, and lasting, claim to fame came in 1934 with the publication of his book *Music Ho!* which provides a fascinating, and startlingly subjective insight into music of the time. Musically, *Horoscope* was an accomplished work, written during a period of comparative calm, but the combination of hard days at the theatre and a tempestuous emotional life too often led to excessive drinking and the dissipation of his remaining energies on trivialities. In 1935 their son, Christopher, was born (later to achieve fame as the flamboyant manager of the pop group 'The Who'), but the marriage was under strain and two

years later the couple divorced. The next eight or so years were dominated by a deep and passionate affair with Margot Fonteyn which ended only shortly before his second marriage, to the artist Isobel Delmer.

On the outbreak of war, The Sadler's Wells Ballet embarked on the first of many provincial and later foreign tours which included a narrow escape from Holland in 1940 following the German invasion. It was a punishing schedule. In 1943-44, for instance, there were forty-eight weeks of performance. After the war, Lambert's major task was to train a largely inexperienced orchestra for the reopening of the Royal Opera House and from this point Covent Garden became the home of the ballet company.

During the winter of 1946-47, Lambert was at his lowest ebb, physically and mentally. As a student he had enjoyed a captivating personality, great charm and radiant good looks, reminiscent, some said, of the young Winston Churchill. Pictures of him in later years, when ill health and immoderate drinking had left their mark, tell a different story. Indeed, for a while he was accustomed to carry around a photo of himself as a young man which he would take out of his pocket and contemplate in a disconsolate way. Alcohol was not the only factor. He began to suffer blackouts which were later attributed to undiagnosed diabetes. No longer trusted to give consistently good performances at Covent Garden, he offered his resignation as its musical director in 1947.

Four years later, after a concert, Lambert invited a couple of friends to join him in a last round before closing time. It was indeed his last round. The following day he was taken ill and died in the London Clinic on 21st August. In common with a good number of British composers of this century, Lambert was very fond of cats and once gave a radio talk on 'Cats in Music'. During a memorial concert given by the BBC in 1952, a large black cat appeared on the platform and stayed until the final applause, when it strode off into the darkness.

E J Moeran
1894–1950

'So I'll go down to some lonely waters,
Go down where no-one they shall me find.'
– Norfolk folksong

Ernest John Moeran was born on the last day of the year 1894 at Springrove Vicarage, Isleworth, in Middlesex, the second son of a clerical family; his mother hailed from Norfolk and his father was an Irish Protestant priest from County Cork. Little has been written about his early life, but 'Jack', as he was known to friends, moved as a child to Norfolk, where his father was the vicar at Bacton, a village on the Norfolk coast. Apart from periods at boarding school, Moeran lived there until the outbreak of war.

After a spell at Suffield Park Preparatory School at Cromer, where he first took violin lessons, the young Moeran was sent to Uppingham School and received his formative education in music under the guidance of Robert Sterndale Bennett. When he left in 1912, he played second violin in the orchestra and was one of the school's finest pianists. It was at Uppingham that he first began composing – three quartets and a cello and piano sonata – music which he later destroyed. Living in the secluded environment of an evangelical household, the opportunities to hear sophisticated music were few and for a while it seemed that the boy might have followed an engineering line: his enthusiasm for railways and fast trains remained with him all his life. Instead he developed an interest in the folksongs of Norfolk still sung in the local inns by villagers, and over time immersed himself in the melodic idiom of the sand dunes and marshes of East Norfolk to the extent that his later music resonates with

155

local landscape. Many of these tunes he collected and arranged, though he rarely quoted any in his work. While other enthusiasts may have been swept along by the current fashion for rediscovering their musical heritage, Moeran was one of the few composers who used the idiom as if it was his native language.

In 1913 Moeran enrolled as a student at the Royal College of Music, but left to join the army on the outbreak of war. He enlisted as a motorcycle despatch rider and was commissioned early in 1915, serving as an officer in the Norfolk Regiment. He used this opportunity to extend his collection of folksongs, but was soon sent to France on active service and in 1917 was seriously wounded at Ballecourt. Several pieces of shrapnel were lodged too near the brain for removal and he was eventually discharged in January 1919. Later that summer, Arnold Bax recalled meeting Moeran at a dinner party in London and described him 'as charming and as good looking a young officer as one could wish to meet', although few knew that his severe head wounds had required the fitting of a metal plate. Nothing daunted, his interest in motor cycling continued after the war and he became a frequent competitor in long trials, winning a gold medal in the 1922 London to Land's End rally of the Motor Cycling Club. He also retained a great and abiding love of steam trains and everything concerning railways, being able to recognise the class of locomotive just by the sound of its approach. He shared this enthusiasm with his friend Patrick Hadley, who once gave an entertaining interval talk on the Home Service in which he referred to the roaring exhaust of a blue Claud Hamilton engine racing through the music of Moeran's Symphony in G minor.

After the war Moeran took up a teaching post at his old school but, like Butterworth before him, he felt that his musical training was incomplete and in 1920 resumed his studies at the Royal College of Music. For three years he studied composition with John Ireland, for whom he had the greatest respect: 'He gives unstintingly of his very best to those who come under him ... (who) soon discover a very human personality and a warm friend.' Before that period was over he had already had songs and some orchestral pieces published and had begun arranging the folksongs on which he had been nurtured. By mid-decade he was known and respected as a significant musical figure in the metropolis and in those early days was a steady and prolific worker. In 1925, however, Peter Warlock invited Moeran to share his cottage in the Kentish village of Eynsford, an arrangement which lasted for three years. Despite their firm friendship, and the undoubted impact of Warlock's musical and literary influences, the open house atmosphere dominated by the pub did not suit Moeran's more sensitive nature and composition became intermittent.

Leaving Eynsford in 1928, Moeran lived with his parents in Norfolk and Herefordshire, and from 1934 onwards spent much time in Kenmare, County Kerry. The Southern Irish coast and its Atlantic breakers was the inspiration for his only symphony, which he completed in 1937, although he acknowledged the influence of the Norfolk landscape in the second movement. The success of this and the Violin Concerto, written at Valentia Island the following year, encouraged Moeran to write more. His Sinfonietta was similarly steeped in the landscape, in this case the windswept moorlands of the Radnorshire hills where the composer often walked with a small sheet of manuscript paper in his pocket to jot down ideas. The Cello Concerto, his last major work, was written as a wedding gift to his wife, the cellist Peers Coetmore, whom he married at the end of the war.

Writing in 1939 about his planned Second Symphony, Moeran said: 'I may say I think I have hit on a winner for my opening subject, thanks to the view from Moll's gap looking across to the Reeks and Killarney Lakes ... on a brilliant spring morning.' It has been suggested that he was working on this symphony at the time of his death a few weeks before his fifty-sixth birthday. Despite his intention to withold any references to violent seascapes, he was out walking in a violent Atlantic gale, watching the effect of the storm on the sea, when he was seen to fall into the water from the end of Kenmare Pier. A boat put out immediately, but the swell prevented rescue and he was later found dead. A subsequent post mortem revealed a cerebral haemorrhage which may have been caused by the severe head wound received in 1917. Other reports cite a possible heart attack, or even suicide given some evidence of his mental instability in his later years. Whatever the true causes of his death, the violently changing moods of this part of the Atlantic coast had a great influence in originating and shaping Moeran's music, and he died where he would have wished to die – 'in "The Mountain Country" which he loved so well' – the epitaph on his headstone in Kenmare churchyard.

It is clear from the accounts of those who knew Jack Moeran well that he had an attractive and easy-going personality combined with compassion and a sense of humour. An unpretentious man with a gift for friendship, he appeared shy in company and, again like Butterworth, could be brusque in speech and manner; but he was also able to walk into a village pub and make friends with natural ease. This trait helped him in collecting folksongs in both Norfolk and in Ireland, where he won the hearts of the Kenmare people. Although he was convivial company, he preferred comparative seclusion and would unexpectedly take himself off from time to time, no one knew where, so that much of his music was written away from the distracting if pleasant company of his many friends. He succeeded in finding many such opportunities to respond to the landscapes he so loved, but his untimely death robbed us of a composer whose music was taking flight.

Roger Quilter

1877–1953

'Play the opening bars of almost any of his songs,
and you are left in no doubt as to who wrote them.'
— Mark Raphael

Roger Quilter was born on November 1, 1877, at the maternal family home in Brighton, six days before his friend Henry Balfour Gardiner. His father, Sir Cuthbert Quilter, 1st baronet, was a landowner and prosperous businessman – the founder and director of the National Telephone Company – as well as a politician. His mother was blessed with artistic taste and her children's personalities were shaped by her own sensitivity and aesthetic outlook. Music was a dilettante accomplishment in the Quilter household, but it was she who encouraged her third son to pursue his talent, though he needed no such prompting to cultivate his abiding love, poetry, which he once said meant more to him than music.

Initially his education followed a familiar route for a child of his background: preparatory school at Farnborough, followed by a spell at Eton, which he heartily disliked. Oxford or Cambridge would have been the next logical step, but on the advice of a perceptive friend, Quilter enrolled instead at Hoch's Frankfurt Conservatoire, intending to make music his profession. There he studied for nearly five years with Ivan Knorr along with his new companions: Percy Grainger, Norman O'Neill, Balfour Gardiner and Cyril Scott. These became known as the Frankfurt Group, whose impact has hardly reverberated through the halls of music history, but their exploits as students abroad are entertainingly revealed in Scott's autobiography *My Years of Indiscretion*. Academic life was, nonetheless, a very serious affair for Quilter, who received rigorous and

159

demanding tuition from Knorr, so that he left Frankfurt well grounded in the science and practice of theory and composition.

On returning to London he first came to the attention of the London public as a composer of songs late in 1900 with settings of his own verse, *Four Songs of the Sea*, which he dedicated to his mother. He was fortunate around this time to meet the tenor Gervase Elwes, who became an outstanding interpreter of Quilter's songs and did much to establish his reputation. Elwes's tragic death in 1921 deprived Quilter of a close friend and champion. Seventeen of the songs were later to be recorded by the high baritone Mark Raphael, who became another fine exponent of his music.

Despite a small number of excellent songs written over the next twenty years, it was the *Three Shakespeare Songs*, the song cycle *To Julia* and the *Seven Elizabethan Lyrics* – written between 1905 and 1910 – which established Quilter as one of the foremost songwriters of his generation. Peter Warlock sent him copies of some of his earliest published songs, on which he had written: 'To R.Q. without whom there would have been no P.W.' Equally successful were the light orchestral pieces which Henry Wood performed at his Promenade Concerts, including *A Children's Overture*, a sequence of skilfully linked nursery tunes, inspired by Walter Crane's illustrated book of nursery rhymes.

During the First World War, Quilter gave concerts in military hospitals and founded a chamber music club which continued for a few years after 1918 in the Lindsey Hall, Notting Hill Gate. But though he lived to be 75, Roger Quilter had already reached the peak of his career. He lacked the physical and mental stamina to explore more ambitious themes after 1910, preferring to follow the tried and tested formulas which had served him so well. He suffered from a stomach ulcer in his late thirties which involved an unsuccessful operation and a considerable period of convalescence. He never fully recovered and for the remainder of his life endured ill-health which was probably compounded by the mental anguish arising from several homosexual attachments. A lifelong bachelor, extremely shy and sensitive, Quilter lived quietly in London, first near Marble Arch and later in St John's Wood. For all his reserve, his friends knew him as a wit and even a practical joker with a keen sense of ironic humour. He would often tell of the question put to him by a fashionable lady when he had finished playing some of the songs which had made him famous: 'Mr Quilter, are you fond of music?'

Composing did not come easily despite the apparent fluency and grace of his music, but by the mid-1930s audiences were being introduced to a wider range of song, including the new English song-writers such as John Ireland, Peter Warlock, Gerald Finzi and Benjamin Britten. Heir to a handsome income, Quilter never had to seek a livelihood, and he neither taught nor held any musical appointment. Instead, when not choosing to compose, he gave a great deal of his time and waning energies to assist fellow musicians less fortunate than himself. Where money and influence were not needed, he provided encouragement and advice, and was a founder-member of the Musicians' Benevolent Fund, on whose executive committee he remained until his death.

On his seventy-fifth birthday the BBC broadcast a concert of his work which Quilter was able to attend, but during the following year his health again deteriorated. Twice he had been admitted to a private mental hospital and he eventually died, quite insane, on September 21, 1953.

Alan Rawsthorne

1905–1971

'And he'll say, as he scratches himself with his claws,
"Well, the Theatre's certainly not what it was".'
– T S Eliot: *Gus, the Theatre Cat*

Alan Rawsthorne was born on 2 May 1905 in the family house at Haslingden in Lancashire, where he and his sister spent a happy childhood. When he was four the family moved to Sykeside House, which had a garden large enough to contain a spinney and endless outdoor games. His father had qualified as a doctor but, inheriting a private income, never practised and instead devoted himself to his young wife and children. Their education was in the hands of a governess until 1914, when Alan attended a boys' preparatory school in Southport which provided a somewhat narrow curriculum based on arithmetic and Latin grammar, but at least he was able to begin piano lessons.

During this time, however, he was often ill, frequently staying away from school for long periods, and even when he later attended a private day-school he continued to suffer from bouts of rheumatism which forced him to study at home with a private tutor. He always said this was the greatest piece of good fortune as the time spent at home when he was unwell gave him ample opportunity to read widely and play the piano, but apart from one or two piano miniatures he made few serious attempts at composition.

His parents were initially opposed to his following a musical career and in 1922 Rawsthorne entered the Dental School at Liverpool University, but quickly became bored and frustrated and soon abandoned the course, never again, according to his friend Constant Lambert, to 'practise dentistry, even as a hobby.' Various plans were considered, but a career in music was still felt to be too precarious, so the following year he entered as a first-year student at the School of Architecture. This was an improvement on dentistry, but as time went on he felt more and more that his life must be in music and after lengthy family discussions he finally entered the Royal Manchester College of Music to study composition alongside the cello and piano.

It was a wise move and at last Rawsthorne could give his undivided attention to his true vocation. Fellow students soon realised his genuinely creative talent and his early compositions were much in demand as he gained a reputation as an enthusiastic and promising student. Lessons continued until the summer of 1929, when he wrote to Bax asking for advice in composition. When he declined, Rawsthorne decided to continue his studies abroad with Egon Petri and the following year left for Poland. On the whole it was a useful experience, but left Rawsthorne with no clear idea of how best to pursue a musical career. He was by now an accomplished pianist and contemplated a future in the concert hall, but he needed above all to compose.

On his return from Europe, Rawsthorne was offered his first, and only, full-time post as a pianist and composer at The School of Dance Mime at Dartington Hall in Devon, where he stayed for two years. During the Christmas holidays he returned to his London circle and to Jessie Hinchliffe, a young violinist he had known since his Manchester days. It was she, together with his sister Barbara, who nursed him back to health following a car accident in the narrow Devon lanes, and they were married soon after he left Dartington Hall in 1934.

The couple settled in London and Rawsthorne earned a living by scoring other people's music and arranging music for BBC ensembles. During the rise of Fascism and the Spanish Civil War he was firmly on the Left and involved himself in providing 'occasional' music for the Socialist movement. It was during this period that he met Constant Lambert at a concert and the two became firm friends. Musically they had much in common and Lambert's influence confirmed Rawsthorne's developing personal style, which was beginning to attract some notice. Yet it was not until 1938, when he was 33, that Rawsthorne achieved wider recognition with his *Theme and Variations* for two violins, first performed at the Wigmore Hall in January of that year. This was followed by the orchestral *Symphonic Studies*, a far more ambitious score, which received its first performance in Warsaw in 1939. It was an immediate success.

Despite the acclaim, Rawsthorne remained a private person and seemed, outwardly at least, somewhat aloof and preoccupied, often restricting his conversation in company to short witty asides. Although firmly committed to the telephone, he was in many ways more than a little detached from modern life. He never, for example, drove a car; indeed, his large black hat, signet ring, bow tie and silver-knobbed cane suggested more the romantic artist of a previous era. He scorned buses, preferring to travel by taxi to pubs, restaurants and drinking clubs which extended from a well-trodden nucleus around Oxford Circus and Baker Street in a vapour trail to Hampstead, Bristol and Saffron Walden.

He attended the Warsaw première of his *Symphonic Studies* in April, but with Europe poised on the brink of war he was confronted with the realities of the world, whether he liked it or not. In 1941 he was called up for military service and officially spent the war writing scores for government documentaries, though he still found time to pursue his own career, notably with a rewrite of his first piano concerto. On one occasion, at the start of a performance of the work in Liverpool, the conductor mistakenly began conducting a piece by Liszt, much to the bewilderment of both orchestra and pianist. Moments later, the kettle drum broke loose and rolled slowly down the orchestra steps, to the huge delight of the audience, after which Rawsthorne felt he might be better advised returning to the comparative calm of army life. But in 1940 he lost his first violin concerto, together with other manuscripts, when his Bristol flat was destroyed in an air raid and he had to begin again, eventually completing it eight years later. It was only with the end of the war that he was able to devote all his energies to composition once more, and within some five years Rawsthorne was among the more prolific instrumental composers of an English generation that included Walton and Tippett.

While his music flourished, Rawsthorne's domestic circumstances were troubled. It was no secret that he had a serious alcohol problem and around this time landed in University College Hospital with a drink-related illness. Further emotional upheavals involved his divorce from Jessie, for whom he felt great affection and to whom he owed so much, and his subsequent marriage in 1954 to Isabel Lambert, widow of his close friend Constant Lambert. Together they moved to a cottage in Little Sampford near Saffron Walden – a home they shared with about 28 cats – and inspired by this new-found stability the next ten years were undoubtedly among the most fruitful in his creative life. In 1961 he was awarded the CBE and his work was regularly featured at festivals and by the BBC. Even with the increasing burden of composition, he also found time to travel abroad and in 1963 visited the Soviet Union with his old friend Alan Bush, whom he had first met in Berlin some 30 years earlier.

Rawsthorne rarely conducted his own music: his own natural reticence may explain this, but when he did he greatly enjoyed himself. Yet he was never the showman and his retirement from the concert platform probably went unnoticed. In fact both he and his music grew more introspective in his final years, dogged as they were by a number of serious illnesses brought on by his extraordinary capacity for remaining sober despite absorbing vast quantities of alcohol. A reticent figure, Rawsthorne was always uncomfortable in a world where changes were taking place at a pace unsuited to a man possessed of a uniquely Edwardian elegance and refinement which set him apart from most of musical society. Quiet, unhurried, and always courteous, his conversation nevertheless had a sharp edge: he chose his words with the same precision as he did his black and white notes, so beautifully set out in the immaculate manuscript of his scores. He worked feverishly throughout the winter and spring of 1970-71 to complete a commission and later that year braved the summer heat to attend a degree ceremony at which he was awarded his third Honorary Doctorate from British universities. He was taken ill soon afterwards and although he rallied briefly in June, he died on 24 July at the age of 66 and was buried on a beautiful summer morning in Thaxted Church.

Franz Reizenstein

1911–1968

*'The general public will decide in the long run which kind of
twentieth-century music it wants to hear.'*

Something of a prodigy, Franz Reizenstein displayed remarkable gifts as
a pianist and composer from an early age, twin pursuits which occupied
the two halves of his musical personality and career over his relatively
short life. Born in Nuremberg, he came from an artistic and musical
family and in 1930 was encouraged by his father to attend the Berlin
State Academy, where he studied composition with Hindemith. For the
next four years he aligned himself artistically with the established norms
of tonal composition, refusing to be drawn towards the more
experimental schools of thought that began to be rife in Europe in the
1930s.

As soon as Hitler came to power in Germany, Reizenstein was forced
to realise the evils of Nazism, particularly for those of Jewish birth, and
in 1934, at the age of 23, he left and came to England, where he
eventually became a citizen. His choice was no doubt influenced by the
fact that an uncle on his mother's side lived at Kingston. Here he studied
composition with Vaughan Williams at the RCM and took piano lessons
privately with Solomon. These were years of considerable difficulty for
him and he struggled to devote time to composition and recitals while
striving to earn a living.

On the outbreak of war he was interned on the Isle of Man, along
with others of non-British birth whose naturalisation papers were not
quite in order, but he managed nevertheless to arrange and perform
concerts at his camp. During this time, Vaughan Williams helped him as

much as he could, as he did so many of his pupils, by writing on his behalf and putting arranging and editing work his way. On his release he volunteered for the army but was disqualified on medical grounds and spent the remainder of the war as a railway clerk, giving charity concerts in his spare time.

The first two years after the war were spent writing for films before embarking on the central and most productive period of his life, beginning with the *Scherzo* and ending with the Second Piano Concerto: between these two are included most of the major compositions by which he is chiefly known. Despite his years of hardship, Reizenstein took great delight in promoting his own brand of practical humour, which found a natural outlet in the diversions of the musical cartoonist Gerard Hoffnung in the 1950s. For these entertainments he contributed witty and extremely successful pastiche works, notably the *Concerto Populare* (Piano Concerto to end all Piano Concertos), and *Let's Fake an Opera*. In 1958 he took up teaching at the Royal Academy and in 1964 became professor of piano at the Royal Manchester College of Music.

The last years of his life were prolific and his appearances in concerts and radio performances became more frequent, though it was America, not for the first time, which most readily acknowledged the proven worth of a British composer, and Reizenstein spent six months in 1966 as visiting professor of composition at Boston University. (He was only employed to teach composition in England during evening classes at Hendon Technical College.) Though fundamentally a deeply serious musician, Reizenstein radiated humour and geniality and his death at the age of 57 robbed the country of a naturally gifted composer.

Edmund Rubbra

1901–1986

'I never know where a piece is going to go next ... When I begin, my only concern is finding a starting point that I can be sure of.'

The son of a Northampton factory worker, Edmund Rubbra was encouraged in his musical interests by his parents, both of whom loved music. His mother was a good amateur singer and it was she who first gave her eight-year-old son piano lessons, enabling him to demonstrate the instrument in his uncle's music shop. On leaving school at 14 he progressed from office boy to railway clerk, teaching himself as much as he could in his spare time and discovering the music of Debussy and Cyril Scott. He was so taken with Scott that at 16 he single-handedly promoted a concert in Northampton devoted to the composer's works. Hearing of this extravagant gesture, Scott offered him free lessons and for several months Rubbra travelled to London every fortnight to work with him at both piano and composition.

At 19 he won a scholarship to Reading University, where Howard-Jones and Holst were his principal teachers, and the following year won a further scholarship to the RCM, where he continued with the same teachers and with R O Morris, who introduced him to counterpoint. By the time he left the college in 1925 he had composed a number of songs and small choral works, but as with most of his contemporaries from working-class backgrounds he was forced to take whatever work came his way. This included teaching, playing for a travelling theatre group, and music journalism. He continued to compose slowly, mostly vocal works already marked by the religious mysticism and lyricism that characterised him. It is interesting to note that Rubbra's brother also

distinguished himself, as the chief designer of aeroengines for Rolls Royce, and was part of the team that made the Merlin engine used in the Spitfire.

In the early 1930s, Rubbra moved gradually out of his formative stage into a more personal harmonic style with such works as the First Violin Sonata, followed by the First String Quartet and the *Sinfonia Concertante* for piano and orchestra. Rubbra thus gradually enlarged the range and size of his structures, each work slightly larger than the one before, culminating in three of his eleven symphonies written by 1938, by which time he was regarded as one of the major English composers of his generation.

The outbreak of war interrupted Rubbra's composing career and he joined the Royal Artillery as an anti-aircraft gunner. Fortunately the war years were not entirely without music for him as he kept up his piano-playing, especially on BBC broadcasts, and in 1942 he and two fellow soldiers, cellist William Pleeth and violinist Joshua Glazier, formed a trio to tour camps giving concerts. They became so well known that they continued afterwards, and not until 1956 did pressure of other engagements compel Rubbra to give it up. After the war another opportunity came his way when Jack Westrup, Professor of the newly-formed Music Faculty at Oxford, invited him to join the academic staff, which he did in 1947. The following year he converted to Roman Catholicism, having picked up the broken thread of his composition with an Anglican *Canterbury Mass*. In 1961 he joined the Guildhall School of Music to teach composition and throughout this period he composed intensively, with outstanding achievements in almost every field except opera and ballet.

He once said that his musical ideas often occurred at unusual times or places, as with the opening of his Fifth Symphony, which came to him while waiting in a bus queue. He retired from Oxford in 1968, having received a great many prestigious awards, and died peacefully in Gerrards Cross aged 85.

Cyril Scott

1879–1970

'My Years of Indiscretion'

At one time Scott was regarded as an English counterpart of Debussy, though it is difficult now to see where the resemblance lies. Gifted with melodic invention, an original sense of harmony, and a natural instinct for the orchestra, he had in him the main requirements for a good composer but his insistence on mingling miniatures with his more serious music relegated him to comparative obscurity long before he lived out his 91 years.

Scott was the youngest of three children born to educated parents living in Oxton, a small Cheshire village. His father, a cultivated businessman, was a fine Greek scholar but it was from his mother, an amateur pianist, that the boy inherited an interest in music including, it is said, perfect pitch. After he had received some piano lessons, his father somewhat reluctantly agreed to allow his wife to accompany the 12-year-old Cyril to the Hoch Conservatory in Frankfurt to study under the Neapolitan pianist Uzielli and the composer Humperdinck. He returned after eighteen months and received intermittent instruction from one Herr Welsing, who as often as not arrived for lessons late or not at all, prompting Scott's second visit to Frankfurt in 1895. This time he studied with Ivan Knorr and became friends with a group of young compatriots which included Grainger, O'Neill, Quilter and Balfour Gardiner, who were to be referred to as the Frankfurt Group. It was during this period that he initiated a close friendship with the German poet Stefan George, many of whose verses he later translated.

Scott left Frankfurt in 1898, returning to Liverpool to earn his living as a pianist and teacher. Two years later he completed his *Heroic Suite*, which was performed in Manchester and Liverpool by Richter, but he later withdrew it, as he did his first symphony, which had received its German première the same year. His London debut, at the old St James's Hall, came in 1901 with a performance of the Piano Quartet in E minor, and created something of a stir when Fritz Kreisler agreed to be the violinist. A second symphony, which he later reworked as *Three Symphonic Dances*, was conducted by Wood at a Promenade Concert in 1903, but alongside such serious compositions the lighter songs and piano pieces attracted as much attention. Grainger, as pianist, popularised some of the early music, though it was probably Kreisler's violin transcription of his well-known piano piece *Lotus Land* that brought the composer to the fore.

A new influence at this time on the already impressionable Scott was the art of Melchior Lechter, a stained-glass window designer and mystic, and before long he was taking a deep interest in occultism, oriental philosophy and other fashionable mysticisms. A self-proclaimed agnostic and freethinker, he began to dispense with key-signatures and bar-lines and developed a reputation as a 'modernist' composer, a view no doubt encouraged by his flowing hair and artistic appearance. By the start of the war, Scott's music had certainly created considerable interest in Europe, at all events a higher reputation than in England. His most outstanding achievement during this period was the Piano Concerto which Beecham introduced at the British Musical Festival in 1915. Exempted from military service on medical grounds, he was eventually conscripted for an administrative post from which he was excused by the personal intervention of Lloyd George.

In the early 1920s, Scott returned from a successful concert tour of the United States to find that his housekeeper had committed suicide in his apartment. The shock perhaps increased his obsession with spiritualism, reinforced by his abiding interest with Indian philosophy, which led to his becoming a Vedantist and eventually a follower of the

Higher Occultism. He came to depend on the advice of a spiritual contact known as Mahatma Koot Hoomi, on whose suggestion he married the novelist Rose Allatini in 1921. He also became absorbed in the study of osteopathy and homeopathy, and was to write successfully on all these topics as well as on the mystical properties of his music. His literary output included several volumes of poetry, a large number of unpublished plays, and two autobiographies.

Between the wars, Scott's music was performed largely on the continent, a notable success being the production of his one-act opera *The Alchemist* at Essen in 1925. Nor was he ignored in England, where large-scale works for chorus and orchestra were heard at the 1936 and 1937 Norwich and Leeds Festivals, but by now his music had begun to lose much of its appeal. Though he continued to compose virtually to the end of his life (partly on the advice of another occult sign), and wrote three more operas, several ballets and a considerable quantity of orchestral and chamber music, his music attracted less and less notice. The outbreak of war had dispersed his family and after some years of a lonely existence he regained a measure of domestic stability and began to see a gradual reappraisal of his best work. He died a contented man, assured by the spirit world that his music would not lie neglected for long.

Humphrey Searle

1915–1982

'Riverrun, past Eve and Adam's, from swerve of shore to bend of bay...' – James Joyce: *Finnegan's Wake*

Humphrey Searle was arguably Britain's first important exponent of the now rather discredited twelve-note style of Schoenberg, even though his own music doesn't seem to have worn well with the passage of time. After leaving Winchester in 1933, he read Greats at Oxford before proceeding to the RCM, where he studied, somewhat hesitantly, with John Ireland and Gordon Jacob. After consulting other musicians, including Walton, he eventually spent a year at the New Vienna Conservatory and encountered Webern, who influenced him considerably. During this formative period he had no doubt that the path indicated by Schoenberg was the one that music was destined to take, but he felt the musical atmosphere in England at the time to be too narrow.

Returning to London from Vienna, he resumed his studies at the College before taking a job with the BBC as a programme producer. In 1940 he joined the Gloucester Regiment and was briefly involved in training paratroopers before working for the Intelligence Corps, which found him in Germany at the end of the war helping Hugh Trevor-Roper round up information on the fate of Adolph Hitler. He returned briefly to the BBC but left in 1948 to work freelance for three years, when he became music adviser to Sadler's Wells Ballet. An enthusiast for promoting new music, he was also for a time general secretary of the International Society for Contemporary Music.

A distinguished Liszt scholar, he found time among his many other activities to complete a new catalogue of Liszt's works and, together with his friends Lambert, Walton and Sacheverell Sitwell, established the Liszt Society in 1950. The most important products of this interim period were three ambitious choral-orchestral works, two based on poems by Edith Sitwell (*Gold Coast Customs* and *The Shadow of Cain*) and a setting of the final section of Joyce's *Finnegan's Wake (Riverrun)*. After this trilogy, Searle set about the task of applying his style to large-scale orchestral pieces, which include five symphonies, and operas. The influence on his music of Webern and Schoenberg encouraged a radical style not then in vogue in Britain, and Searle remained an unfashionable though vigorous and prolific composer, never daunted by the music establishment's neglect of his large output. He gave up the Sadler's Wells post in 1957, the year his first wife died, but later served a year at Stanford University, California, as composer-in-residence, and in 1965 joined the teaching staff at the RCM, where he numbered several promising composers among his pupils.

A shy man, Searle's integrity and cosmopolitan outlook won respect among his many friends and students, yet for all his reserve and professional detachment he loved conviviality, and his humour is readily apparent in the splendid settings of Lear's *The Owl and the Pussy Cat* and T S Eliot's *Skimbleshanks the Railway Cat*. He died in London aged 67.

Ethel Smyth

1858–1944

*'What the devil does a twopenny-halfpenny whippersnapper like
you mean by talking like this of your betters?'* – Edvard Grieg

Ethel Smyth was born in London, the daughter of a Major-General from
whom she no doubt inherited her forthright and militant outlook (her
mother called her a 'stormy petrel'). Her first home was at Sidcup, a
spacious house which she shared with her brother and three sisters,
parents and grandparents before the family moved to Frimley near
Aldershot and an even grander house surrounded by thirty-two acres of
grounds.

There is no evidence during those early years that music was among
Ethel's interests until the memorable day at the age of twelve when she
heard a Beethoven sonata played by a governess who had studied at the
Leipzig Conservatory. The Army, the Navy, and the Church were the
professions most frequently adopted by the family, so her declared aim
to give her life to music was not taken seriously. Her resolve was
stiffened when a paternal friend, Alexander Ewing, admired for
composing the popular hymn *Jerusalem the Golden*, recognised the girl's
musical talent and told her parents that she must be trained. General
Smyth would have none of it and declared, rather melodramatically, that
he would rather see her dead. For nearly two years there was a truce,
during which Ethel threw herself into the social diversions of her class
and even became fleetingly engaged to William Wilde, Oscar's brother.
She then resumed the struggle with her father, deploying tactics familiar
to most parents of teenage girls by refusing to speak to anyone and
spending most of the day in her bedroom with the door locked. Through

all this she had the consolation of knowing that her mother was secretly on her side and that she had influential friends who openly supported her. Eventually her father relented and under the charge of her brother-in-law she left home in 1877 for Germany. She was just 19.

Having achieved her ambition, however, Smyth did not relish her humble position as one of 300 students at the Conservatory and turned to private tuition with Heinrich von Herzogenberg, whom she followed to Berlin. She wrote a good deal of music during this period and was encouraged by such luminaries as Brahms, Tchaikovsky and Dvořák, all of whom accepted her as a promising and serious composer. Nevertheless, the few performances of her first chamber music compositions given in Germany were thought to be 'deficient in the feminine charm that might have been expected of a woman composer.' This was the first time she had to face the fact that her sex might prevent her music being judged solely on its merits. Her belief was unshaken by the bad notices, and soon after her return to England in 1888 she made her debut with an orchestral work in four movements, modestly titled *Serenade*, followed in the autumn with an overture, *Antony and Cleopatra*. The full extent of her ambition and achievement was realised at the Albert Hall in January 1893 with the performance of her Mass in D. The audience and most of the critics were impressed and one of Smyth's hunting friends called it 'slashing stuff.' Although well received, it was in many ways ahead of its time and audiences had to wait another 31 years for a second hearing.

From 1894 to 1898, Smyth spent a good deal of time and energy trying to secure a production of her first opera, *Fantasio*. A familiar figure dressed in tweeds, hat crammed down and smoking hard, she traipsed from one opera house to another, hounding the main European producers. When finally it was performed at Weimar, the orchestration was the only thing the critics praised, and rather than see it gather dust she destroyed all the scores printed and threw the ashes on the compost heap in her cottage garden. She had better luck with *Der Wald*, premièred at Berlin in 1902, and at Covent Garden later the same year, but it was *The Wreckers*, her third opera and probably her major achievement, which finally established her reputation. At one point she wrote to a friend, 'I feel awfully full of power – deadly sure of what I am doing.' Once again she fought hard to gain a hearing for the work, but finding champions in the likes of Mahler and Beecham, *The Wreckers* was eventually performed in England at His Majesty's and later at Covent Garden. It created a deep impression, prompting one critic to observe that it was a wonderful achievement, for a woman. Good old-fashioned misogyny again.

The honorary doctorate Smyth received from Durham University in 1910 was small compensation for such faint praise and not surprisingly she found herself drawn into the Women's Suffrage Movement. It seems strange that she should have been so indifferent to the cause until then. One possible reason was that although she had been born and brought up in a society in which the inferior status of women was taken for granted, she had not much experience of its disadvantages. In her childhood and youth she had been able to hold her own with boys in games and sports, and after winning the battle with her father her self-confidence never wavered. Able to make her way with all sorts of social advantages, she was apt to think that the Suffrage Movement was unnecessary. It took 30 years to realise that it was one of the most significant and beneficial movements of her age and at an all-Smyth concert at the Queen's Hall she conducted her *March of the Women*, which became the Movement's musical theme. Nor were her activities confined to wielding a baton; to the mortification of her family she was arrested and sentenced to two months' imprisonment for hurling a stone through the window of a Cabinet Minister's house. Shortly after, Beecham recalled visiting Holloway to find a group of women marching round the courtyard singing their marching song at the top of their voices while its composer conducted with a toothbrush from an overlooking window.

During the years she devoted to the Suffragist cause, Smyth's output was rather larger than it had been when she was touring Europe fighting for performances of her operas, or indulging her twin passions for sport and friendship. The war meant another break with music, but the situation after 1918 was more favourable to English composers than it had been in the early days of her career, and few were as successful as she was between 1920 and 1926. She had by now begun writing prose and her first two volumes of autobiography met with great popular and critical success, further stimulating interest in her music.

Ethel Smyth became a Dame of the British Empire in 1922 and during the 1920s frequently appeared as a conductor as well as attending concerts of her own work. Her last major composition, *The Prison*, a choral symphony first heard in 1931, was written at a time of increasing deafness which made further musical endeavours virtually impossible. More entertaining books based on her own experiences followed and she remained a larger-than-life personality until her death from pneumonia in 1944. The obituary notices recalled a composer, a writer, a feminist, a fighter, and a great character. Had she chosen or been able to devote more time to the first, there may have been a greater body of work against which her true merit could be judged.

Michael Tippett

1905–1998

'I have to sing songs for those who can't sing for themselves.'

Michael Tippett was born in Pimlico on 2 June, 1905, after which he and his brother Peter spent a happy childhood in Wetherden, a small Suffolk village between Bury St Edmunds and Stowmarket. His father was of Cornish descent and had made sufficient money through the shrewd backing of various enterprises, including London's Lyceum Theatre, to be able to retire from the legal profession at a comparatively early age. Isabel Tippett was herself a spirited woman, joining the suffragette movement and chaining herself to a railing, for which she was arrested in 1913 and subsequently imprisoned for a fortnight. Her commanding personality helped to shape her son's attitudes and certainly taught him to stand by his own beliefs.

In many ways the Tippetts were conventionally middle-class, living comfortably in Wetherden and able to employ a cook, a governess, two maids and a gardener, as well as a chauffeur to drive the only car in the village. Yet within this protected environment both parents were exceptionally energetic and resourceful, well ahead of their time and remarkable in encouraging their children to seek their own independence. On at least one occasion he accompanied his mother to London's East End to work alongside her in the soup kitchens, an experience which instilled in him a lifelong social conscience. His own early education included piano lessons from a succession of local teachers and he would spend many hours practising before giving impromptu 'recitals' to the family with the flourish of an accomplished performer. Talented, but not exceptional, Tippett later abandoned thoughts of becoming a scientist and announced his intention of becoming a composer. Although not opposed to the idea, there were few opportunities to cultivate their son's aptitude and in due course he was sent to a prep school in Swanage, where his brother was already a pupil. He was moderately content there, particularly enjoying Greek and Latin, but with the outbreak of war the family finances began to decline and by 1918 the cottage at Wetherden was sold and the Tippetts moved to France. Turning misfortune to their advantage, the couple supported themselves from the proceeds of property investments and thereafter lived in a succession of small hotels and rented apartments around the continent. It was a nomadic existence tolerated by both parents, but this loss of a permanent home was felt keenly by the boys, who spent their holidays travelling alone across Europe to wherever their parents were staying. This was no small matter for a boy prone to travel sickness whose private cure for it (marmalade) could hardly compensate for the upheaval faced every school holiday.

In 1918, Tippett won a scholarship to Fettes College in Edinburgh and started there in the September. Piano lessons resumed and he was able to pursue his musical interests through the school orchestra, as well as continue his study of the classics; but his enjoyment was outweighed by the harsh regime which was prevalent at the school in those days. His mother had wanted him to acquire the robust health associated with a well-bred family, but the atmosphere at Fettes was particularly austere and forbidding and not at all to Tippett's liking. Bullying and sadism were commonplace, and when he wrote to his parents in all innocence about sexual practices at the school, they promptly removed him. His scholarship had paid for the fees, so his father was obliged to find a cheap alternative and finally arranged for him to attend Stamford Grammar School in Lincolnshire. He quickly found life more congenial, making many friends and rapid progress in his studies, taking up science and advanced mathematics in the Sixth Form. Apart from playing the piano for school assemblies, there were no official musical activities at the school, so he depended upon lessons from the aptly named Mrs

Tinkler, an influential local piano teacher who had previously taught Malcolm Sargent, also an ex-pupil of Stamford School.

During the period immediately after the war there were few opportunities for those living in the provinces to hear much music of importance, so it was hardly surprising that a symphony concert attended by the young Tippett given in Leicester should have made a profound impression on him. Sargent was conducting and the impact of this direct contact with symphonic music confirmed his intention that, come what might, he would devote the rest of his life to music. His father wrote for advice from Stamford's headmaster and Sargent himself, both of whom replied that the idea was absurd, but faced with his son's determined path he decided that the only thing to do was for Tippett to train as a concert pianist. More lessons with the redoubtable Mrs Tinkler followed, then, quite by chance, his parents met a professional musician on a train who advised a period of study at the Royal College of Music and in April 1923 he enrolled as a student under Charles Wood.

Unlike some of his contemporaries, Tippett was unusually well prepared for his formative years at the RCM. In several respects he was out of the ordinary. He was an accomplished French speaker from the age of nine and had acquired an awareness of European peoples and customs which were markedly less insular than those around him. He had inherited a perceptive intelligence and an instinct to challenge received ideas; among friends he was an entertaining conversationalist, vivacious and good-humoured, and at the age of 18 was ready to assimilate all that life in a capital city could offer. As well as developing an appetite for music of all kinds and styles, he read widely, went to concerts and the theatre, and discussed politics, psychology and philosophy into the small hours. Despite gaining two minor awards, he enjoyed little real success as a composer but Tippett never underestimated the time it would take for him to find his own musical voice. He knew exactly what he wanted and was prepared to wait, much as Vaughan Williams had done. (He always maintained that he learned most about orchestral composition by standing alongside Adrian Boult every Friday for four years while Boult took the senior conducting class.) At the end of his days at the RCM he sought peace and quiet away from the whirl of London life and in 1929 managed to land a job conducting a small choir in Oxted, Surrey, where he was to remain for the next twenty-two years.

For some time he tried to supplement his modest income by teaching French at a small prep school in Limpsfield but soon realised that the job interfered with his ambitions to compose, and devoted himself instead to working with local music societies. This in itself called for a degree of ingenuity to overcome the somewhat primitive conditions of the local Barn Theatre where Tippett attempted to mount operas and concerts. The orchestra was forced to play under the stage (wearing wellingtons because of the water level) while the singers above remained in touch through 'hear holes' drilled through the stage floor. Not for the first time, enthusiasm and endeavour won the day and with just enough money to build himself a small and rather inelegant bungalow in the neighbourhood, Tippett found the solitude needed for thinking out his own music. He cultivated a routine of composing in the morning, followed by a long walk in all weathers, and ending the day either working with his choirs or writing music again.

Of the works of this period, nothing was published and little remains, for after attending a concert of his own compositions at the Barn he found himself agreeing with the *Daily Telegraph* critic who suggested that 'Michael Tippett will probably prefer to put all behind him and go on to fresh ideas.' The concert had revealed his lack of individuality and he promptly scrapped most of the things he had written to date. Stoically, he made up his mind to return to college and made arrangements through the RCM to have private lessons with R O Morris, with whom he studied fugue for eighteen months. More music emerged from this renewed period of study but it was again rejected by Tippett, and it was not until the second half of the 1930s that he began to write works that have been allowed to survive. At this early stage, the BBC showed no interest in his music and to begin with he had difficulty in finding a publisher, so that at the outbreak of the Second World War, Tippett was still largely unknown.

Yet he had been busy during those years in other ways. In 1932 he became the conductor of the South London Orchestra, which rehearsed regularly at Morley College and gave concerts in schools, churches, hospitals and parks. The players were recruited mainly from the ranks of unemployed instrumentalists who had lost their jobs in cinema bands with the arrival of the 'talkies'. Most of them were twice Tippett's age but quickly recognised in him a musician of exceptional ability, possessed of a remarkable capacity to convey what he wanted. For some concerts he even persuaded a number of eminent soloists to give their services for free and such names as Harriet Cohen, Myra Hess and Solomon appeared on the programmes. He also worked for the Royal Arsenal Co-operative Society's Educational Department, writing and arranging music for special performances given by schoolchildren, and for the ironstone miners at Boosbeck in Cleveland he wrote a ballad opera, *Robin Hood*, which was performed in 1933.

The most profound effect on Tippett of these North Yorkshire work camps is illustrated by an incident which occurred during a hike through mining areas in the Tees Valley. Stopping for a picnic of bread, cheese and apples, a group of malnourished children appeared, seized upon the discarded crumbs and apple-cores and ran off eating them. Such first-hand experiences of the miserable conditions at Boosbeck reminded him that if he was to remain an artist of integrity, he must be ready to take sides and commit himself. When the realities of the communist and fascist menace abroad became more apparent, he aligned himself for a while with Trotskyism, but espoused an explicitly pacifist rather than political viewpoint. Surrounded by terrible events at home and abroad, Tippett wondered whether in all conscience he should continue writing music, but throughout this time he was working towards a position where he could begin on the composition that was to announce to the world that an important composer, with something very much of his own to say, was at hand. Early in November 1938 a 17-year-old Polish Jew, driven to desperation by the Nazi persecution of his mother, shot dead a German diplomat in Paris, causing one of the most violent Nazi pogroms of the Jews in Europe. Just two days after the outbreak of war, Tippett began to compose his response – *A Child of Our Time*.

With the onset of hostilities and the suspension of adult education, Tippett lost the income from his co-operative choirs but when Morley College was destroyed by bombs in 1940, he was asked to take over as Director of Music, organising classes from a neighbouring school. Once again, his enthusiasm triumphed and within a year he had built up the choir from eight voices to thirty, and to over seventy by the end of the war. In terms of public musical activity, this was his golden period, during which he continued to work on his oratorio despite the air raids going on around him: an experience which hastened his decision to take up an open commitment to pacifism. He had long held opinions that

enabled him to claim a conscientious objection to war service and was granted exemption on condition that he did some form of work on the land or in hospital. He refused to do either, arguing that the best way he could serve the community was through music. He was eventually brought to trial in 1943 and sentenced to three months' imprisonment, much to the delight of his mother, who spoke of this time as her proudest moment.

His spell in Wormwood Scrubs was brightened by a visit from Britten and Pears, who encouraged him to arrange a performance of *A Child of Our Time*. It was subsequently given its première the following year and confirmed Tippett's reputation as a new force in British music. If it caused something of a stir in this country, its full impact was perhaps not appreciated until it could be played in those parts of Europe which had endured war-time occupation. Meanwhile, the post-war success of Britten's *Peter Grimes* did much to direct the attention of British composers to the importance of opera as a medium. Tippett was present for its first performance, at Sadler's Wells, and as soon as his own first symphony was finished, he started work on *The Midsummer Marriage*. His activities at Morley were increasingly distracting him from composition and he resigned in 1951 to concentrate on his opera, which was six years in the making. Already earning a small income from BBC talks, he managed to support himself by further broadcasts and that winter moved from his Oxted cottage to a large, dilapidated house in Wadhurst with its hilltop view over the Sussex countryside. *The Midsummer Marriage* was eventually accepted by Covent Garden and produced there for the first time in January 1955, the month of his fiftieth birthday.

Its reception was mixed, to say the least. Press reaction ranged from grudging admiration to outright derision, and most declared themselves completely baffled; one of the mocking headlines that greeted the work – 'Tree Takes a Bow' – says it all. But the publicity raised Tippett's profile as a composer, and when it was given a radio performance eight years later, hard on the heels of his second opera, *King Priam*, the tide had turned in his favour. Colin Davis heard the broadcast on his car radio and determined one day to record the work, which he did to tremendous acclaim in 1968.

In 1960 he moved from Wadhurst to a house in the village of Corsham, Wiltshire, where his music room overlooked a large rectangular lawn and beyond to the woodlands of Corsham Park. When not playing croquet on this lawn with friends, Tippett continued to give lectures and interviews, write articles, and compose, including three further operas and the huge oratorio *The Mask of Time*, which he completed in 1982. He also made time to conduct amateur orchestras, most notably the Leicestershire Schools Symphony Orchestra, for whom he also wrote *The Shires Suite*. Under his leadership the Bath Festival enjoyed a revival of its fortunes in the 1970s and included a two-day blues and pop festival which attracted a quarter of a million people. Some of the items on the programmes of these events reflected Tippett's growing interest in the USA following his first visit there in 1965 and the subsequent popularity of his music in that country.

As he grew older, Tippett did not find composing any easier. It was always for him a painstaking process, but greater financial security had enabled him to maintain his routine of writing in the morning and walking in the afternoon, during which he would sift musical ideas in his thoughts. When, in 1970, plans were approved to build a multi-storey car park close to his house in Corsham, he moved once again, this time to a house outside Chippenham, where he continued to write, read, travel and compose. Failing eyesight curtailed some of these activities, but in 1991 his autobiography, *Those 20th Century Blues*, was published, in which he wrote candidly about his homosexuality and his wish to see in the new millennium. It was not to be, and he died with just two years to go.

Tippett's merit has been recognised slowly but surely. There were none of Walton's 'entertainments' or Vaughan Williams's 'big tunes' to launch his career; indeed, his music has long remained challenging and technically difficult, with only comparatively few works establishing a firm place in the international repertory. But after Britten's death in 1976,

Tippett was self-evidently the country's leading composer. He was knighted in 1966 and became a Companion of Honour in 1979, having already gathered a worthy collection of honorary degrees and prestigious awards. His most recent honour, and the one which reflected his eminence most clearly, was the Order of Merit, conferred by the Queen in 1983. He always wore such acclamations lightly, however, and would speak about his music in a detached manner as if it were by another. Producers of his operas who asked him for advice would usually be answered with: 'Oh, I don't know, love. Do what you like, it's no good asking me.'

Ralph Vaughan Williams

1872–1958

'I don't know whether I like it or not, but it's what I meant.'

Ralph Vaughan Williams was born in Down Ampney on 12 October 1872. His father's side of the family was of Welsh extraction and included among their number several distinguished and gifted lawyers. His mother was both a descendant of Josiah Wedgwood and a niece of Charles Darwin, and from an early age the young Vaughan Williams displayed two main characteristics common to both sides of the family: original views forthrightly expressed, and a capacity for sheer hard work. The youngest of three children, he spent most of his life in the Dorking and Leith Hill area or in London, and although born in Gloucestershire he always thought of himself as a Londoner. The move from Down Ampney actually came as early as 1875 on the death of his father, the Rev Arthur Vaughan Williams, leaving his wife Margaret to return with her young family to Surrey.

He grew up with his mother's relatives in the family home at Leith Hill Place overlooking the Surrey Downs and the Sussex Weald. Surrounded by trees, rhododendrons and azaleas planted by his grandfather, the terrace commanded a fine view across to the twin windmills above Hassocks some twenty miles away, an English landscape which seeped into the young boy's consciousness. Domestic discipline, though kindly, was also strict. Margaret taught her children to respect the needs of others whatever their position in life and in doing so profoundly influenced the character of her younger son, so that compassion and consideration remained indelible features of his personality throughout his life.

Ralph's early interest in music was encouraged by his mother, who went so far as to install an organ for him in the entrance hall of Leith Hill Place, an event less than appreciated by the family servants, who were frequently cajoled into pumping the bellows for him. Even then he had developed his lifelong habit of rising early to devote some time to music before breakfast, struggling with the rudiments of piano-playing, which he disliked, and trying his hand at composition under the watchful eye of his Aunt Sophie. At the age of seven he began to learn the violin and the following year took a correspondence course in music at Edinburgh University, passing both the preliminary and advanced examinations.

In 1882 Ralph was sent to a preparatory school in Rottingdean, where he continued piano and violin lessons before joining his brother at Charterhouse in 1887. Here he played second violin in the school orchestra and sang in the choir, but the most important event of his school career came the following year when he approached the formidable figure of Dr William Haig Brown, the Headmaster, for permission to give a concert of his own compositions in the school hall. To his surprise, approval was granted and the Vaughan Williams Trio in G was performed to an audience of masters and their wives. It was actually performed by a quartet as the composer took the precaution of getting another boy to help out with the violin part, but he was encouraged when the mathematics master, James Noon, took the boy to one side and told him that he must continue with his composing.

In the days when it was only just becoming respectable for a young man from a prosperous middle-class background to take to music as a profession, there seems to have been no family opposition when in 1890 Vaughan Williams chose to devote two years to study at the Royal College of Music before going up to Trinity College, Cambridge. He was taught composition by Parry, who succeeded in broadening his pupil's knowledge of music but failed to discover his musical 'character' and found nothing in his composition exercises to suggest the great composer he later became. It was a view shared by his tutor at Cambridge, Charles Wood, who confessed that he, too, held out no hopes for Vaughan Williams as a composer. Whilst at Cambridge, he continued weekly lessons at the RCM but these early years were a hard struggle to master his craft and determine his musical direction.

Despite obtaining a good second in the history tripos, Vaughan Williams's actual achievement at Cambridge was not considered impressive, so in the autumn of 1895 he returned for a further period of study to the RCM. Tall, imposing, serious minded and somewhat reserved, even shy, he did not easily make friends and was overshadowed by most of his fellow pupils. It was during this second period of study, however, that he met and became friendly with the man who was to have more influence than anyone on his music – Gustav Holst. Almost at once they began to give each other composition lessons, playing and criticising the earliest sketches of their works and rewriting passages together. These sessions they called their 'Field Days', which continued until Holst's death nearly 40 years later. There was hardly a work by either composer that the other did not see during that time.

Holst was not Vaughan Williams's only friend during this period, although he was far and away the most important. They were the nucleus of a small group of students, including John Ireland and Thomas Dunhill, which used to meet in a small Kensington teashop to discuss everything under the sun; he once said that he learnt more from those conversations than from any amount of formal teaching. He had also grown to know Adeline Fisher, whom he had first met as a boy, and despite some misgivings on her family's side they were married in October 1897. He decided to spend a further period of study abroad and the couple extended their honeymoon stay by some months in Berlin, where he worked with Max Bruch. On their return, he and Adeline lived in rooms in Westminster before buying 10 Barton Street, their home for the next seven years. Thus throughout his student days and in the early years of his married life, while he was developing his musical character, the sights and sounds of London formed the daily background to his existence. It was during this period that he virtually completed his formal musical education when he took his doctorate in music at Cambridge, becoming Dr Vaughan Williams, the title he proudly carried to the end of his days.

The turn of the century years were full and important. Though not compelled to earn a living, his private income never deflected him from his routine of working eight hours a day and destroying much that he wrote as unsatisfactory. By 1902 performances of his works began to attract some notice, but he had still to achieve that distinctive voice which he knew ought to be his. With Holst, he recognised that the way ahead would be found, not in writing 'second-hand music' borrowed from abroad but in re-awakening the English tradition, and it was in this way that events in 1903–4 provided the opportunity for Vaughan Williams to forge his own musical identity. He had already begun to collect folksongs in earnest in 1903 after hearing the lovely *Bushes and Briars* sung by a shepherd at an old people's tea party at Ingrave in Essex. Horrified that these beautiful tunes were in danger of disappearing, he began to collect songs in earnest, visiting various parts of the country and over the next ten years he gathered over 800 songs and variants. The orchestral *Three Norfolk Rhapsodies* written during 1905-6 contained some of the fine tunes he had collected at King's Lynn, but the extended work *In the Fen Country* which followed did not quote any actual folk-tunes, drawing instead upon the contours of the songs he had gathered and shaped to his own musical style. By absorbing the essence of English folksong in this way, Vaughan Williams had at last liberated his strong and original musical personality.

His interest in folksong happily coincided with a second event of almost equal importance when he was asked to edit a new hymn book, the main task to provide music for the verse, which involved rediscovering forgotten tunes and weeding out Victoriana. He was told it was a two-month job but, tackling it with his customary zeal, it took him two years, during which he wrote some tunes himself, persuaded friends to write others, and adapted forty from folksongs. Not surprisingly the quality of both words and music ensured its success and by the time of its golden jubilee, five million copies had been sold. In its own way the *English Hymnal* was to play an important part in the renaissance of English music and represents some of the composer's most enduring work. With its completion Vaughan Williams set off for France to acquire the lightness and colour he felt his music needed. He met briefly with Delius before spending three months in Paris studying orchestration with Ravel, and returned to complete the big choral work which became *A Sea Symphony*. He also wrote two other works, which had their first performances within a week in September 1910: the *Fantasia on English Folk Song* and one of the glorious masterpieces of English music, the *Fantasia on a Theme by Thomas Tallis*. The inspiration for the piece may have been Tudor, but its personality is pure Vaughan Williams. It was his first work which was recognisably and unmistakably his own and no one else's. These were busy years for RVW. He was not only active in writing music, collecting songs and attending concerts, but he also found time to encourage local choirs and amateur orchestras, notably with the Leith Hill Festival established earlier by his sister Margaret. English musical life was still dominated by Elgar, but within this period Vaughan Williams had emerged as a distinctive voice and by 1914 he had behind him a considerable body of work.

Although he was nearly 42 when war broke out, Vaughan Williams immediately enlisted as an orderly in the Medical Corps and served in France and on the Salonica fronts, later returning to France as an artillery officer. Military service, like folksong collecting, brought him into contact with people from very different backgrounds to his own, but his complete lack of pretension won their respect and in some cases their lifelong friendship. As with so many of his contemporaries, the impact of the war on his imagination was deep and lasting, but he was psychologically robust and able to withstand the losses and devastation of those years. Returning to England in 1919 at the age of 46, and knowing that many of his younger colleagues were dead, he was looked up to as a 'senior' composer, although he knew himself that his music

was still in its formative stage. Thus there was no flood of new music from his pen and he chose instead to revise his pre-war work while accepting an invitation to join the staff of the RCM.

By 1920 he had completed *The Lark Ascending* and within two years his war requiem, the *Pastoral Symphony*, received its first performance in London. This was just the beginning of a hectic few years of composing during which the seminal force of folksong poured forth in a series of personal works which left the world of *Norfolk Rhapsodies* far behind. Over the next decade or so, Vaughan Williams reconciled all manner of musical activity – practical, educational, administrative and advisory – with some of his most powerful work, so that by 1930 he had taken Elgar's place as the principal public figure in music. While other composers in the 'twenties were busy experimenting with new dissonant combinations, Vaughan Williams pursued his own line of development, carefully assimilating contemporary ideas but remaining fiercely independent. To his closest friends Vaughan Williams's warm and excitable nature was well known, but to the world at large he often appeared gruff, solitary and aloof, given to occasional explosions of terrible anger. The public image was only half true. Both Vaughan Williams and Holst were anything but men of solitude and while neither suffered fools gladly, they both enjoyed the company of vast numbers of friends from all walks of life. They were never happier than when making music and revelling in their 'Field Days', which made the death of his friend in 1934 so distressing. Vaughan Williams wrote no music *in memoriam*. That was not his way; but he felt the absence of Holst's criticism and encouragement to the end of his days.

With Holst's death Vaughan Williams was left as the only one of his generation of English composers who represented genius, confirming his status as leader of the 'English school'. In 1935, having previously refused a knighthood and other honours, he accepted the Order of Merit – because it involved 'no obligation to anyone in authority' – but official recognition had no effect on either his outspokenness or his versatility.

In the same year Adrian Boult conducted the vigorous and uncompromising Fourth Symphony, provoking both ecstatic and hostile reactions from audiences more familiar with the gentler music of earlier years.

When war broke out in 1939, Vaughan Williams had been unable to join the armed forces so he busied himself collecting salvage and addressing envelopes (in his almost illegible handwriting). Fortunately he soon found a more productive way to serve his country by writing music for films, beginning with the *49th Parallel*, a medium he found particularly stimulating. But the most important work was unquestionably the Fifth Symphony, first performed in 1943 and taken up by orchestras in England and America.

In the post-war years Vaughan Williams learnt to his dismay that he had become the Grand Old Man of English music, a phrase he detested, saying that he was neither grand nor old. Nevertheless, the special affection which everyone – musician and man in the street – had for him, was such that he was asked to lend his support to all sorts of gatherings and organisations. Those groups who sought to enlist only his name soon found, however, that he took his duties as president or chairman very seriously. He thrived on incessant labour and, showing total disregard for the calendar, devoted himself to composition and good causes.

The 1950s also brought important changes in his personal life as well as his music. In 1951, Adeline died at the age of 80, having been an invalid for many years; and in the same year the inept production at Covent Garden of his morality *The Pilgrim's Progress* wounded its composer more deeply than anything else in his career. In 1953 he married Ursula Wood, a close family friend, whose husband had been killed in the war, and left the White Gates near Dorking, where he had been living since 1929, for central London. Apart from deafness, he enjoyed good health and as he approached his eighty-second year he was at work on a big choral work for Christmas with two more symphonies before him. Late in 1954, he and Ursula arrived in New York for his third and last visit to the States. As usual his energy was inexhaustible and even after a hectic day sightseeing he insisted that the whole party should go to the top of the Empire State Building to see the sunset.

He was now not only a public figure but a beloved institution who remained fiercely independent in mind and body. He possessed a battery of hearing aids, the largest of which he referred to as his 'coffee pot', but regularly went out of his way to attend performances of new works by promising young composers. He also remained a landmark on the conductor's rostrum, instantly recognisable by his massive frame, shock of white hair and his uniquely untidy appearance – largely the result of his preference for tweed suits of uncertain fit. He found time for everything, and if inadvertently interrupted while working, he would lay it aside saying 'I like to be disturbed'. Nor was he ever too busy for the important details of life, as when receiving a letter from a nine-year-old boy commenting on how much he had preferred a Haydn symphony to a work by Vaughan Williams in the same programme. The composer wrote back:

Dear Tom,

... I am glad you like Haydn. He was a very great man and wrote beautiful tunes. I must one day try to write a tune which you will like.

Yours affectionately,
R Vaughan Williams

He retained this unquenchable zest for life until his death, which came early in the morning of 26 August in 1958 after a normal working day. He suffered a heart attack and died as he would have wished – suddenly and peacefully and at home. On his desk were an opera and a setting of carols.

William Walton

1902–1983

'Composing has never come easily to me, and the older I get the
more difficult it seems to become.'

The audience was aghast. Someone called the fire brigade, Edith Sitwell
was not allowed to take a curtain-call (for her own safety), and Walton's
name – for better or worse – was made. His misfortune was to compose
this highly individual masterpiece at the start of his career before the
impact of the later works could provide a measure of his true worth. Yet
for all its hornpiping, fanfares, parodies and eccentricities, *Façade*
contains fascinating insights into a post-First World War era of sudden
and violent change. For Elgar the party was over, an uninvited guest in
his former home. When he met Walton in 1932 for the first and last time,
it was in the lavatory at the Three Choirs Festival, where he complained
that the younger man's Viola Concerto murdered the poor instrument.
Yet he shared striking similarities with Walton: both were born in
provincial towns to parents with musical backgrounds but reduced
means; neither received a formal musical training; and each was
eventually absorbed into the music establishment.

Walton was born in Oldham, the second of four children. His father
taught music at Hulme Grammar School and for twenty-one years was
organist and choirmaster of St John's Church, Werneth, where William
and his brother sang on Sundays. Charles Walton was a strict
disciplinarian with a violent temper who would rap his son's knuckles
with his ring when mistakes were made, but for all that William's
childhood was not unhappy. He learned to play the piano and had violin
lessons until his father stopped them because he was careless about

practising, but a newspaper advertisement for probationer choristers at Christ Church, Oxford, caught Charles's eye and an application was made. William was nine when Mrs Walton and her son arrived at the college for the auditions. In fact they arrived too late, having missed the train because their fares had been drunk by Charles in the pub the night before and had to be borrowed from the local greengrocer. Fortunately, the organist was persuaded to listen and William was accepted on the spot.

Walton soon left the Oldham board school, which he detested, and joined the Christ Church Cathedral choir school, staying there for six years until 1918. He survived the first term, quickly losing his Lancashire accent to avoid discrimination from the other boys, and joined in the rigorous routines of practices and services which served as an education during the war years. To avoid being sent back to Oldham when his voice broke, Walton turned to composition and sufficiently impressed the Dean, Dr Strong, who paid the balance of the school fees himself in order to retain his promising pupil. He stayed on to the great age of 16 under the general supervision of Hugh Allen, who could bring orchestral scores vividly to life by playing them on the organ, and spent hours in the Radcliffe Camera, working through an extensive music library containing a large number of scores by Debussy, Ravel, Stravinsky and Prokofiev. Through studying these, Walton mastered his technique of orchestration, but all the time at the expense of Latin, Greek and Algebra, necessary requirements for his degree, which he repeatedly failed, and in 1920 it was decided he had better leave Oxford.

If these had been formative years in his musical education, Oxford also provided friendship of a more tangible kind, notably with the poet Siegfried Sassoon and Sacheverell Sitwell, at 21 the youngest brother of Osbert and Edith. They hailed the young Walton as a musical genius on the strength of his Piano Quartet and their own remarkable percipience, and invited him to live with them at Swan Walk in Chelsea and later in Osbert's house in Carlyle Square. Initially he was to stay just for the vacation but remained for almost fifteen years, scrounging a living from his adopted family, which enabled him to devote his days to composition without the need of regular work. Far from leading the life of a dilettante, Walton worked extremely hard, spending most of his time shut in his attic room with a hired piano and bags of black cherries. The Sitwells, meanwhile, through their social position, provided an aesthetic background otherwise unthinkable to the boy from Oldham, introducing him to wealthy patrons, literary figures, and influential music circles. They knew everybody who was anybody but, although reserved and awkward, Walton was never overwhelmed in their company and retained always a strong belief in his own ability. For their part, the Sitwells liked having him around and were at pains to cultivate his prodigious talent in any way they could. All in all it was a very satisfactory arrangement.

When the first, private, performance of *Façade* was given, the invited audience allegedly talked all through the recitation and concluded that both Walton and Edith were off their heads. Subsequent performances provoked general feelings of indignation, even hostility, which made the work famous overnight. While the Sitwells courted such publicity, Walton knew that for all its being called an 'entertainment', *Façade* merited serious consideration as an important work and was deeply offended when Howells accused him of 'fooling around'. Despite such reactions, however, he acquired enough wealthy sponsors to allow him to go on composing at his own deliberate pace. In the spring of 1925 he accompanied the Sitwells to Spain, where he revelled in the rhythms of the Catalonian national dance and wrote the overture *Portsmouth Point*, although he later claimed the main theme came to him while travelling aboard a No 22 bus in London. The fact that this work by a young English composer was selected for an international festival in Zurich was sufficient to reinforce the general view of Walton as belonging to the avant-garde. It also helped to establish his reputation at home, not least as a conductor of the work since no one else could do it. A glass of brandy given to him by Thomas Beecham before he ascended the podium at the first London performance may have helped.

In the 1920s and 30s very few people ever commissioned works: they just suggested something should be written for so-and-so. In 1928, Beecham had done just that, proposing a work for Lionel Tertis, who had single-handedly restored the viola to the ranks of solo instruments and had elicited major works from Bax and Vaughan Williams among others. On finishing the piece, Walton sent it to Tertis, who promptly rejected it by return of post. Hurt and disappointed, Walton contemplated turning it into a violin concerto – all that work for nothing; but Hindemith took up the work, which received its première at a Henry Wood prom concert in 1929. Indeed, so successful was it that later violinists of the stature of Menuhin and Nigel Kennedy transferred to the viola in order to play it.

Walton was still living in Carlyle Square, uncertain what to do after this latest triumph. He was always jealous of other people's successes and given the chance believed himself to be capable of better. So after his friend Constant Lambert scored a major hit with *The Rio Grande*, Walton was prompted to emulate and outdo it and when approached in 1929 to write a work for the BBC, he seized his chance. The fact that Lambert and Hely-Hutchinson had also been contacted spurred him to complete the assignment, most of it written in the stables of Sacheverell's house in Northamptonshire. Despite the distractions of Imma von Doernberg, a widowed baroness, with whom he was now living in Switzerland, *Belshazzar's Feast*, the work in question, was ready for its first performance in Leeds, to be conducted by Malcolm Sargent. Dedicated to Lord Berners, it was a riotous success and critics acclaimed it as a landmark in British choral music, rivalled only by Elgar's *The Dream of Gerontius* some thirty years earlier.

A symphony was to follow, although it took some three years to complete the first three movements. Interest in its progress was intense and Walton was eventually persuaded to allow a first performance of the incomplete work to go ahead at Queen's Hall late in 1934. The audience was overwhelmed by its impact and eager for the composer to finish it. In the meantime he had been deserted by Imma, his first real love, and found solace in the company of Alice Wimborne, whose husband,

Viscount Wimborne, was an extremely wealthy steel magnate. In truth, they lived independent lives and although twenty-two years older than Walton she looked far younger than her age and they enjoyed a close relationship until her death in 1948. The inspiration to complete the symphony and finish the last movement came from Patrick Hadley, who supported Walton in his decision to wait until he had the right material for a satisfactory conclusion, and after its first complete performance, in 1935, it was Alice who gave a grand party which included royalty. A more telling post-concert gathering occurred after the new symphony's second performance, at Oxford, where, addressing an undergraduate musical society, Walton revealed his inherent dislike of pomposity and posturing when replying to a solemn question about his inclusion of a fugue in the last movement. Stuck for ideas he had rung Lambert, who had suggested the device, recommending a couple of good pages on the subject in Grove's *Dictionary*: he had simply read the entry and written the fugue.

The Symphony crowned a remarkable decade for Walton during which he had produced the three masterpieces on which his reputation was secured. Further recognition of his stature came when he was asked to write a royal march for the Coronation of George VI. As majestic as Elgar's ceremonial music at its best, and containing a 'big tune' of which Walton was never ashamed, *Crown Imperial* was played in Westminster Abbey to accompany the entry of the Queen Mother. 1937 ended with Walton undergoing a hernia operation, but to convalesce Alice took him to the beautiful Villa Cimbrone overlooking the sea above Ravello, where he worked doggedly on a violin concerto in a little room above a crypt. As usual, writing it gave him a lot of trouble, especially the last movement again, but once completed he let it be known that the work expressed his feelings for Alice. Had the war not intervened she would have built a house on the cliff for them both, a dream palace which Walton spent effortless hours planning, even building a replica out of matchboxes glued together. (He smoked at least twenty pipes a day, so was not short of building materials for his model.) It had been his intention to conduct the first performance of the concerto in the United States but was forced to change his plans when war was declared in September.

Initial attempts to help the war effort were less than successful when he attempted to drive an ambulance, and after running it off the road once too often he just waited to be called up. In the event, he was exempted from military service on condition that he would write music for films deemed to be 'of national importance'. He had written some film music earlier – notably for *As You Like It* with Laurence Olivier in 1936 – and during the war years wrote the music for *Went the Day Well?* and *The First of the Few*, Leslie Howard's film about the man who designed the Spitfire. In all he wrote music for half a dozen films in this time, the most memorable being his second collaboration with Olivier, on *Henry V*, which was first shown in November 1944. It includes the two beautiful episodes for strings, *Passacaglia: Death of Falstaff* and *Touch her soft lips and part*, both of which have found their way from the cinema to the concert hall.

After the war Alice and William left London for a holiday in Capri, but on the way she became ill and entered a nursing home in Lausanne. The doctors diagnosed cancer of the bronchus and she died the following April after suffering alarming distress which haunted Walton for the rest of his life. Work was his therapy and he continued with his opera *Troilus and Cressida*, resumed work on a violin sonata, and undertook considerable revision of the score of *Belshazzar's Feast*.

Later in the year he sailed to Buenos Aires as a delegate to an international conference, where he met Susana Gil, the attractive twenty-two-year-old daughter of a well-to-do Argentine lawyer, who was organising a press conference for him. After only two weeks, he and Susana were engaged, much against the wishes of her family and much to the alarm of Walton's friends in London. Impulsive and irresponsible it may have been, but the marriage lasted for thirty-five years until his death, and despite the age-gap, he and Susana remained ideal partners. Shortly after returning to London, they rented an old convent on the

island of Ischia in the Bay of Naples, loaded up Walton's treasured Bentley with the essentials for a six-month visit, and remained there for the rest of his life in the house and gardens of La Mortella.

Still regarded as a distinguished composer in England, Walton was paid the princely sum of £50 in 1952 to write a march celebrating the Coronation of Elizabeth II, for which he wore his Oxford gown of Doctor of Music awarded ten years earlier. For the same occasion Gordon Jacob had favoured Court Dress, in order to stock his hat with sandwiches, whereas Walton filled his with miniature bottles of scotch to sustain himself through the long ceremony. The following year saw the first performance at Covent Garden of *Troilus and Cressida*, which was well enough received but tinged by feelings of disappointment that Walton had written an old-fashioned opera in a tradition then held to be outmoded. The Cello Concerto which followed fared a little better, but 1956 was a time of immense change in the British musical outlook and composers like Bax, Ireland, Rubbra and others found themselves out in the cold. Walton was among them. Already at home in his Mediterranean retreat, he and Susana occupied themselves planning and building their magnificent house and gardens at Ischia. The only problem with living abroad was that he increasingly had the feeling that England had forgotten him, although in 1961 he returned to Oldham to become its 14th honorary Freeman.

Walton was always regarded as a reluctant rather than a compulsive composer, but in fact he was businesslike and methodical in his approach, following a regular routine of starting work after an early breakfast, writing until lunch and then again in the evening. Never a prolific composer, he made a habit of writing at least something every day, if only a couple of bars which he would usually destroy. Works which saw the light of day included the Second Symphony and the *Partita*, as well as the *Variations on a Theme by Hindemith*, one of his finest pieces which deserves wider recognition. Remote from his native country, Walton complained that *all* his music deserved wider acclaim, yet he had already enjoyed his fair share of public renown. Apart from his knighthood in 1951 and the Order of Merit in 1967, he received a clutch of doctorates, was made an honorary fellow of the RCM and the RAM, and was awarded the Gold Medal of the Royal Philharmonic Society among others.

In 1965 doctors in London detected a shadow on his left lung and a second opinion confirmed cancer. (He immediately told his wife to throw away all his pipes and he never smoked again.) The operation was successful but after a few months the cancer returned and there followed three months of painful ray treatment which left him exhausted. He recovered from the ordeal and returned to Ischia with Susana to continue work on his second opera, *The Bear*, which was performed the following year at Aldeburgh.

Around this time he also agreed to compose music for a feature film about the Battle of Britain and, determined to write something rousing and patriotic, threw himself into the project. Everyone connected with the film was delighted with the finished score except United Artists, who claimed never to have heard of Walton and approached Ron Goodwin for a re-write. Walton's anger and hurt was shared by Olivier, who threatened to have his name removed from the credits unless they retained some part of the original music. Eventually the producers agreed to use just five minutes of the air-battle sequence, but nothing more. They also refused to release the score until the intervention of the then Prime Minister, Edward Heath, when it was restored to the OUP in 1972. Notwithstanding this fiasco, Walton was to collaborate with his friend Malcolm Arnold on the score for David Lean's film *Lawrence of Arabia*, but after drinking a fair amount over lunch, they decided it would need hours of music and declined.

Fortunately, the composer enjoyed good health for his 70th birthday celebrations and spent six months of 1972 travelling through the UK for concerts in his honour, culminating in a dinner given at Downing Street attended by seventy-five guests which included the Queen Mother. Over the next few years his health gradually deteriorated and he was eventually confined to a wheelchair. In 1981, Tony Palmer filmed a moving television profile of Walton which contained archive material and a long interview with the composer, but soon after he became increasingly delicate and endured considerable physical hardship. Rumours of a third symphony persisted, but two years later he awoke early feeling unwell and died peacefully in Susana's arms. On his piano were left a sheet of music-paper with a few notes sketched on it, together with his rubber, pencil and spectacles, left there the evening before he died. Today they are still just as he left them.

Peter Warlock

1894–1930

'One should make no concessions,
and insist on everything or nothing.'

A well-known portrait photo taken when he was about thirty shows hair
slicked straight back, with lean, sensitive features marked by a neatly
trimmed beard and a thin smile. It conveys an impression of a quietly
assured man at ease with himself – a respected scholar and critic with a
growing reputation as a composer of brilliant songs. It was only a few
years later that he was to die of gas poisoning at his Chelsea flat, a
coroner's jury unable to decide whether or not it was a case of suicide.

Philip Heseltine was born into a prosperous family and although his
father, a solicitor, died when he was two years old, his mother remarried
and he enjoyed an amicable relationship with his stepfather. It has been
suggested that the early loss of his father may have contributed to his
later instability, but his friend E J Moeran thought it was more likely an
overpowering maternal influence which accounted for Heseltine's early
shyness and the later conflicts and tensions which permeated his
personality.

There was no evidence of musical interests in his family and it was
not until he was sent to prep school in Broadstairs that he first showed a
liking for music. After winning a scholarship to Eton, he was fortunate
in his music master, Colin Taylor, who noted in this pale little boy '…
something arresting, something apart, something strikingly different from
the ordinary run of our music students.' It was Taylor who introduced
Heseltine to the music of Delius, whom he eventually met via an artist
uncle living not far from the composer's home at Grez-sur-Loing near

Paris. Delius soon became a personal friend and for some years afterwards his mentor both in matters of music and life. This friendship with Delius was to last until his death, but it was between the ages of sixteen and twenty-three that it was of primary importance to him. Though he took no formal lessons from him, Delius's paternal and musical influence was decisive, and Heseltine determined upon a life in music.

Leaving Eton in 1911, he spent some months in Germany before entering Oxford, at his parents' insistence, to study Classics. A dreary life in the Civil Service beckoned and he wrote in desperation to Delius, who advised him to abandon all other pursuits and devote himself to music. As expected, Oxford proved too stifling for a man of Heseltine's eclectic tastes. He therefore indulged himself in a series of motorcycles and devoured literature that was unlikely to be on the recommended reading lists. It was also around this time that he first exhibited signs of a dual personality : an innate gentleness alternating with mood-swings towards a more reckless and vitriolic posture.

At the outbreak of war the following summer, Heseltine declared himself a conscientious objector (although he was officially classed as medically unfit for military service), and left Oxford to settle in London, thinking perhaps that he might study composition with Holst. Instead, he briefly enrolled at London University to read English, but in 1915 was appointed music critic to the *Daily Mail*, a somewhat limited role in wartime Britain, and he resigned after six months. It was during this period that he met D H Lawrence, was immediately impressed by his work and ideas, and strove mightily for the publication of *The Rainbow* which was then proscribed. The friendship was short-lived, Heseltine claiming that, for all his talent, personal relationships with Lawrence were impossible. Nothing daunted, his next enthusiasm arose from a meeting in the following year with that curious figure Bernard van Dieren (1884–1936). In fact, van Dieren's music probably had greater impact on Heseltine than even Delius and together with his close companion, Cecil Gray, he became a champion of van Dieren's music in the teeth of almost universal critical hostility. Marriage to Minnie Lucy Channing, an artist's model, did little to diminish Heseltine's growing instability. They divorced in 1924, but not before Lawrence featured them as 'Halliday' and 'Pussum' in *Women in Love*. (Such was the magnetism of his personality that he was depicted in five other novels, including the young man 'Coleman' in Aldous Huxley's *Antic Hay*.)

When he wasn't providing inspiration for other people's writing, Heseltine himself liked to employ obscure pseudonyms : 'Bulgy Gogo', 'Mortimer Cattley' and 'Rab Noolas' among others served their turn; but by now he was regularly using the name 'Peter Warlock' by which, as a musician, he is generally remembered. There is some evidence for the view that the two names represent opposing aspects of his character: the quiet, introspective scholar, Heseltine, and the acerbic, mischievous, scurrilous Warlock, whom one glimpses riding his motorbike stark naked through the English countryside at night. Certainly the two contrasting moods of his music – an extrovert, rumbustious joviality, and a refined, meditative lyricism – reflect the duality of his personality, but further attempts at classification under the two names are fruitless. The notion that Philip Heseltine committed suicide to kill off Peter Warlock, as Gray suggested, is almost certainly untrue. In particular company and in certain situations he seemed determined to assume a markedly different personality from the reserved and thoughtful Heseltine, but those who knew him well were constantly reminded of his courtesy and sincerity; they understood, too, the complexity of a man who was in many ways ahead of his time.

Despite setbacks, his enthusiastic passions remained a feature of his personality. During a year spent in Ireland, where he met and later fell out with Yeats, Heseltine immersed himself in the study of Celtic languages. He also became a fanatical student of the occult in all its forms, a destructive activity which probably exacerbated his volatile changes of mood. Nevertheless, his year in Dublin was in other ways especially productive and he returned to London with a collection of manuscripts which demonstrated both his growing confidence and individual style. Among them were carols and several exquisitely poignant songs which received immediate acclaim when published in 1919. Thereafter he found it convenient to issue his compositions under the name of Warlock and to reserve his own name for literary and critical purposes. His writing came in sudden bursts of frantic creativity, followed by long periods of sterile inactivity, but still he found time to pursue his literary interests. In 1920 he founded a promising but short-lived musical journal, *The Sackbut*, and for the next decade continued to edit and transcribe large quantities of Elizabethan and Jacobean music, writing articles and books, and promoting the music of his favourite composers.

He lived for a while in the family home in North Wales until 1925, when he cajoled E J Moeran to share a cottage with him in the Kentish village of Eynsford. There they enjoyed an anarchic lifestyle involving heroic quantities of beer which did little for the immediate creativity of either composer, although Moeran provided an illuminating insight into his friend's methods of composing:

For weeks he would be sunk in gloom, unable to think of a note ... When the black mood passed he would write a song a day for a week. He went to the piano and began fumbling about with chords and whistling, quite undisturbed by conversation from the next room.

Heseltine left Eynsford in the autumn of 1928 and returned to Wales, but was disillusioned and frustrated with his lot. Alternating moods of hope and depression characterised 1930 and on a fine winter's morning eight days before Christmas, he put out his cat before dying from gas poisoning. Accident or suicide? No one is sure.

Shorter entries

Richard Addinsell

1904–1977

Addinsell had intended to study Law and was for a brief time at Hertford College, Oxford, but became distracted by the possibilities of music for the theatre and after a short course of study at the RCM produced a score for Clemence Dane's play *Come of Age*. Encouraged by this, he chose to study abroad for a while, mainly in Berlin and Vienna, before visiting America in 1933 to provide music for Eva Le Gallienne's production of *Alice in Wonderland*. He stayed to work in the Hollywood studios but returned to England in 1941 to collaborate as composer and accompanist with Joyce Grenfell for her one-woman shows, at the same time continuing to write almost exclusively for the theatre, radio and the cinema.

Among his better-known film scores are *Goodbye Mr Chips*, *The Prince and the Show Girl*, *Blithe Spirit*, and Jean Anouilh's *The Waltz of the Toreadors*. But the piece which guaranteed Addinsell immortality was a one-movement piano concerto in the style of Rachmaninov which became known as the *Warsaw Concerto*, written for the film *Dangerous Moonlight*. Addinsell worked for six months on the nine-minute concerto, which was then recorded and edited into the already finished film. When it was shown at the Regal Cinema in Marble Arch in 1941, it caused an avalanche of enquiries about the music, which has since become one of the most successful film scores of all time.

William Alwyn

1905–1985

Alwyn was born in Northampton, four years after Rubbra and sixteen years before Malcolm Arnold. 'It is odd,' he had written, 'that a boot-manufacturing provincial town ... should have produced three composers', and indeed Northampton provided little encouragement from a musical point of view. His father moved there from London to open a small grocery business and although well read (he called his shop 'The Shakespeare Stores') there was no particular interest in music in the family. Alwyn, however, showed musical leanings and was given lessons in flute and piano by local teachers, who encouraged his first attempts at composition, written at the age of eight.

He went to Northampton Grammar School, where he displayed outstanding promise in both music and painting, but left at the age of 14 to help in his father's shop. Fortunately his piano teacher managed to persuade his parents of his rare talent and they sent him to the RAM, where he won a flute scholarship and encountered the enlightened teaching of John McEwen, who opened his eyes to the possibilities of modern music. When he was just 18 his father died suddenly and Alwyn had to abandon his scholarship and earn a living. He endured a brief spell at a prep school in Haslemere before playing the flute in theatre orchestras and summer resorts while teaching piano at a shilling an hour in London's East End. He was eventually rescued from the bandstand at Eastbourne and taken on as a flautist with the London Symphony Orchestra, where he played under Elgar and Vaughan Williams. When McEwen was appointed Principal of the Royal Academy in 1926, Alwyn was invited to join the staff as a professor of composition and remained there until 1955. His output in those early years was prodigious: he had already nearly equalled the Beethoven canon of string quartets by the time he was 30 and had completed an oratorio setting of Blake's *The*

Marriage of Heaven and Hell in its entirety by 1936. The Concerto for Piano brought him a measure of fame and popularity, but by 1939 he had concluded that his music lacked form and disowned most of what he had written until then, concentrating his energies on acquiring real technique.

Alwyn is still chiefly remembered, like his colleague Malcolm Arnold, as a composer of film music with the implied disapproval that the words 'film composer' usually evoke. This may be the reason why Alwyn's music is not so well known as that of his contemporaries, as if all his other music must be contaminated by contact with the cinema industry. His first encounter with screen writing came in 1935, when he was asked at short notice to compose music for a programme on air travel, and when war broke out he was selected for special duties as a composer for feature films and documentaries. His contribution to the war effort seems to have been very effective for he held the dubious honour of having his name on Hitler's official 'black list'.

With the war at an end, his services as a film composer were in great demand and for the next fifteen years or so he earned a substantial part of his livelihood in this way. Of his more than 60 film scores, perhaps the most important are those for *Odd Man Out, The Fallen Idol*, and the wartime documentaries *Desert Victories* and *Fires Were Started*; in 1958 he was made a Fellow of the British Film Academy. Having 'bought time', in his own words, for his more important compositions, he retired to Suffolk to compose what and when he liked. Alwyn was also a poet, an artist, an authority on Pre-Raphaelite painting, and a skilled translator of contemporary French poetry. He died in Southwold in 1985, since when his five symphonies and much more besides have been recorded.

Richard Arnell

b. 1917

Arnell was born in London during a Zeppelin raid on Hampstead, from which he survived unscathed, and went on to lead a versatile life both in England and America as composer, conductor, writer, poet, film maker and teacher. Following a public school education, he studied for three years at the RCM with John Ireland until, in 1939, he travelled to New York and found a publisher for his compositions. In 1943 he was appointed music consultant to the American offices of the BBC and stayed there for two years before returning to London to teach composition, theory and orchestration at Trinity College. His music had earlier caught the ear of Thomas Beecham, who included some of it in his programmes, noticeably the concert version of Arnell's most famous work, *Punch and the Child*, performed by the New York City Ballet. He later wrote operas, further ballets and a number of symphonies, as well as works for television and other media.

Arthur Benjamin

1893–1960

Along with Grainger, Benjamin was one of the first Australian-born composers to win international fame. After a general education at Brisbane Grammar School, he won a scholarship to the RCM, where he studied with Stanford and specialised in piano. He remained there until the outbreak of war in 1914, when he joined the British army and was sent to France. Later he flew in the air force and was shot down and captured by the Germans. After the war he went back to Australia to teach piano at the Sydney Conservatory, but the desire to compose prompted a return to London, where his first published work, a string quartet, appeared in 1924 and won a Carnegie Award. Two years later, Benjamin joined the staff of the RCM as a professor of piano, and included among his students the young Benjamin Britten.

Though he could be serious, as in the Violin Concerto of 1932 or the tragic mood of his only symphony, written at the close of the last war, the title of an earlier orchestral work, *Light Music Suite*, indicates Benjamin's more usual direction. His first opera, *The Devil Take Her*, displayed his warm sense of humour and was enthusiastically promoted by Beecham, but his orchestral music has fared much better. As an examiner and adjudicator, Benjamin travelled to various parts of the globe, which explains his several Caribbean-based works, of which the 1938 *Jamaican Rumba* became an instant favourite. It made his name known throughout the world and astonished many who discovered that he was not a dance-band leader but a professor at the RCM.

After the war he wrote a more ambitious opera, *A Tale of Two Cities*, which was premièred in 1953 by the BBC, who then broadcast his television opera, *Mariana*, three years later. Benjamin also wrote film music, including Hitchcock's *The Man Who Knew Too Much*, and at the time of his death was working on an adaptation of Molière's *Tartuffe*.

Richard Rodney Bennett

b. 1936

Bennett was born into a household that was already very musical – his mother, a pupil of Holst, was both a composer and pianist; his father, Rodney Bennett, a well-known author of children's books. Their son showed early signs of an exceptional musical and creative talent, writing music from the age of five, and by fifteen completing his first string quartet. The following year he wrote a *Theme and Variations* for violin and viola which he regarded as his first serious composition. He was then attending Leighton Park School in Reading before gaining a scholarship to the Royal Academy to study with Lennox Berkeley and Howard Ferguson. Bennett's music began to appear in concert programmes almost as soon as he set foot in the door, and several other works were professionally performed in London while he was still a student. His interest in modern music, however, was not encouraged by the RAM so he formed his own small music society which revelled in the attractions of the twelve-note technique.

Elizabeth Lutyens was a strong influence at this time, but in 1957 a further scholarship, awarded by the French Government, enabled him to study with Pierre Boulez in Paris for two years. Unimpressed by Bennett's apparent superficial fluency, Boulez was the first musician to confront him with the need to adopt a ruthless approach to technique. He was always grateful and, given his exceptional facility, could well have opted for the temptingly fashionable internationalism of the 1950s; however, his flirtation with *avant-garde* techniques was short-lived and with his return to England in 1959 he decided that this sort of thing was not for him.

Once in London it was not long before he established himself as the most spectacular rising star of the new generation of British composers. He had always enjoyed working with singers (as a child he would accompany his sister's singing), and in 1961 came the breakthrough when he was commissioned to write *The Ledge* – a one-act opera for Sadler's Wells. Concertos and symphonies followed, and in keeping with some of his contemporaries, he turned to writing film music in order to support himself, a medium for which his exceptional versatility was admirably suited. He has since written effective scores for over thirty-five films, including *Far From the Madding Crowd* and *Nicholas and Alexandra* (for which he won Academy Award nominations), as well as *Billion Dollar Brain, Murder on the Orient Express*, and *Yanks*. His most recent success has been Mike Newell's hugely popular *Four Weddings and a Funeral*.

During the 1960s, Bennett's enthusiasm for jazz prompted him to write serious concert works in a sophisticated jazz style, but his main interest in this genre was predominantly vocal, dedicating such works as *Jazz Calendar* (initially a ballet) and *Soliloquy* to the singer Cleo Laine. He has held academic posts as professor of composition at the RAM from 1963-5, and Visiting Professor at the Peabody Conservatory in Baltimore from 1970-71. He was made a CBE in 1977 and two years later escaped the drudgery of teaching and committee work to settle in New York, where he remains an eclectic composer, more admired by the general public than by the fashion-conscious.

Like Noel Coward, Bennett has always taken his light music seriously and to underline this point he more recently resumed his association with the Royal Academy, holding the International Chair of Composition, while pursuing a successful career as a cabaret pianist and singer. He now lives on Upper West Side and revealed in a recent 'Desert Island Discs' programme that he wouldn't live anywhere else, adding that if he could only take one record, it would be Walton's Violin Concerto.

York Bowen

1884–1961

So often associated with his more illustrious contemporaries at the Royal Academy in the early 1900s, it comes as a surprise to discover that Bowen lived for 77 years and remained a prolific composer throughout his life.

He was born in north London at Crouch End, the youngest of three sons, and from an early age displayed a remarkable musical talent. For two years he studied with Alfred Izard at the Blackheath Conservatoire, where he accumulated numerous prizes and medals before winning a scholarship to the RAM in 1898. Initially reluctant to leave Izard, he became a student of Tobias Matthay and Frederick Corder, concentrating mostly on the piano, viola and horn. Although a gifted player, he soon turned his attention to composition, and a piano concerto was performed at Queen's Hall as early as 1904 which confirmed his reputation as a distinguished student.

Two more concertos followed and by 1912 two symphonies had already received favourable public notices, when his career as a composer was interrupted by the outbreak of war. He enlisted as a horn player in the regimental band of the Scots Guards, and served in France before eventually being invalided home with pneumonia in 1916. After a frustrating few years, he somehow managed to pick up the threads of his former life and quickly established his name as a brilliant concert pianist. Everything he did had a professional touch and as his fame spread he continued to compose freely, including among his works a number of symphonies, orchestral suites and overtures, concertos for both horn and viola, and a quantity of chamber music.

Despite this prodigious output, Bowen is remembered chiefly for his smaller piano compositions, notably the *Twenty-Four Preludes*, which have been described as the finest pieces for solo piano ever written by an

Englishman. After a promising beginning, he drifted into relative obscurity, his later years clouded by financial concerns, until his sudden death in November 1961. However he may be judged, Bowen's accomplished technique and imaginative range ensures him a place among Britain's unsung minor composers whose time has yet to come.

Geoffrey Bush

1920–1998

Born in London, Bush inherited from his parents a love of literature, teaching, puzzle-solving and sport. His father, Christopher Bush, was a novelist and not especially musical yet his son was accepted as a choirboy at Salisbury Cathedral at the age of eight, where his encounter with 400 years of English choral music made an indelible impression. More specifically, the Salisbury years taught Bush how to write for voices. Music was all around him and he absorbed it as effortlessly as children learn a foreign language when they live abroad.

His time at Lancing College, where he was taught by the influential Jasper Rooper, also had a profound effect on his development. By this time, Bush had been composing for a number of years and at the age of 13 had a five-minute *Winter Ballet* performed in Bath by none other than his aunt's dancing class. Rooper, meanwhile, arranged for his pupil's work to be glimpsed by Vaughan Williams, who offered sound advice: 'Don't be afraid of writing a tune, then stopping it and starting another. The critics won't like it, but that's the way to write music.' Bush took note, but a more permanent relationship developed around this time with John Ireland, whose music he greatly admired, and school holidays were spent attending informal composition lessons at Ireland's Chelsea studio.

It was Ireland who drew Bush's attention to a scholarship being offered at Oxford and in 1938 he won a place to study Classics and composition at Balliol College. Musically, he found himself more-or-less fending for himself, but was greatly helped and encouraged by the celebrated organist Sir Thomas Armstrong (then in charge of most of Oxford's performing activities), who diligently promoted the younger man's early compositions. From these formative encounters, Bush developed an acute ear for sung harmonies and learned to write music that was both challenging and rewarding to perform, using as few notes as possible to create his musical effects. Economy and understatement long remained hallmarks of Bush's style.

At Oxford also he met John Gardner, some of whose works had already received regular performances, and Bruce Montgomery, a musician now known more for his novels written under the alias of Edmund Crispin. Together, Bush and Montgomery gave joint concerts of their music at the Wigmore Hall, and collaborated on plots for detective fiction which, alongside bridge and tennis, remained one of Bush's lifelong hobbies. The war interrupted this pleasant existence and five years were spent as assistant warden at a hostel for unbilletable evacuee children in Wales. In 1947 the ever-popular *Christmas Cantata*, written while still a student at Oxford, was first performed there, and following his marriage three years later, Bush moved to London and was eventually invited to be Visiting Professor in Music at King's College in 1969.

Apart from composing, Bush was an ardent champion of English music, about which he has wrote widely and broadcast frequently. Besides composition, most of his remaining time was taken up teaching adults and for 30 years he was staff tutor in music at the Extra-Mural Department of London University. Like his music, Bush's lectures were well-informed, elegantly presented and succinctly expressed. He may have appeared to some as austere and forbidding, but as one commentator noted, the twinkle in his eye was never far away. Beneath a disciplined exterior, Bush concealed the generous nature which is so clearly evident in his music. He died peacefully at home in February 1998.

Rebecca Clarke

1886–1979

Rebecca Clarke was born in Harrow, the daughter of a German mother and an American father, a colourful character about whom she reminisces entertainingly in her memoirs. Music-making was part of the daily family life and she learnt the violin from the age of eight. In 1902 she entered the RAM to study under Percy Miles, but when he eventually proposed marriage her father insisted that she leave. Back at home, Clarke started to write songs which attracted the attention of Stanford and in 1907 she became the first female composition student at the RCM. It was on his suggestion that she switched to the viola, on which she became a notable player, and after her father had thrown her out of the house in 1910, she was forced to make her own living as a professional viola player. Within two years she became one of the first women to be employed by Henry Wood in his Queen's Hall Orchestra, but it was during the 1920s and 1930s that she established a sound reputation as the founder member of a piano quartet, the English Ensemble.

Most of her compositions date from this period and met with some success, although by 1930 Clarke was completing fewer scores and her popularity waned. She had lived in America for a number of years following a concert tour in 1916, and was there again visiting relatives when war broke out. She was forced to remain in the United States and after marrying the pianist James Friskin, a former student friend, she lived in New York from 1944 until her death 35 years later. During that time she virtually stopped composing and performing, preferring to give only the occasional lecture or broadcast.

Clarke's total output comprised 58 songs – many remarkably ahead of their time – and 24 instrumental chamber pieces, of which her Viola Sonata, written in 1919, has recently been cited as one of the finest ever written for the instrument.

Arnold Cooke

b. 1906

Arnold Cooke, a modest man who has never sought the limelight, is nonetheless a prolific composer with some 130 works to his credit. These include two operas, six symphonies, several concertos, five string quartets, and a host of smaller pieces for various combinations of instruments and voices.

He was born in Yorkshire, where the family owned a carpet manufacturing business. He won an entrance exhibition to Repton School, where his musical talents, including composition, were encouraged.

Cambridge followed; there he read history but later switched to music, with Edward Dent as his principal composition teacher.

In 1929 Cooke joined fellow composer Walter Leigh in Hindemith's composition class at the Berlin Hochschule für Musik, and there encountered a much broader musical education than would normally be found in England.

Cooke taught at the Manchester School of Music from 1933-38 and then moved to London. He served in the Navy during the war, and it was while on a Norwegian escort vessel that he heard the first performance of his Piano Concerto, broadcast by the BBC.

Cooke later taught composition at Trinity College of Music in London, retiring in 1978.

Clarity of expression, transparency of texture and clear orchestration are hallmarks of his output, which has not latterly enjoyed the exposure it certainly merits.

Benjamin Dale

1885–1943

Benjamin Dale was born in London and studied under Corder at the RAM, where he revealed a precocious talent. An overture inspired by Macaulay's *Horatius* was performed when he was only 14, and the Piano Sonata, probably his best-known work, was composed in 1902 while Dale was still a student. The last two movements of his Suite for Viola and Piano, written when he was 21, were among the most popular pieces in the repertory of the distinguished viola player Lionel Tertis.

In August 1914, Dale was in Germany and held prisoner there until the end of the war, an experience which severely affected his health. Examining duties which took him to Australia and New Zealand in 1920 revived his spirits somewhat and he composed a Violin Sonata, followed by the festival anthem *A Song of Praise*. He continued to immerse himself in his work at the RAM and the Associated Board to such an extent that he had little time left for composition. His meticulous self-criticism resulted in a small output, leaving audiences wondering what might have been.

Walford Davies

1869–1941

John Davies was a devoted lover of music; he played the flute and the cello and brought up his large family to make music together. Walford was the seventh of nine children, of whom the boys at least grew up playing on any instruments they could find, forming themselves with a cousin or two into 'The Boys' Band.' Walford himself was experimental from the first, untuning the piano before a failed attempt to retune it, and improvising a storm symphony on the family harmonium while a brother adjusted the gas bracket to represent lightning.

When he was twelve, Walford left Oswestry to become a chorister at St George's, Windsor, where he was apprenticed to the great organist Walter Parratt until the sudden death of his father in 1885. Help was at hand and it was arranged for the boy to become the Dean's secretary for a while before gaining a scholarship in composition at the RCM. No sooner had he settled in and begun to earn a living as a church organist than he fell seriously ill with peritonitis and endured a long convalescence. His first year at the RCM, though interrupted, was not wasted, however, since he had already impressed Hubert Parry with his natural gifts, and in 1895 he was taken on as a teacher of counterpoint.

After completing a doctorate at Cambridge and serving in other London churches, Davies began, in 1898, a notable twenty-year career as organist and choirmaster at the Temple Church. Here he showed remarkable imagination in his choice of music for the services and set rigorous standards for choral singing and organ-playing. He also ensured a higher standard of general education for the boys by transferring them to the City of London School, where they were given the best and, unlike many cathedral schools, there were no 'extras' to be debited to parents.

He continued to compose and through the good offices of Elgar got his first commission, to write a festival work, *The Temple*, which

received a mixed reception at the Three Choirs in 1902. His next major work, *Everyman*, followed two years later and was better received, though his *Festival Overture* for the Lincoln Festival and a *Symphony in G* produced at Queen's Hall both died a death. No doubt they deserved a better fate, but Davies was far happier with smaller orchestral works and fared better with his *Holiday Tunes*, written for Henry Wood's Promenade Concerts. These were unpretentious, fresh and characteristic of himself, none more so than *A Solemn Melody*, which he dashed off for a commemoration service of the birth of Milton at Bow Church in 1908. Later he offered the work to Wood and to his surprise it was received at a Prom with such loud applause that Wood had to break his rigid rule against encores and repeat it. It became a regular feature of every Promenade season and beyond doubt Davies's most popular instrumental work. It was also played at the coronation of George V in 1911, as well as the initial concert of the Promenade season given at the Albert Hall after the destruction of Queen's Hall in 1941.

During the war, Davies initially busied himself enthusiastically with music for and among the troops and from the outset seemed to be not a little touched with 'war fever' in his desire to assist. Well-meant patriotism clouded his better judgement and he became increasingly fascinated by the idea of The Front, almost wishing himself to be a combatant, until he was eventually invited to spend a few days with the Third Army Headquarters. When he was taken up the line to see what it was really like, he discovered what he most needed to learn: that soldiers were driven more by the need to survive than any heightened sense of valour. Chastened, but lacking none of his original zeal, Davies found himself posted with the rank of Major to the undefined position of musical director within the newly-formed Air Ministry. In February 1919 a Memorial Service for members of the RAF was held in Westminster Abbey followed by a public concert at Queen's Hall, during which Davies's second lasting contribution to the nation's music was played: the official Royal Air Force March Past.

After the war, Davies was given an endowed chair at the University of Wales in Aberystwyth, from where he formulated musical policy for Welsh schools. As the network of festivals, concerts, lectures and classes spread over Wales, Davies rushed from point to point, exhorting, inspiring, teaching and conducting. Knighted in 1922, he was named Gresham Professor of Music two years later, a year that proved to be a landmark in his life when he was invited to attend an advisory committee on music set up by the BBC. The upshot was his first broadcast for children from Savoy Hill, on 4th April, given during school hours so that it might become a regular feature of the school curriculum. What emerged was that Davies's ability to communicate did not evaporate before the microphone. He had the same voice, the same touch on the piano, the same easy, confidential manner: 'There's a little girl on the back row who's not attending; I expect she's tired,' he might suddenly remark, and little girls on back rows across the country would look up in disbelief. The series continued for ten years, during which he gave 428 broadcasts, directed 75 children's concerts from the studio and wrote 60 sets of concert notes for use in lessons.

He was made musical adviser to the BBC in 1927, the year he returned to Windsor as organist, and in 1934 he succeeded Elgar as Master of the King's Musick. From 1926 onwards he broadcast another educational series for adult listeners, followed by a series on English church music. During the first week of the war he reached his 70th birthday, a respectable age for retirement, but instead he dedicated his remaining years to the war effort, resuming his school broadcasts to catch the ears of evacuees scattered around the country. Within eight months, however, he became ill with pleurisy and died in the early spring of 1941. His last words might well have been 'Good night, listeners all.'

Peter Dickinson

b. 1934

Peter Dickinson, one of the most original and versatile British composers, was born in Lytham St Anne's, Lancashire, in 1934. He went up to Cambridge as organ scholar of Queens' College, and then spent three formative years in the USA, initially as a graduate student at the Juilliard School of Music, New York. From that time onwards his music has been regularly commissioned, performed and recorded in this country and abroad.

After returning from America, Dickinson spent some years teaching in London and Birmingham, and from 1974-84 was the first Professor of Music at Keele University, later moving to Goldsmiths' College, University of London, to head the music department there. He is now head of music at the Institute of United States Studies at London University. At all periods he has been active as a pianist, notably in recitals, broadcasts and recordings with his sister, the mezzo-soprano Meriel Dickinson. He also broadcasts regularly on musical and literary subjects.

Dickinson's wide range of interests, and his specialist research into Lennox Berkeley, Erik Satie, Charles Ives, Lord Berners and writers such as W H Auden, James Joyce, e e cummings and Stevie Smith, came into focus in his own music. Many of his compositions, such as his piano concerto, demonstrate his affection for aspects of popular music and jazz.

In 1987 the South Bank Show (ITV) made a 50-minute documentary about him. Several of his larger works have been recorded.

Bernard van Dieren

1884–1936

Though born in Holland, the Dutch origin is misleading: his father was half French and his mother entirely so. Van Dieren learnt to play the violin at an early age, and greatly enjoyed art and literature, but trained initially as a scientist and supported his early attempts at composition by working in a laboratory.

In 1909 he came to England and eked out a precarious existence with his wife Frieda, writing criticism mainly for continental newspapers and magazines. It wasn't long, however, before his cause was taken up by a handful of friends and devoted admirers, including Warlock, Lambert, Cecil Gray and Moeran, who considered him to be one of the greatest musicians of his generation. (Walton had also been an early follower, but in retrospect concluded that van Dieren's music was 'so invertebrate that it would hardly stand up.') It has to be said that they probably admired him more as a radical free-thinker and enigmatic personality than as a composer, but they did their best to bring his music before a sceptical public. Arthur Bliss referred to him as a latter-day Leonardo da Vinci, so diverse were his inventive interests, and he was indeed a skilled linguist, chemist, art critic (he wrote a book on Epstein), as well as a composer of songs and chamber music.

In the early 1930s the BBC broadcast several of his works and a revival seemed imminent, but his health was ever precarious, not helped by his ability to subsist on tumblers of neat gin, and continuous illness kept him mostly confined to his house in St John's Wood. In 1935 he published a collection of musical essays called *Down Among the Dead Men*, whom he joined a year later at the age of 51. An exotic splash of colour in his own time, sadly he is now almost entirely forgotten.

237

Thomas Dunhill

1877–1946

Dunhill was born in Hampstead, the third son and fourth child of Henry Dunhill, a manufacturer of sacks, ropes and tarpaulin in the Euston Road, and his wife Jane, who kept a music shop. He went to school locally and later to Kent College, Canterbury, when the family moved to nearby Harbledown.

As a boy he showed great promise when he entered the RCM at the age of 16 to study piano with Franklin Taylor and composition with Stanford, staying on after 1899 to teach harmony and counterpoint while also acting as assistant music master at Eton. In 1907 he founded a series of London concerts dedicated to presenting unknown and forgotten chamber works by young British composers, including some of his own, and it was as a composer of chamber music that he first made his mark. He also wrote a symphony and other orchestral works, two ballets and a one-act opera, *The Enchanted Garden*. His most successful effort was an operetta to a libretto by A P Herbert called *Tantivy Towers*, which was not far removed from the style of Sullivan. It enjoyed a long run and was followed by *Happy Families* two years later in 1933, but neither achieved national acclaim for its composer, who, nonetheless, wrote much excellent music for educational purposes, and continued to work as a teacher, lecturer and adjudicator for the rest of his life.

Dunhill's musical standards were high and he never compromised for the sake of popularity. When adjudicating at music festivals, for example, he always came to the point, telling competitors exactly what he thought, but was able to lighten criticism with entertaining remarks and was always willing to help and advise young composers and performers. He enjoyed a simple life which included a great love of the country. In 1942 he remarried after the death of his first wife and lived at Scunthorpe, where he died in March 1946.

Ernest Farrar

1885–1918

If Farrar is remembered at all it is usually as the one-time friend and teacher of the young Gerald Finzi. But leading musicians of the day held him in high regard and, like his exact contemporary George Butterworth, he was among the more promising composers of his generation.

He was born in Lewisham but soon moved to Micklefield, where his father was the vicar. After attending Leeds Grammar School and Durham University, he was awarded an open scholarship to the Royal College of Music in 1905 to study composition with Stanford, who later described his young pupil as 'very shy, but full of poetry.' While there he became friendly with Frank Bridge, who subsequently dedicated his Piano Sonata to Farrar's memory, a year after Finzi had done the same with his first extended work, the *Requiem da camera.*

After a period as organist of the English church at Dresden, Farrah returned to Yorkshire and was chosen from some seventy applicants to become organist of St Hilda's in South Shields, County Durham, before moving to Christ Church, Harrogate, in 1912. The following year he married Olive Mason and remained in Harrogate until joining the Army. When Finzi and his mother went to live there, she asked Julian Clifford, who conducted the local orchestra, to recommend a teacher for her son, so Gerald studied with Farrar for two happy years. They shared not only lessons but walks on the moors, concert-going and companionship. It was not to last long and in December 1915 Farrar enlisted as a private in the Grenadier Guards. They met occasionally when Farrar was on leave in Harrogate, but on receiving a commission in the Third Battalion Devonshire Regiment, he left for France on 6th September 1918. He wrote every day to his young wife, up to and including two letters on September 15th, three days before his death. After just two days at the front he was killed by machine-gun fire leading his men in the Battle of Epehy Ronsoy.

Benjamin Frankel

1906–1973

Benjamin Frankel was born in London and displayed his talents as a violinist from an early age. His theory teacher was the Hammersmith Public Library, from which he consumed every available book on music until apprenticed to a watchmaker with the prospect of a very different career. When he was sixteen, Frankel managed to spend six months in Germany as a piano student of Victor Benham and on his return gave up his apprenticeship and paid his way at the Guildhall School of Music by playing piano and jazz violin in cafés and nightclubs. He eventually won a composition scholarship and was able to concentrate his energies studying with Orlando Morgan.

Between the wars, Frankel emerged as a jazz musician and composer of film music, also orchestrating and conducting West End musical revues and comedies. These included Noel Coward's *Operette*, Beverley Nichols's *Floodlight*, and many C B Cochran shows. He was 28 when he wrote his first film score and over the next three decades produced more than 100 scores for the cinema; *The Man in the White Suit* was a notable example of his ability to define character in musical terms, as was the theme 'Carriage and Pair' from *So Long at the Fair*, which is still played today. His success in these fields enabled him to devote much of his life to more serious music and his reputation increased suddenly after the war, when his works began to be more widely performed.

It was during the 1950s that he turned to twelve-note serialism and a rush of creativity which continued until shortly before his death. There followed eight symphonies between 1958 and 1971 (a ninth remained uncompleted), as well as a full-length opera, a ballet, five string quartets, concertos for violin and viola, and much else besides. From 1958 he was principally resident in Switzerland, but died in the city of his birth in the winter of 1973.

Henry Balfour Gardiner

1877–1950

From the first, Balfour Gardiner showed a notable talent for music which was encouraged by his family. He learnt the piano from the age of five and within four years had begun composing, prompting him to leave Charterhouse in 1894 and go first to the Hoch Conservatory in Frankfurt to study composition and piano. From his two years of study with Ivan Knorr he returned, as his friend Grainger said, 'a magnificent pianist ... and one of the most inspired composers of his generation.'

In 1896 he resumed his formal education at New College, but returned to Frankfurt for vacations and for further study after leaving Oxford. From 1900 onwards, Gardiner decided to devote his time to composition and produced a steady output of music, including a symphony, an overture, and any number of smaller pieces. Important among these early works are a quartet and a quintet for strings, and a ballad for chorus and orchestra called *News from Whydah*, written in 1912, which gained him wide popularity. An even greater achievement at this time was the remarkable series of eight concerts which Gardiner financed and organised at Queen's Hall, conducting many of them himself. His ready appreciation of other people's work helped considerably to introduce the music of his English contemporaries, particularly that of Bax, Holst and his fellow students from Frankfurt: Grainger, Quilter, Scott and O'Neill. His enterprising spirit and his inherited wealth enabled him to initiate and support a number of influential musical activities which enhanced the music of his generation. He arranged, for example, the first performance of *The Planets* in 1918 for Holst's benefit, and made it possible for Delius to continue to live in France by buying his house in Grez-sur-Loing.

At the outbreak of war in 1914, Gardiner's own career was at its height and he returned from the army five years later with every intention of resuming it. He found, however, that in the intervening years the musical climate had changed and the warm romanticism of the Edwardian age had given way to a more austere and intellectual atmosphere. It was a mood foreign to Gardiner's temperament and, chastened by an almost pathological self-critical outlook, he suddenly renounced composition and devoted himself to country pursuits, which he had the means to enjoy, and after 1924 wrote no more music. His decision disappointed but did not surprise his many friends, who recognised Gardiner's determined nature and refusal to be influenced by majority opinions. When asked after the war what style of music he composed, he replied, 'Oh, the style of 1902, I suppose.' He died unmarried, but with many friends, at Salisbury aged 73.

John Gardner

b. 1917

Gardner was educated at Wellington School, where he received his first counterpoint lessons from Gordon Jacob. Note was taken of his musical talent, and in 1935 he went as organ scholar to Exeter College, and studied with Walker and Armstrong. He distinguished himself in the musical life at Oxford and on graduating four years later was appointed chief music master at Repton School.

The war intervened and in 1939 he enlisted in the RAF, serving as a military bandmaster for a time but spending the last two years of combat as a navigator in Bomber Command. In 1946 he joined the newly formed Covent Garden Opera Company as rehearsal director and assistant conductor. He had written numerous works before the war but withdrew them all, presenting his first major composition, a symphony, at the Cheltenham Festival in 1951. The work's success led to various commissions, including a full-length opera for Sadler's Wells, *The Moon and Sixpence*.

Meanwhile, he had resigned his position at Covent Garden in 1952 to become a music tutor at Morley College, where he was appointed director in 1965. Thriving on a heavy workload, he also taught at the RAM and in 1962 succeeded Howells as director at St Paul's Girls' School in Hammersmith. Since then he turned increasingly to vocal music, combining jazz and pop elements to otherwise traditional idioms, and, while retiring from St Paul's in 1975, is still actively composing.

C Armstrong Gibbs

1889–1960

The first half of the 20th century saw a great flowering of English songwriting. While Ivor Gurney's settings were not recognised until later, Warlock, Finzi, Ireland, Moeran and others were particularly active; equal among them was Cecil Armstrong Gibbs, who contributed songs of abiding worth to the long tradition of settings of English poetry.

Although born into a prosperous middle-class family, Gibbs's childhood was blighted by the death of his mother when he was barely two years old, after which he was brought up by a succession maiden aunts. His father insisted on an English public school education to 'toughen up' his sensitive son, but Gibbs survived and at Winchester began to develop his considerable musical talent. He initially studied history at Cambridge before taking a further degree in music, receiving help and tuition from Edward Dent and Charles Wood. He greatly enjoyed his five years there and made many friends, among them Bliss and Vaughan Williams, but on leaving in 1913 Gibbs turned to teaching rather than composition and obtained a post at Copthorne School in East Grinstead. His application for war service was rejected on medical grounds, so two years later he joined the staff of The Wick, his old preparatory school in Hove, where he taught Classics, History and English. He still took every opportunity to write music for the boys' choir and in 1919 was commissioned by the retiring Headmaster to compose a special work for the school. Gibbs approached Walter de la Mare, who obliged with a specially written script for the occasion, and with Edward Dent overseeing rehearsals and a young Adrian Boult invited to conduct, *Crossings* enjoyed an illustrious pedigree. Impressed by the quality of the play's incidental music, Boult persuaded Gibbs to enrol at the RCM, where he flourished and between 1920 and 1933 produced much of his best work, notably with settings of de la Mare's poetry. Throughout this

244

period he taught part-time at the RCM, became active as a festival adjudicator, and continued to write music which chimed with the public mood. Exquisite songs like *Silver*, *The Fields are Full* and *Nod* were all written early in his career and contain a magical chemistry of music and words which he seldom recaptured in later years.

Pyschological problems stemming from his early childhood led to a nervous breakdown in 1929, but the years that followed saw the publication of solo songs, chamber music and choral music which confirmed Gibbs's reputation as a practical, unpretentious composer. The outbreak of war in 1939 prevented the première of his choral symphony *Odysseus*, due to take place at the Albert Hall, and Gibbs spent the next few years promoting musical events in and around Windermere.

It is not difficult to see why he was drawn to the far-away realms of de la Mare's poetry: despite his impressive public presence, Gibbs lacked confidence and relied on the strength of his wife, Honor, and his own religious convictions to support him in a world which seemed to him increasingly hostile. This was never more so than in 1943 when his son, David, was killed on active service in Italy.

As soon as the war was over, the couple returned to Danbury and, 'retiring' from professional music activities, Gibbs busied himself conducting the local choral society and attempting larger-scale compositions. His slow waltz entitled *Dusk*, written some years earlier, soon made its own way in the world, but while his music generally cannot claim immortality, Gibbs will be remembered for his songs, many of which have established their place in the repertoire.

It was shortly after the Danbury Choral Society gave a farewell performance in his honour that he died of pneumonia at the age of 71.

Alexander Goehr

b. 1932

Walter Goehr, a pupil of Schoenberg and later an active influence in the performance of new British music, fled with his family to England from Germany when his son was a year old. Alexander had lessons from his father before studying composition from 1952-55 at the Royal Manchester College, where he was a friend and contemporary of Harrison Birtwistle, Peter Maxwell Davies and John Ogdon. After this he spent a year studying with Messiaen in Paris before returning to London to work as a copyist and translator until 1960, when he joined the BBC as a programme producer of orchestral concerts.

He has travelled widely and taught at Morley College, and at Yale and Cambridge Universities. His interest in musical theatre and multimedia concepts led to brief periods as musical director of the Music Theatre Ensemble and of the Leeds Festival, but the song cycle *Sing Ariel*, premièred at Aldeburgh in 1990, and the symphonic *Colossos or Panic*, heard at the 1994 Proms, provide possible starting points for new listeners. Since 1976 he has been Professor of Music at Cambridge University.

Eugene Goossens

1893–1962

The name Eugene Goossens spans three generations. Eugene the grandfather came to England from Belgium and became a successful conductor, as did his son, Eugene II. Eugene III was the eldest son of the family; his younger brothers were Adolphe, a horn player who was killed in World War I aged 18, and Leon, the celebrated oboist. His sisters Marie and Sidonie were equally well known as harpists. Eugene was born in London, and at the age of six, by which time his family had moved to Liverpool, he was sent to the Muziek Conservatorium in Bruges. Returning to Liverpool a year later, he attended the Liverpool College of Music for three years until a scholarship led him to the RCM. There he was a pupil of Stanford, who secured a performance of his *Chinese Variations*, which Goossens himself conducted at the College in 1912; later he made his Prom debut as a conductor with the same work.

For a time he played the violin in the orchestra at the Haymarket Theatre and from 1912 to 1915 in the Queen's Hall Orchestra, but after being rejected for military service on health grounds, he began to concentrate on conducting. In 1916 he became a protégé of Thomas Beecham and quickly gained a reputation for being able to take on demanding or unfamiliar works at short notice. Within five years he was sufficiently well known to form his own orchestra, which gave the English première of Stravinsky's *The Rite of Spring*, as well as further concerts introducing contemporary British music.

Goossens was now becoming known as a composer in his own right: his choral work *Silence* was performed at the Three Choirs Festival at the request of Elgar, and during the 1920s he was regarded as a member of the British *avant-garde*. In 1923, George Eastman, head of the Kodak Company, decided that Rochester in New York State needed an orchestra, and hired Goossens to direct it. In the eight years which

Goossens spent there, he established its reputation as one of the leading orchestras in the United States. During this time, he would conduct at Rochester in the winter months, returning for the summers to London, where he continued to fulfil ambitious engagements as conductor and composer.

In 1931, Goossens was appointed conductor of the Cincinnati Symphony Orchestra, a position he held for fifteen years until he left to become director of the New South Wales Conservatory and resident conductor of the Sydney Symphony Orchestra. During that time he did more than anyone to put Australia on the musical map. In recognition of his success there he was knighted in 1955, but a year later returned to England in disgrace, having been detained by customs officers for carrying what was then regarded as illegal pornographic material in his luggage (although evidence has since emerged to suggest that he was wrongly accused). He continued to conduct in this country and made a number of guest appearances with orchestras overseas but, while returning from a visit to Switzerland, he was taken ill on the plane and died in Hillingdon hospital shortly after his 69th birthday.

Goossens's considerable achievement as a conductor seems to have overshadowed his compositions, and his own music has fallen into neglect, though for a period between the wars his reputation was equal to that of Bax, Bridge, Walton and others.

Julius Harrison

1885–1963

Harrison was born at Stourport in Worcestershire, the same year as Butterworth, and attended Queen Elizabeth's School before studying with Bantock at the Midland Institute. After gaining some experience as an operatic conductor with the Beecham Opera Company, he joined the British National Opera Company and continued to enjoy a distinguished career conducting at Covent Garden, the London and Liverpool Philharmonic Orchestras, the Hallé, and others. In 1930 he was appointed permanent conductor of the Hastings Municipal Orchestra, a position he held for ten years until deafness brought about his retirement.

Although he had always composed (the *Requiem for Archangels* dates from 1919), Harrison now devoted himself entirely to composition. His output, influenced by Elgar, included orchestral pieces, an opera entitled *The Canterbury Pilgrims*, chamber music, a cello concerto, and many choral works, among them his Mass in C and the *Requiem*, written in 1957. His best-known works were probably the *Worcestershire Suite* and the rhapsody *Bredon Hill*, which evoked a rural idyll of the west of England.

Victor Hely-Hutchinson

1901–1947

Born in South Africa the year his father was appointed governor of Cape Colony there, Hely-Hutchinson returned to England ten years later to follow the traditional educational route of Eton and Oxford before joining the RCM. After gaining a doctorate, he lectured for four years at Cape Town University, then joined the staff of the BBC, first in London, and from 1933 in Birmingham as Midland Regional Director of Music, later succeeding Granville Bantock as professor at the university.

In 1944 he followed Arthur Bliss as music director of the BBC, but his appointment was tragically cut short by his death at 46. Hely-Hutchinson is remembered chiefly for his light music: songs set to texts of Hilaire Belloc and Edward Lear, as well as parodies of such composers as Handel. It has been said that his music, having served its turn, left little impression, but his *Carol Symphony* on familiar Christmas carols continues to delight listeners of all ages.

Alun Hoddinott

b. 1929

Hoddinott comes from Bargoed in Glamorganshire and was educated at Gowerton Grammar School before taking a degree in music at University College, Cardiff. He also studied privately with Arthur Benjamin in London and in 1951 joined the staff of the Welsh College of Music and Drama, where he stayed for eight years. Returning to University College as a lecturer, he was appointed professor of music there in 1967, the year in which he founded the Cardiff Festival specialising in contemporary music. A Welsh *composer* rather than a *Welsh* composer, Hoddinott's Op 1, a String Trio, dates from his twentieth year, but was preceded by a large corpus of juvenile compositions which he has withheld from publication. His early maturity owes much to the benefits of self-tuition which created these rejected works; certainly his earliest compositions are remarkably assured and, although influenced by Walton and others, already reveal a personal style.

Hoddinott's admiration for both Bartok and Rawsthorne emerges in later works, and he has also experimented with serial techniques, but in the end he must be regarded as an eclectic composer who has developed his own powerful individuality. Unusually prolific, and writing mostly to commission, Hoddinott's output ranges across opera, choral, symphonic and chamber works, though he is by no means averse to writing in a lighter vein. He was awarded the CBE in 1983.

Joseph Horovitz

b. 1926

Writing in the *Musical Times* some 40 years ago, one critic noted that Horovitz's music was 'refreshingly independent of all the commonest influences and mannerisms of the younger English composers'. The word 'English' is important for a composer born in Vienna, although he emigrated to this country at the age of 12 and cites Warlock, Moeran, Delius and even van Dieren as early influences on his own musical development.

After studying literature and music at New College, Oxford, Horovitz went to study with Gordon Jacob at the Royal College of Music, where he won the Farrar Prize with a score for a one-act ballet, and thereafter to Nadia Boulanger in Paris, under whose tutelage he composed his Oboe Sonatina and Violin Concerto. His name first became known in the 1950s with his light ballets, such as *Les Femmes d'Alger* and *Alice in Wonderland.* Other notable successes in this unusual genre, which he has made singularly his own, are *Concerto for Dancers* and *Let's Make a Ballet.* Horovitz himself conducted performances, and his two works for the Intimate Opera Company, *The Dumb Wife* and *Gentleman's Island,* never fail to please audiences.

The Hoffnung Music Festival concerts were ideally suited to a facet of the composer's style which many regarded as witty and ingenious rather than merely light. Though his five string quartets, and the *Fantasia on a Theme of Couperin,* show him to be more than capable of serious expression, his collaboration with Alistair Sampson in a series of brilliant parodies have ensured him lasting recognition. Of these, *Metamorphoses on a Bedtime Theme* presented a television commercial for Bournvita in the manner of Bach, Mozart, Verdi, Schoenberg and Stravinsky, while *Horroratorio* ridiculed the old oratorio tradition in a work which celebrated the wedding of Frankenstein and Dracula. Equally well-known is his later *Jazz Harpsichord Concerto,* with its comic juxtaposition of two entirely different styles, which underline Horovitz's versatility and musical energy, and which Vaughan Williams used to say was the main justification of a composer. *Captain Noah and his Floating Zoo,* to a libretto by Michael Flanders, is another work to have acheived numerous performances.

William Hurlstone

1876–1906

Like his good friend Coleridge-Taylor, William Yeates Hurlstone has slipped into relative obscurity which neither man deserves. Certainly at the time of his early death, Hurlstone was highly regarded by his contemporaries and even featured in a *Daily Mail* article of August 1904, when he was numbered among a group of 'promising composers who may help to bring back the golden age of English music'.

Hurlstone was born at 12 Richmond Gardens in Fulham, where, despite their former distinguished artistic background, the family lived in comparative poverty – circumstances which may have contributed to the boy's chronic bronchial asthma. Even so, he enjoyed an active childhood, producing a weekly periodical, *The Boys' Half-Holiday*, written and illustrated by himself, and from an early age revealed a remarkable musical talent which his parents, both amateur musicians, were quick to nurture. When he was only eight they invited Parry to hear him play and the following year he published a set of five waltzes for the piano. Poor health prevented a career as a concert pianist but composition remained his passion and in 1894 he won a scholarship to the RCM. It was here that he met Coleridge-Taylor and the two would travel into London together from South Norwood immersed in the relative merits of their favourite composers. Each enjoyed the patronage of a local worthy and it was at the home of one of these that Hurlstone first met the businessman and amateur violinist Walter Cobbett, who later commissioned many chamber works by British composers.

While excelling as a composer of chamber music himself, Hurlstone found it necessary to publish some trifling songs and drawing-room pieces to support his meagre livelihood as a teacher – an occupation he detested; but before long, public attention was drawn to his *Variations on a Swedish Air* which was performed at the first concert of the Patrons'

Fund at the Royal Academy in 1904. A few years earlier he had played his own Piano Concerto at St James's Hall and delighted concert-goers with his 'Fairy Suite for Orchestra', *The Magic Mirror,* based on *Snow White and the Seven Dwarfs.* His reputation was gaining momentum when he was appointed Professor of Harmony and Counterpoint at the RCM at the age of 28.

For a while he seemed to have shaken off the debilitating effects of financial hardship and looked forward to a flourishing career as a musician. Not a man to take himself too seriously, he enjoyed the friendship and respect of his contemporaries at the RCM, who recognised the sincerity and simple charm of his music which reflected his own engaging personality. Everyone who knew him anticipated a brilliant future, but four months after his 30th birthday he died of the illness that had dogged him throughout his life. By a strange coincidence his beautifully pathetic *Litany* for female voices was sung by the Magpie Madrigal Society on the evening of his death, before the news was widely known. As with Butterworth, we are left to wonder what delightful music he might have written.

Daniel Jones

1912–1993

Jones began composing and writing poetry as a child, encouraged by his parents, who were both musicians. Initially he studied English literature at Swansea, but in between degrees he attended the RAM, taking lessons in composition from Harry Farjeon, brother of the poet Eleanor Farjeon, and in conducting from Henry Wood. In 1936 he won the Mendelssohn Scholarship and spent a year in Rome, Vienna, and other musical centres in Europe. During these pre-war years he also belonged to a group of artists and writers which included his school friend Dylan Thomas, who had used Jones as a character in a short story, *The Fight*. In return, Jones made many settings of Thomas's early poems and on the poet's death became literary trustee of the estate, constructing *Under Milk Wood* from the unfinished manuscripts, and in 1971 editing the *Complete Poems*.

Jones was already attracting attention as a composer when war intervened and from 1940 to 1946 he served as an officer in Army Intelligence. Settling in Swansea, he turned increasingly to orchestral composition, particularly symphonies (he wrote twelve), and bravely wrote a sonata for three kettledrums which explored the development of complex metrical patterns. In 1950 he won the first prize of the Royal Philharmonic Society with his *Symphonic Prologue*, and four years later the radio version of *Under Milk Wood*, with Jones's music, won the Italia Prize. He was awarded the OBE in 1968 and died in Swansea exactly 40 years after Thomas.

John Joubert

b. 1927

Like Hely-Hutchinson, Joubert was born in Cape Town and educated there until he was 19, when he came to England to study at the RAM under Howard Ferguson. It was during his final year in London that he wrote his Op 1, the First String Quartet, although he had begun composing much earlier. His music was first introduced in his native South Africa, but his reputation became more widely established after he won the Novello anthem competition in 1952 with his innovative choral work *O Lorde, the Maker of Al Thing*. The carols *Torches*, written in the same year, and *There is no Rose*, two years later, quickly became part of the repertory of cathedral and parish choirs, for whom Joubert has since written extensively. At this time he was lecturing in music at the University of Hull, leaving there in 1962 to teach at the University of Birmingham, where he stayed for twenty-four years, producing operas, symphonic and chamber works besides his highly regarded music for voices.

Walter Leigh

1905–1942

Walter Leigh was born in London and educated at University College School, after which he won an open scholarship to Christ's College, Cambridge, where he studied with E J Dent. After graduating in 1926, he went to Berlin to continue his musical training with Hindemith for a further three years, and his first published works date from this period. A short spell as musical director of the Festival Theatre in Cambridge enabled him to go on composing and he rapidly developed an affinity with the stage. His comic opera *Jolly Roger* ran for six months at the Savoy Theatre in 1933 and he was soon commissioned to write the music for several revues, stage productions and films, especially documentaries. In addition, he composed chamber works, notably the *Concertino for Harpsichord and String Orchestra*, which dates from 1936 and remains his most popular work.

Everything was set for a promising career but, after enlisting early in the war, Leigh was killed in action in Tobruk, ten days before his 37th birthday.

Kenneth Leighton

1929–1988

Leighton has tended to be thought of as a Scottish composer and certainly the last twenty-five years of his life were largely spent in Edinburgh, first as University lecturer in music and from 1970 as Reid Professor. He was actually born in Wakefield and was very much the Yorkshireman. Although he composed a great amount while still at school, music was never his only interest. He was an outstanding Classicist, and in fact it was with a Classical rather than a Music Scholarship that he went up to Queen's College, Oxford, in 1946.

After that, music took pride of place and he became a student of Bernard Rose, with whom he studied composition until 1951. It was Rose who first drew Finzi's attention to his symphony of 1949 and Finzi, much taken with it, performed the work with his Newbury String Players. Encouraged, Leighton wrote his suite *Veris Gratia* for the NSP, who gave the first performance in May 1951. When published, it was dedicated to Finzi's memory. The same year, and with a considerable portfolio of compositions to his credit, Leighton won a Mendelssohn Scholarship which enabled him to study in Rome with Goffredo Petrassi. The effect of this release from Oxford was electric and he forged a powerful and personal style which was more highly chromatic than formerly, with essays in serial technique and a general absence of conventional tonality.

In 1955 he returned to England and took up a composition fellowship at Leeds University before accepting the appointment at Edinburgh, where he later died, at the height of his powers, aged 59.

George Lloyd

1913–1998

Lloyd's career was remarkable for his courage in overcoming adversity; in fact, given his life and circumstances, it is astonishing that he should have continued to compose at all.

He was born in Cornwall to a comfortable family whose large house overlooked St Ives Bay. His father, William Lloyd, was an amateur flautist and an enthusiast for Italian opera; his mother played the violin and viola, and would invite other local musicians to give weekend concerts in their spacious artist's studio. George started to play the violin himself when he was five and began composing at the age of 10, but recurring bouts of rheumatic fever interrupted his formal education. After just two years at prep school he was allowed to concentrate on a musical career, studying with Albert Sammons and at the RAM with Farjeon.

His was a prodigious talent. By the time he was 22, Lloyd had written two symphonies, the first premièred by the Bournemouth Symphony Orchestra in 1933, the second at Eastbourne two years later, quickly followed by a third. He came to prominence, however, with his first opera, *Iernin*, which was performed in Penzance before transferring to the Lyceum in London in June 1935. Three years later his second opera, *The Serf*, was seen at Covent Garden before touring to Liverpool and Glasgow. Lloyd was still only 26, with a highly promising musical career ahead of him, when war broke out and he enlisted as a bandsman in the Royal Marines.

While on Arctic convoy duty in 1942 his ship, *Trinidad*, was destroyed by a rogue torpedo fired from an allied ship, leaving Lloyd as one of the few survivors. The trauma and severe shell-shock he suffered led to a complete breakdown in his health, compounding difficulties he had already endured in childhood, and any attempts to resume his career were abandoned. He moved with his wife to her native Switzerland,

261

where he tried in his Fourth and Fifth Symphonies to come to terms with his devastating wartime experience, but a further breakdown followed. In 1952 he withdrew to a small farm near Sherborne in Dorset to grow carnations. When this failed, he took up mushroom farming, which proved more successful.

Lloyd continued to compose intermittently, rising at 4.30 each morning and writing for three hours before work on the farm, but was largely ignored by the BBC and concert promoters. When, in 1956, he showed the score of his hard-won Sixth Symphony to a musical colleague, he was told that the work had 'no contemporary significance'. There was simply no interest in music like his among the British musical establishment. Some years later he was told by a senior Radio 3 executive that he was on the blacklist: 'I sent off scores,' he said. 'They came back, usually without comment.'

The tide began to turn, slowly, in the 1970s. The BBC accepted his Eighth Symphony in 1969 (although it waited another eight years to be broadcast), and his Sixth Symphony was given at the Proms in 1981. Belated recordings of his music began to emerge, bringing Lloyd to the attention of a wider public, many of whom were seeking refuge from the serialism and dissonance of so many of his contemporaries. In 1970 he was awarded the OBE and enjoyed a remarkable Indian summer in the last two decades of his life. New works were written, older pieces were rediscovered. All were greeted with enthusiasm which encouraged him greatly in his later years. 'I like the sort of thing the average person likes,' he said. 'I will write what pleases me.'

Elisabeth Lutyens

1906–1983

A composer of 12-tone music at a time when it was barely understood in Britain, Lutyens struggled hard for her music to be heard. Often battling with alcoholism, depression and the pressures of raising a family, she was determined to remain true to her chosen profession.

She was born into a distinguished family. Her father, the architect Sir Edwin Lutyens, whose most familiar work is perhaps the Cenotaph in Whitehall, and her mother, Lady Emily Lytton, encouraged their daughter's musical leanings and she started to learn the violin when she was seven, later taking up the piano. Both parents insisted, however, that she completed her formal education before being allowed to study music in Paris for a few months in 1923, after which she travelled with her mother and sister in Europe, India and Australia. Lutyens returned to England in 1926 and enrolled at the RCM, determined to become a composer. Her composition teacher was Harold Darke, who arranged for several of her works to be played at the College, but it was the violinist Anne Macnaghten and the conductor Iris Lemare who first provided the opportunity for professional performances of Lutyens's early work in a series of concerts in the 1930s featuring music by unknown British composers. Her first public performance was the ballet *The Birthday of the Infanta*, which Constant Lambert conducted.

Lutyens married the singer Ian Glennie in 1933 and continued to compose while bringing up three young children. By the end of the decade, however, she had met Edward Clark, founder of the North Eastern Regional Orchestra in his native Newcastle, and one of the leading figures in contemporary music circles at the time. Despite their age difference (he was considerably older) she eventually moved in with him. The following years were difficult for Lutyens. She now had four children to provide for and with Clark unable to find regular employment, money was scarce. In 1943 she began to earn a meagre living copying music, eventually moving into radio and films, writing nearly 200 scores which provided a source of income needed to support her more 'serious' work.

By now she was absorbed in the challenge posed by her use of serial techniques, a style which ultimately led to her isolation in the post-war years. It was an all-demanding approach to composition, through which

only the strongest musical personality could assert itself. Her self-belief, however, could admit no compromise and during this period she felt that she had finally found her true voice and produced some of her most individual music. Notoriously outspoken, she fought hard to have her work played, adding to the pressure she was already under. She began to spend time in London pubs, usually in the company of writers and musicians like Dylan Thomas and Alan Rawsthorne, and in the early 1950s suffered a nervous breakdown. With help from her family and Ian Glennie, she recovered, gave up drinking, moved away from Clark and concentrated exclusively on composition.

A changing musical climate in the 1960s meant that her work began to be heard more frequently and, championed by the new BBC regime of William Glock, Lutyens wrote some of her finest pieces. Her star was in the ascendant and throughout the 1970s and into the 1980s she continued to compose and to be even more outspoken in her views on music and the establishment. She was awarded the CBE in 1969 and three years later published her autobiography, *A Goldfish Bowl*. She once said her life consisted of 'Innumerable compositions, two husbands, three lovers, four children, one abortion, and *nobody* knew'. Nowadays she is seen by many as a courageous and uniquely inspired pioneer.

John McCabe

b. 1939

It was once said of John McCabe that he could write music on a train or during a Test match, an observation confirmed by his steady flow of works for orchestra, wind and brass, chamber ensembles, organ, piano, choral and theatrical. If a definition was needed for an all-round musician, then McCabe would be one of the first names to come to mind.

He was born in Huyton, Liverpool, and endured an isolated childhood after an accident prevented him from going to school until he was 11. He spent those early years reading, playing the piano and listening to records of music by Bax, Moeran, Rawsthorne and Copland. By the time he was well enough to attend the Liverpool Institute High School for Boys in 1950, he had composed no less than 13 symphonies and an opera based on themes from Mussorgsky. This remarkable juvenilia was followed by a silence of some five years, broken only shortly before going to Manchester University, where he studied with Proctor Gregg and began to compose seriously. He then entered the 'old' Royal Manchester College of Music as a piano pupil of the late Gordon Green and a composition student with Thomas Pitfield, before spending a further year at the Munich Hochschule on a German government scholarship.

On his return to Britain in 1965, McCabe was appointed resident pianist at Cardiff University, where he remained for three years. In the meantime, it was Manchester's orchestra, the Hallé, which launched his career as a composer, when in March 1963 Martin Milner was the soloist in the First Violin Concerto. Two years later, Maurice Handford conducted the work that put McCabe on the map, *Variations on a Theme of Hartmann*, which led to a Hallé commission for a symphony, eventually conducted by Barbirolli at the Cheltenham Festival of 1966. It became clear to many listeners that here was a composer who was closer to the main stream of twentieth-century music than to what would be for him the arid reaches of avant-garde fashions. He was in touch with his audience. As a man of his time, McCabe has dallied with serialism, enjoyed the company of rock and jazz, and become acquainted with minimalism. Nothing in his music can be taken for granted and with a catalogue of over 150 works constantly being added to, on top of his successful career as a concert pianist, McCabe is one of the busiest of living composers, and one of the very best.

John McEwen

1868–1948

Although born in Hawick in the border country, McEwen's early life was spent in Glasgow, where his father was a Presbyterian minister. In 1888, McEwen graduated with an arts degree from Glasgow University and took music lessons while holding successive choirmaster appointments at St James's Free Church and Lanark Parish Church. In 1891 he went to London and two years later studied at the RAM before returning to Scotland as choirmaster in Greenock and teacher of piano and composition at what is now the Royal Scottish Academy of Music. Three years on he was invited back to the RAM as professor of harmony and composition and remained there for almost forty years.

Both as a teacher and an administrator, McEwen's attitude was progressive, and his appointment as principal in 1924 was welcomed by students, who found him sympathetic to the new ideas which were then fermenting in all the arts. His career, on the surface, was one of absolute academic respectability. An ardent champion of new music and selfless in helping other composers, he was particularly energetic in promoting the development of British music and became one of the founder members of the Society of British Composers. For one so occupied with education and administration, McEwen's own compositions were impressive and covered opera, choral works, symphonies and numerous string quartets, songs and piano pieces.

Little is known of his personal life, but it is evident from this list that McEwen made a determined attempt to be a major composer. The pressure of maintaining his academic responsibilities, while finding time for his own creative work, resulted in persistent insomnia and in 1913 he succumbed to a break-down in his health. The RAM released him from his duties and he retired to a fishing village in the Bay of Biscay; although he recovered and returned to England refreshed, his reputation as a composer soon went into decline. However, he seemed indifferent to furthering his own career and never wrote for the major festivals, one of the most successful ways of getting your music performed.

The first of his works to receive national acclaim were the Border ballad *Grey Galloway* and the *Solway Symphony*; other fine examples of his strong musical personality have not deserved the neglect they have suffered. McEwen was knighted in 1931 for his services to the RAM, from which he retired five years later, but continued to compose until 1946. He died at his home in London in the following summer.

Elizabeth Maconchy

1907–1994

Though born of Irish parents, Elizabeth Maconchy's early childhood was spent in Broxbourne, Hertfordshire, before the family moved back to Ireland after the First World War. Within a few years her father died and her mother brought the family to London, where Maconchy entered the RCM at the age of just 16. There she was first taught the piano by Arthur Alexander but gradually began to concentrate on composition, studying initially with Charles Wood and then with Vaughan Williams. Maconchy was soon regarded as one of the College's most brilliant students, winning several prizes and having her work played at College concerts.

In 1929 a fellowship took her to Prague, where her first major work, the *Piano Concertino*, was performed the following year. Back in

London, Henry Wood played her suite *The Land* at a Promenade Concert in 1930, and later that year she married the Irish scholar William Le Fanu, the younger of their two daughters being the composer Nicola Le Fanu. During the 1930s, Maconchy became known in England and on the continent for her chamber music, which was performed at the ISCM Festivals in Prague and Paris, and at concerts devoted to her works in Krakow and Warsaw.

In 1932, the year that her Piano Concerto was broadcast by the BBC, Maconchy developed tuberculosis, the disease that had killed her father, and she left London for Kent to cure herself by living in a hut at the bottom of the garden. In spite of this isolation, her music continued to be performed and broadcast throughout the 1930s, although the difficulties of bringing up a young family during the war years severely curtailed her composing. She said that she had to learn to compose between feeds as well as making clothes, growing vegetables and keeping hens, but still she managed to write four of the thirteen string quartets by which she is best known, and a number of other chamber and orchestral pieces. After the war she was able to devote more time to her craft and produced a great deal of music, including operas and a symphony.

Maconchy seems to have had an easier time than her more radical and outspoken contemporary Elisabeth Lutyens in getting her music heard in the 1950s, but neglect came later and it is only recently that interest in her work has begun to grow again. She was made a CBE in 1977 and ten years later a DBE. She died in Norwich aged 87.

Nicholas Maw

b. 1935

Born on Guy Fawkes night in Grantham, Maw grew up in Lincolnshire and came to London at the age of twenty to study composition with Lennox Berkeley at the RAM. In 1958 a French government scholarship enabled him to study in Paris with Nadia Boulanger and on his return Maw embarked on the fairly typical life of a young composer. Editorial work, lecturing and teaching formed the background, and often the interruption, to his composing. His first real impact came with *Scenes and Arias*, written in an outburst of creative excitement in 1961-62 for the Proms, which determined the course of his writing for the next eight years. During this time he was also Fellow Commoner in Creative Arts at Trinity College, Cambridge, and from 1972 was visiting lecturer in composition at Exeter University.

Maw's strengths as a composer reached a superb climax in the symphonic poem *Odyssey*, which was fifteen years in the making, finally appearing in truncated form at the 1987 Proms. A violin concerto for Joshua Bell and orchestral works, including *Shahnama* and *Dance Scenes*, have further extended the scope and character of Maw's work and consolidated his reputation.

Thea Musgrave

b. 1928

Forty years of composition reveal Thea Musgrave to be one of the most steadily innovative of post-war composers in this country. An ability to reflect critically on her own work, combined with a discriminating awareness of current musical trends, have produced a diverse and developing series of compositions. She was born in Barnton, Midlothian, and after reading music at Edinburgh, where she was firmly grounded in the classical tradition, she studied for four years with Nadia Boulanger in Paris – one of the comparatively few British composers to do so. During the summer of 1953 she was at Dartington Hall as a pupil of William Glock, the school's director, who introduced her to the music of Schoenberg and Charles Ives, which had a particular impact on her own development. At the same time, her music began to arouse interest in Scotland and she fulfilled her first commission with the *Suite o' Bairnsongs*, followed by a BBC commission, the *Cantata for a Summer's Day*.

It was for her a period of artistic awakening. She took more than a decade to find a truly individual voice, but in the mid-1960s Musgrave began work on an uncommissioned three-act opera, *The Decision*. The libretto was about a 19th-century Scots miner, who was trapped for 23 days in an Ayreshire coalmine, and his lover, the pit-foreman's wife, who dies in childbirth. The opera was completed in 1965 and its first performance at Sadler's Wells two years later proved a turning point.

In the succeeding eight years the twelve or more major compositions from the second and third Chamber Concertos of 1966 to the opera *The Voice of Ariadne*, premièred in 1974 at Aldeburgh, represent a remarkable achievement in the music of her generation. Four years earlier she had married the violist Peter Mark, for whom she wrote her Concerto for Viola and *One to Another* for viola and tape. She joined him on the staff of the University of California and in 1977 had an outstanding success with her opera *Mary, Queen of Scots*, which was taken up later by the New York City Opera and followed two years later by her version of Dickens's *A Christmas Carol*. Even though she has transferred her main scene of activity to the United States, Musgrave remains a major force in British contemporary music.

Norman O'Neill

1875–1934

Son of a talented and successful Victorian painter, Norman O'Neill was born in London and spent a comfortable childhood in Kensington. At 14 he began music lessons with Arthur Somervell and four years later, on the advice of the violinist Joachim, it was decided he should go to study under Knorr at Frankfurt. There he met Gardiner, Grainger, Quilter and Scott, and also Adine Ruckert, whom he married. On his return to England, the O'Neills settled in London – she as head music mistress at St Paul's Girls' School, where she brought Holst on to the staff, and he as Musical Director of the Haymarket Theatre, where he worked for many years.

It was here that he made his mark, and as a conductor and composer did more than anyone at that time to raise the standard of theatre music. In addition to incidental music for over fifty plays, O'Neill wrote five ballets, chamber music, choral works and overtures, but unfortunately, with the rare exception of one of his orchestral suites, his music is hardly ever heard today. He died after a road accident at the age of 59.

CW Orr

1893–1976

If Charles Orr's is still less than a household name, it is not through lack of admirers. He was born in Cheltenham in 1893 and, like many other composers who hailed from this part of England, was strongly influenced by the countryside he knew and loved as a young man. He came to music relatively late after a projected military career had been abandoned because of ill-health, and following his discharge from the army in 1917 he enrolled at the Guildhall School of Music. His early compositions impressed the likes of Heseltine, Bax and Goossens, while he reserved a special admiration for the music of Delius, whom he came to know well and who, in return, offered help and encouragement.

In 1930 he moved away from London and returned to the Cotswolds, where he lived for the rest of his life. He developed a form of deafness which effectively closed his composing career, and his few works, nearly all of them songs, are confined to a brief period in the 1920s. Nevertheless, while a minor composer compared with such redoubtable figures as Vaughan Williams and Britten, Orr captured the very essence of Housman's verse in a handful of memorable songs which more than earn him a place alongside the more familiar names in this book.

Robin Orr

b. 1909

Robin Orr (no relation to C W) had an early opportunity to enjoy music-making when his father, an amateur organist, built and installed an instrument in the family home in Brechin near Montrose. After schooling in Edinburgh he went to the Royal College of Music at the age of 17, where Arthur Benjamin taught him piano. Organ studies continued under Alcock and in 1929 he was elected organ scholar of Pembroke College, Cambridge, where he studied this time with Dent and Rootham. Graduating in 1932, he went to Siena to complete his composition tuition with Alfredo Casella and later with Nadia Boulanger in Paris.

In 1933 Orr was felt to be suitably qualified to be appointed as director of music at Sidcot School in Somerset, and three years later joined the faculty of music at Leeds University. He returned in 1938 to Cambridge as organist of St John's College, remaining there for the next 18 years, apart from a period of war service as an RAF officer in photographic intelligence. He left to become professor of music at Glasgow University in 1956, but returned to Cambridge as professor of music in 1965, eventually retiring 11 years later.

Orr's output is substantial and includes three operas, three symphonies, and a considerable number of works for smaller forces. He was also active as an administrator, being chairman of Scottish Opera from 1962-76 and a director of Welsh National Opera from 1977-83.

Alan Ridout

1934–1996

Alan Ridout was an extraordinarily prolific composer, a high proportion of whose works were written for particular performers, professional and amateur.

He was born in West Wickham, Kent, in 1934. Both his mother and his uncle supported his early desire to become a composer; his father, however, was vociferous in his opposition to this, so that he was permitted to begin formal instruction only at the age of 9. Such was his dedication, however, that he had by the age of 12 already achieved a distinction on the piano in the final grade of the Royal Schools of Music. More important to his future career was that by the same age he had written over a hundred works, covering the same wide range that is evident in his adult music: dramatic music, orchestral works – a symphony and numerous concertante pieces – chamber music, piano music, songs and choral settings.

He was allowed to leave Haberdashers' Aske's School in Hampstead immediately he was 15 to begin some six years' professional music study. Two years were spent at the Guildhall School of Music, where, apart from composition, he continued his piano studies, being chosen to give his first public recital before he was 16; he also studied conducting. His primary interest in composition, however, took him to the Royal College of Music, where he worked for two years with Gordon Jacob and a further two with Herbert Howells.

By the time he left the RCM at the age of 20 a good number of his works had been performed, mainly at concerts of the Society for the Promotion of New Music.

While being in charge of music in a boarding school he continued his studies in composition with Peter Racine Fricker and Sir Michael Tippett. He was then awarded a Netherlands Government Scholarship in 1958, and explored both electronic techniques (his *Psalm for Sine Wave Generators*, realised in 1959, was one of the first pieces of purely electronic music by an English composer) and microtonal techniques.

When Ridout returned to England he decided to undergo a comprehensive study of early music. This was carried out with Thurston Dart, Professor of Music at the University of Cambridge.

At about this time Ridout started teaching at the University of Birmingham, and at the Royal College of Music. He also broadcast a great deal about music for the BBC. This included two series: *Background to Music* (40 programmes) and *Background to Musical Form* (27 programmes). For these he also compiled and wrote the companion volumes.

By 1964 he was teaching at both the University of Cambridge and the University of London, while being professor of theory and composition at the Royal College of Music. His work as a teacher also included spells at the University of Oxford, and teaching composition to musically gifted children.

He spent many years living in Canterbury as resident composer to the Cathedral and latterly the King's School, writing three operas for the choir school and over 45 works for the Cathedral choir.

In 1990, following a heart attack, he stopped teaching entirely, and gave all his time to composing and editing.

John Rutter

b. 1945

Go to almost any service or concert at Christmas time and you are likely to hear at least one of the catchy carols by John Rutter. Pieces like the *Shepherd's Pipe Carol* have proved immensely popular by virtue of their memorable tunes and springy rhythms. His larger works add poignancy to these qualities, also a notable use of colour in his orchestrations.

Rutter was born in London and received his first musical education as a chorister at Highgate School. He went on to study music at Clare College, Cambridge, where he wrote his first published compositions and conducted his first recording while still a student.

His compositional career has embraced both large and small-scale choral works, orchestral and instrumental pieces, a piano concerto , two children's operas, music for television, and specialist writing for such groups as the Philip Jones Brass Ensemble and the King's Singers. His most recent larger choral works, *Requiem* (1985), *Magnificat* (1990) and *Psalmfest* (1993), have been performed many times in Britain, North America, and a growing number of other countries. Among his numerous arrangements and collections, he co-edited four volumes in the widely popular *Carols for Choirs* series with Sir David Willcocks.

From 1975 to 1979 he was director of music at Clare College, whose choir he directed in broadcasts and recordings. After giving up the Clare post to allow more time for composition, he formed the Cambridge Singers, a professional chamber choir primarily dedicated to recording, and he now divides his time between composition and conducting. He has guest-conducted or lectured at many concert halls, universities, churches, music festivals, and conferences in Europe, Scandinavia, North America and Australasia.

Robert Simpson

1921–1997

Robert Simpson was born at Leamington in 1921. At first he intended to become a doctor but gave up medicine after two years and studied harmony and counterpoint with Herbert Howells between 1942-6. After some years as a freelance lecturer and writer, he joined the music staff of the BBC in 1951, the same year as he received the D Mus from Durham University.

Although a composer from the outset, he first came to public notice as a scholar; his special interest in Bach, Beethoven and Sibelius, among others, gave him considerable knowledge of composition which deeply affected his whole outlook. In addition, Simpson spent much of his working life promoting neglected masterpieces and unjustly underrated composers. It is largely owing to his efforts that the works of, for example, Bruckner and Nielsen are now in the standard repertoire, and he did much to resurrect the career of Havergal Brian.

A watershed in Simpson's life came in 1980 when he resigned from the BBC following his dissatisfaction with its cultural policies, and thereafter dedicated most of his time to composition, continuing a remarkable series of symphonies as well as a large quantity of chamber music, much of which has been recorded.

Arthur Somervell

1863–1937

Born at Windermere, Arthur Somervell went to Uppingham School and King's College, Cambridge, where he studied under Stanford. After two years in Berlin at the Hochschule für Musik, he enrolled at the RCM in 1885, after which he became a private pupil of Parry and eventually joined the College's teaching staff in 1894. Within six years he was appointed as inspector of music to the Board of Education and rose ultimately to be chief inspector. In this office, and by his dedicated work for music festivals, he exercised a profound influence over the whole field of musical education in Britain, for which services he was knighted in 1929.

Although Somervell's official duties may well have interrupted his development as a composer, he found time to write steadily throughout his life, producing a number of large-scale works which included a symphony, concertos, Masses, a *Passion*, and several cantatas. But he was most successful with music for church choirs and notable for his song-cycles and songs, particularly his settings of poems from Housman's *A Shropshire Lad*. Despite the degree to which his style became dated after the war, these, and his earlier song cycle *Maud* to poems by Tennyson, have withstood the test of time. He died in May 1937.

Bernard Stevens

1916–1983

Stevens was born in London and received free piano lessons from Harold Samuel, who instilled in his pupil a deep appreciation of Bach which remained with him throughout his life. In 1934 he went to Cambridge, where he studied composition with Edward Dent and Cyril Rootham, graduating three years later in music and literature. Lessons with Donald Tovey followed, then a period at the RCM with Benjamin, Jacob and

Lambert. Stevens's early works were written during his six years in the army, and after demobilisation in 1946 he settled in London, composing for films and amateur choirs. The first of his works to attract public attention actually came the year before: following the end of hostilities, the *Daily Express* quickly announced a competition to find a musical work worthy to celebrate the allied victory, and *A Symphony of Liberation* by Stevens, still only 29, was the outright winner.

Although he shared radical left-wing beliefs with his post-war contemporaries Ronald Stevenson, Robert Simpson and Alan Bush, Stevens was the only one who attempted any kind of consistent engagement with twelve-note serialism. He was nevertheless able to incorporate popular elements into his serious works without undermining his intent, and while his music has not enjoyed a wide following, it by no means deserves to be consigned to obscurity. According to Stephen Johnson, writing in the BBC book of British music, *Fairest Isle*, Stevens, along with Simpson, Arnold, Rubbra, Alwyn, Maconchy and Lutyens, have all found their stars in the ascendant again.

John Tavener

b. 1944

Tavener was educated at Highgate School and entered the RAM on a William Wallace Exhibition, studying composition with Lennox Berkeley and later with the Australian composer David Lumsdaine. While still a student he composed his dramatic cantata *Cain and Abel*, which won the Prince Rainier of Monaco Prize in 1965, and followed this with another biblical cantata, *The Whale*. Written for narrator, vocal soloists, chorus and orchestra – with considerable use of more unorthodox sounds – the work was received with rapturous acclamation and brought Tavener's name to a wider audience, including John Lennon, who was responsible for its subsequent recording in 1970 on the Beatles' 'Apple' label. The work's immediate success opened further doors for Tavener, still only 22, and *In alium* was commissioned by the BBC for a Promenade Concert. Two years later came the *Celtic Requiem*, which incorporates children's singing games and hymn-tunes and is scored for a small orchestra augmented by an electric guitar and bagpipes; the concluding section, *Requiescat in pace*, is set against the playground version of a familiar nursery rhyme:

> *Mary had a little lamb*
> *Her father shot it dead,*
> *Now it goes to school with her*
> *Between two loaves of bread.*

Though its origins may have been sacred, even hardbitten London critics admitted to its infectious high spirits, and while some accused Tavener of gimmickry, his underlying seriousness and sense of purpose demanded that the work be judged on its own terms.

Never a composer to subscribe to any particular school of composition, Tavener has always steadfastly pursued his own path – a path which increasingly led him towards Byzantium and the Eastern Church. His subsequent conversion in 1977 to the Russian arm of the Orthodox Church had a profound effect on his music, which increasingly began to assume a more transcendental quality. When the BBC commissioned a piece for the 1989 Proms, *The Protecting Veil* for cello and orchestra, it emerged as his most popular work to date from an already prodigious output. Currently fashionable, it remains to be seen whether Tavener's music will survive into the next millennium, although the parting hymn *Song for Athene*, sung at the funeral service of Diana, Princess of Wales, will have attracted many new listeners to his music.

Harold Truscott

1914–1992

Truscott was born into a working-class family in Seven Kings, Ilford, just before the outbreak of war. He suffered from a 'club foot', which although corrected by surgery, forced him to wear a hip-brace until he was 12 and ultimately prevented him from joining the services in 1939. Since sport and games were denied him, he turned to literature from an early age but soon switched his attention to music, composing a setting of Robert Louis Stevenson's *Under the wide and starry sky* when he was just 14. Unable to come to terms with his son's total absorption in music, Ernest Truscott suspected him of copying work from other composers and, convinced that Harold was suffering from delusions which may be linked with a form of mental illness, took the drastic step of having him committed to an asylum in Romford. After a spell in hospital and a convalescent home in Kent, neither of which did anything to deter Truscott from pursuing music, his father relented and offered to pay for his son's musical tuition.

In 1934, Truscott briefly attended the Guildhall School of Music, but was largely self-taught and at first earned his living working for the Royal Mail. Later, he was able to enrol for two years on a part-time basis at the RAM, where he received instruction in composition from Herbert Howells, supported by the close study of music scores from his local public library. Truscott first became known in the late 1940s as a broadcaster on the BBC's Third Programme and as a contributor to musical periodicals, where he quickly established a reputation as one of the most knowledgeable writers on music since the war. For much of his life he taught music, eventually retiring as principal lecturer in music at what is now Huddersfield University in 1979, and although he never stopped composing, he made no effort to promote his own work. As a result, little of his music was ever performed and apart from a small piece for cello, none was published in his lifetime.

So secretive was he about his compositions that it was only after his death in 1992 that the quality and quantity of his output came to light. One in particular, the *Elegy for String Orchestra*, written in 1943, was discovered buried amongst Truscott's enormous collection of printed music and appears to have been either forgotten or deliberately suppressed by the composer as he made no reference to it in his work-lists. According to Guy Rickards, who unearthed the work, a performance at any time during the 1950s would have secured Truscott's future as a composer of considerable stature.

Grace Williams

1906–1977

Grace Williams was born in the port town of Barry in South Wales. Her parents were both school teachers who enjoyed music and encouraged their daughter's gifts, which surfaced while still a girl at Barry Grammar School. In 1923 she won a musical scholarship to University College, Cardiff, and on graduating continued her studies with Vaughan Williams and Gordon Jacob at the RCM. During her time there she developed a close friendship with Elizabeth Maconchy and their discussion and criticism of each other's work provided valuable insights for both composers. In 1930, when Williams won a travelling scholarship to Vienna, Maconchy joined her for a while and the two would often be seen together at the opera or enjoying coffee and occasional cigars in local cafés.

Returning to London in late 1931, Williams taught for a time at Camden School for Girls and as a visiting lecturer at Southlands College of Education in Wimbledon. It was during these years that she met Benjamin Britten and the two became firm friends throughout the 1930s, enjoying each other's company and sharing views on the other's music. Williams's own compositions were beginning to be performed and broadcast, and Britten was influential in obtaining commissions for film scores for her. When war broke out they went their separate ways, Britten going off to America while Williams was evacuated out of London with the Camden School to Lincolnshire. Despite the disruption, however, her music received several important performances during the early 1940s. The first of these was her *Fantasia on Welsh Nursery Tunes*, which was to become one of her most popular works, followed soon after by *Sea Sketches* for string orchestra, one of several of her compositions to create vivid pictures of the sea.

Williams returned to London with the school in 1943, but the stress of teaching and composing made her ill and after a brief spell working in the Schools Broadcasting Department of the BBC, she decided to return to Wales and settled in a small flat in her parents' house. In Barry she worked on educational programmes for the BBC and wrote incidental music for radio, television and film, but she aimed always at serious expression and maintained a steady output, including a second symphony, an opera (*The Parlour*), a concerto for one of her favourite instruments, the trumpet, and several works for chorus and orchestra. In 1969 she wrote an orchestral fanfare, *Castell Caernarfon*, which was played on the ramparts of the castle for the investiture of the Prince of Wales, and in 1971 she composed a full-scale setting of the Latin mass, *Missa Cambrensis*, which was written for the Llandaff Festival.

Although renowned for her generous interest in young composers and her own keen sense of humour, Grace Williams always knew and spoke her mind. She refused most of the honours that were offered her, including the OBE, and never married, despite a wartime relationship with a Polish man, claiming music to be her first love. She died in Barry, where she had lived for the past 30 years, aged 71.

Malcolm Williamson

b. 1931

From the age of 12, Williamson studied with Eugene Goossens at the Sydney Conservatory, eventually leaving there in 1951 to take a course of lessons in London with Elisabeth Lutyens. It was his first visit to Europe and it impressed him enough to want to settle there permanently, which he did three years later. He took further lessons with Lutyens, converted to Roman Catholicism, and became fascinated by the music of Messiaen, learning the organ in order to play his works for the instrument. He supported himself during this period working as a nightclub pianist, and for a time wrote large-scale orchestral works which were generally ignored. It was not until he extended his range to include theatre and chamber music that Williamson began to attract attention.

His first two operas, *Our Man in Havana*, produced by Sadler's Wells in 1963, and *English Eccentrics*, premièred at Aldeburgh the next year, were well received at the time, but Williamson then turned to smaller-scale works and a distinctly popularist style, sometimes involving audience participation, which some found facile. Nevertheless, his broad range and capacity to write fluently encompassed a considerable body of work demonstrating his remarkable versatility as a composer, so it was not surprising that he should be chosen to succeed Bliss as Master of the Queen's Musick in 1975, and awarded a CBE the following year.

Forsaking his earlier scores for films such as *The Brides of Dracula* and *The Horror of Frankenstein*, he now turned his attention to some works with royalty in mind, including the *Mass of Christ the King*, dedicated to the Queen. But it has to be said that Williamson has not fulfilled his earlier promise, and while he still has the time and flexibility to develop his appreciable talent, for UK audiences he has become something of a forgotten figure.

Hugh Wood

b. 1932

The younger of two sons in a musical family, Wood was educated at Oundle School and later, after national service, at New College, Oxford. Although he sensed from an early age that he would compose, and enjoyed a good deal of music-making, he read modern history at Oxford and only resolved to take formal lessons once he had left and settled in London. In 1954 he had private lessons in harmony and counterpoint with William Lloyd Webber and subsequently studied composition with Iain Hamilton and Matyas Seiber. During the period 1956-60 he earned his living by lecturing to evening classes for the Workers' Educational Association while supply-teaching in London schools during the day. He went on to teach at Morley College and eventually at the RAM until 1965, when he moved to Glasgow and then Liverpool Universities. From 1977 onwards he lectured in music at Cambridge, and became a familiar voice broadcasting for the BBC, notably about Beethoven and Schoenberg.

As a student, Wood composed several works, with his String Quartet attracting some attention in 1959. These led to his first composition for symphony orchestra, *Scenes from Comus*, first heard at the 1965 Proms. It proved a landmark and was followed three years later by the Cello Concerto, one of his finest orchestral works. Much more was to follow, including perhaps his best-known work, the 1991 Piano Concerto composed for Joanna MacGregor.

Index